Postcolonial English Literature

THEORY AND PRACTICE

Postcolonial English Literature

Theory and Practice

Edited by
DIPAK GIRI

AUTHORSPRESS

Worldwide Circulation through Authorspress Global Network
First Published in 2018
by
Authorspress
Q-2A Hauz Khas Enclave, New Delhi-110 016 (India)
Phone: (0) 9818049852
E-mail: authorspressgroup@gmail.com
Website: www.authorspressbooks.com

Postcolonial English Literature: Theory and Practice
ISBN 978-93-87651-98-2

Printed in India at Krishna Offset, Shahdara

Dedicated to

My Sweet Daughter Diya

Foreword

At a recent seminar held at Deen Dayal Upadhyay Gorakhpur University I took the opportunity of being the Keynote Speaker to express my suspicion that terms or phrases such as "rewriting" or "counter discourse" or "writing back" carry a certain violence, a certain confrontational energy. This energy may be emotionally mobilising but may not be politically productive in the long run, because its oppositionality seems to invoke and reiterate a neat and clear binary; and neat and clear binaries seldom work when it comes to talking about messy things like culture and identity, because there is no such thing as a "pure" culture and no such thing as a "pure" identity. We are all culturally impure, but some of us revel in the notion of being a "pure Hindu" or a "pure Indian" when such purity is just a linguistic lie. Very often language is used to prop up notions of cultural purity. English still continues to be regarded in some quarters as a "foreign" (and therefore untouchable) language. This is why it gives me great pleasure to provide the foreword to this book because it continues the healthy project of engaging with the postcolonial condition using what some still regard as "the coloniser's language."

I congratulate Mr. Dipak Giri for putting together a volume that does not believe in geographical, racial, national, gendered boundaries as unbridgeable. The range of authors discussed here – from Achebe to Roy – is a testimony to the ever-expanding contours of postcolonial writing. The focus on fiction – Dattani being the only playwright dealt with here – seems apposite because sometimes a condition requires the length and breadth of a novel for its adequate treatment. The care with which each contributor has tried to negotiate the tricky terrain of postcoloniality is worthy of note. Volumes such as these are always welcome, because the postcolonial condition is so over determined by innumerable and powerful historical, socio-cultural, and economic forces that careful, tentative but persistent identification of these forces and their impact is always to be undertaken.

I hope that this volume will excite many minds, restart many conversations, invigorate many thoughts, but not in the spirit of loud, confrontational anger. Let us be humbled by the acknowledgement that pure oppositionality is intellectually unhelpful and that dealing with our own postcolonial hybridities with care and understanding may be the way forward.

Niladri R. Chatterjee
Professor, Kalyani University
West Bengal

Contents

Introduction

Impacted by the poststructuralist and postmodernist idea of decentering, postcolonial theory that came into being as a critical theory focusing colonial experience from the perspective of the colonised at the end of the twentieth century, started to challenge the universalist claim of literature. As a theory, it equates with colonial sympathies in the canon, and substitutes the colonial metanarratives with counter-narratives of resistance, by rewriting history and affirming cultural identities through approaches such as nativism, separatism, cultural syncretism, hybridity, mimicry, active participation and assimilation. Supported by an anti-essentialist view of identity and culture, postcolonial theory critiques cultural hierarchies and the Eurocentric modernity. The major theoretical works that are done in the area of postcolonial theory are Franz Fanon's *The Wretched of the Earth* (1961), Edward Said's *Orientalism* (1978) and *Culture and Imperialism* (1993), Gayatri Chakravorty Spivak's *In Other Worlds* (1987), Bill Ashcroft's *The Empire Writes Back* (1989) and Homi K Bhabha's *Nation and Narration* (1990). In literature, indigenous people from late colonised and marginalised countries have found their voices to an increasing rate. They are attempting to assert their own visions, tell their own stories and reclaim their experiences and histories.

If we trace back to history, we see postcolonial literature first made its appearance in Africa and soon spread out all over the continents except Antarctica, most notably Africa, Asia and the Caribbean. Chinua Achebe and Nadine Gordimer set the stage of postcolonial literature. Since then it has been growing in rapid number and many writers from across the globe have started writing their novels, plays and collections of poetry. Chinua Achebe, Nadine Gordimer, Wole Soyinka, Buchi Emecheta, Doris Lessing, V.S. Naipaul, Jean Rhys and Derek Walcott from Africa and the Caribbean, Mulk Raj Anand, Kamala Das, Nissim Ezekiel, Jhumpa Lahiri, Kamala Markandaya, Rohinton Mistry, Arundhati Roy, Michael Ondaatje, Salman Rushdie, Nayantara Sahgal, Raja Rao from South Asia, mostly Indian in origin, Margaret Atwood, Rohinton Mistry from Canada, Peter Carey, A.D. Hope, David Malouf, Judith Wright from Australia, Keri Hulme, Alan Duff from New Zealand, Hanif Kureishi, Graham Swift, Buchi Emecheta from England and Seamus Heaney from Ireland deserve to be noted. Now the area of postcolonial literature has become so broad and ever-expanding that the task of encompassing it in an anthology has become a tough work. Still the present anthology is an endeavour from the part of authors and contributors to comprise the ever-widening area of postcolonial literature into twenty one well written chapters of different perspectives which the authors hopefully see serve the window through which the glimpses of many unexplored regions of this area of study will be caught.

The very first chapter of this anthology is Shilpi Basak's paper proposing to take the problematic issue of selfhood and diasporicity in Jhumpa Lahiri's selected short stories. Attitude to homeland and hostland, sense of rootedness and uprootedness are dealt in detail to understand the nuances of selfhood in diasporic situation. Focus is made on the negotiations of home and host cultures which often culminate the concept of hybridity. It also shows how migrancy effects and affects identity and how the equation changes over generations.

Next Rabi Kanta Roy's paper is an attempt to show an insight of pre-and post-colonialism on Igbo community in late 19th century Nigeria as presented in Chinua Achebe's *Things Fall Apart*. It is argued that the interaction between the Whites and the Igbo people had both negative and positive consequences. That the Europeans greatly influenced the life style of Igbo community is evident in Achebe's novel.

Jointly prepared paper of Dr. Shachi Sood and Dr. Saleem Wani that follows next shows an individual's search for authentic selfhood which is symbolised in his desire to turn his state of unhousement into enhousement in V.S. Naipaul's *A House for Mr. Biswas.* Biswas's desperate desire to have a house of his own is an allegorical representation of the colonial man's desires to locate his place at a strange and alien world

The painful impingement succumbed to a psyche of a man due to economical disturbances, is not to be underestimated in line with that of the traumatic experience getting out of deliberate social discriminations. The former can be sought out, if a considerable effort is practiced consistently, whereas, the later is being dumped upon with layers of interior motives by a section of people in the society. It has created an unbridgeable vacuum both in structural as well as political levels. Mahendran U's paper *The Impact of Binaries in Constituting Social Conflicts: A Reading of A Fine Balance by Rohinton Mistry* is aimed at tracing down such discrimination perpetrated against the disempowered weaker section. Conspicuously, the countless attitudinal prejudices are being sustained with an ulterior impulse. The novel taken for study consists of binaries in countless perspective. However, the major three dimensions such as, political, segregative and economical will alone be elaborated because they prove to be holistic and recurring in nature. If that is carried out, it can be deducted how the binaries get shaped in the form of regulatory mechanisms of the society.

Jointly prepared paper of Dr. Romina Rashid and Asma Zahoor analyses Chimamanda Ngozi Adichie's *Purple Hibiscus* from the religious point of view. Religion from the times immemorial has been one of the major institutions influencing the lives and mindset of people in various communities. This agency has been, however, exploited by many for their own benefit. In the novel, Chimamada Ngozi Adichie has given a considerable space to the understanding of religion. She highlights varied viewpoints in which religion can be comprehended by people simultaneously giving a slice of neocolonial intervention that Britain has made in African states using religion as a tool.

Gouri Kapoor's paper analyses how the experience of migration influences the character development of the protagonists in Doris Lessing's *The Grass is Singing* and Margaret Atwood's *Alias Grace* through a focused textual analysis. In both novels, the mental unhinging of the characters occurs because they are unable to negotiate with the harsh realities they are brought in contact with due to migration. Both of them were compelled to migrate because of the men in their lives. As the migration in their case was more of a compromise than a volitional act, they crumble under the pressures of living in a cultural environment which alienates them and makes them feel like outcasts.

Samiksha Sharma's paper *When the Subaltern React and Create a Space of Their Own: Re-locating Identity in Arvind Adiga's The White Tiger* explores how Balram as a pivotal character, in spite of being born inferior, reacts against it and uses every means to come out of it. Through Balaram, the paper also shows Adiga's concern over the evil face of poverty, exploitation and alienation.

Conforming to the idea that novel deals with the significance of relationships and to what extent is family important in a person's life and to what consequences a person faces when his family life is on the verge of collapse and its after effect, Shweta Verma's paper studies *Family Matters* by Rohinton Mistry by taking into consideration the familial and marital discourse which occurs in the life of the protagonist and his closed ones.

Jointly prepared paper of Tabish Wani and Rumana Nisar effectively highlights the social deprivation and identity issues in Aravind Adiga's *White Tiger*. The paper also brings into light the deprivation of basic rights of citizens like education and health and the exploitation of people by upper hand.

Ragini Kapoor's paper makes a postcolonial ecofeminist study of Margaret Atwood's *The Handmaid's Tale.* Advocating human rights of women and giving a clarion call for the destruction of gender-based injustices, the paper explores the possible ties of combating patriarchal structures of power and domination that refuses a woman's equal claims as an individual in society. It raises a voice for the protection of Canadian environment, organic living, and the deep rooted relation and bonding between nature and humans.

Surabhi K.'s paper tries to address the plights and trauma of a married woman in a diasporic land in the novel *Wife* by Bharati Mukherjee, her journey of rootlessness and gradual assimilation in a hostland during which the life is distorted.

Supriya Mandal's paper shows how eminent postcolonial novelist Arundhati Roy in her much awaited novel *The Ministry of Utmost Happiness* has unwrapped the military insurgency in Kashmir and in tribal area, lambasted the rise of Hindu right wing and portrayed the deprivation of Dalit and the plight of transgender and women. In doing so, she has exhibited the Euro-American imperial policy in India and tried to unmask the Indian political parties' populism that helps them to cope with the common people.

Dr. Prachi Priyanka's paper explores how food is metaphorical as regards identity and isolation in Jhumpa Lahiri's select stories.

Dr. Brajesh Kumar Gupta's paper discusses how Naipaul as a postcolonial writer has written about slavery, revolution, guerrillas, corrupt politicians, the poor and the oppressed, interpreting the rages so deeply rooted in our societies. Naipaul's writing style is characterised by the use of simple yet strong words woven together in grasping narratives that reflect the dark realities of the world we live in. Naipaul very early experienced a profound alienation, both from the close-knit family life of his Brahmin ancestors and from the social and political life of his native Trinidad.

Sujoy Barman's paper, entitled "*The colonialism and the Changes in the Post-Colonial World*" is an attempt to find out the relation through the world, on the basis of power like economical power, power of arms and modern war weapons, cultural power etc. Every country in the world depends on the rest of the world. Some are depending to spread their commercial markets, to create a big consumer society. These are developed countries. On the other hand, the countries who are developing, they are depending over rest of the developed countries for their co-operations in the national progress. This is the twenty first century relation. But at the very beginning of the colonialism, the relation was different when one country dominated others especially for the economical profits, utilisation of the natural resources. As the time advanced, with economical relations, other relations were included. Then culture, religion, language became other parts of the colonialism. And there are found a lot of changes in cultural, socio-economical, political, religious changes when two or more countries come into contact with each other. Behind these changes, there are many reasons. People, from one country, accept the norms and cults of another country. When people do such imitations, there are some reasons. At the same time, there are both negative and positive results, coming from the imitation. The paper "*The Colonialism and the Changes in the Post-Colonial World*" is based on these critical situations of the world. It explores to find out the reasons for imitation by the people, the exact situation after the imitation, its negative or positive effects both on the imitating and imitated people.

The aim of Alik Jha's paper is to explore some novels of Margaret Atwood through the lens of Shamanic Archetype that lays bare Atwood's attempts to break-away from male-oriented myths and archetypes and voices the genuine female experience and at the same time paves the way for the creation of new archetypes which would celebrate female identity and freedom.

Rabindra Sutradhar's article aims to explore the theme of Glocalisation in the light of postcolonial mimicry, hybridity and third space identity in Amitav Ghosh's masterpiece and Sahitya Academy winning novel *The Shadow Lines* and provides examples from the novel the application of some postcolonial elements such as memory, imagination, identity, ambivalence, nationalism, space/place, worlding, Diaspora, hybridity, unbelonging etc. The title *The Shadow Lines* implicitly alludes to the point that there are no clear boundaries amongst people who have lived with hybrid and diasporic identities for a long time. What is more, Ghosh's attempt to project the issue of glocalisation is hinted in the structural pattern of the novel which is divided into two parts, 'Going Away' and 'Coming Home'. Throughout the novel Ghosh throws light on migration, cross-border connection and relationship, cultural interaction, inter-racial marriage, double identity as both coloniser and colonised etc. Most of the characters in the novel as we observe are globe-trotters. They move in so many directions that ultimately the identity of a distinct and discrete homeland and culture become blurred and the world where no boundaries and value of border, religion, race, or caste are acknowledged becomes glocal and there would be occurrences of mimicry and hybridisation.

Amrita Datta's paper describes how Basharat Peer's *Curfewed Night*, an English language narrative by a young Kashmiri Muslim evokes the Kashmir's tumultuous history as lived experiences. The narrator in the narrative cannot consciously or unconsciously able to get rid of his Kashmiri identity and culture. The paper also involves the question of inability to build up connection with so called nationalism and national identity, belonging, location, rights, citizenship, exclusion and oppression.

Tinku Das's article explores the linguistic conflict in postcolonial society through the male protagonist in Anita Desai's *In Custody*.

Saurabh Debnath's paper aims to present a serious discussion regarding the colonial issues that Chinua Achebe has portrayed in *Things Fall Apart*, a unique piece of literary art in the world of fiction. This is Achebe's first and perhaps best-loved novel, published in 1958 in the midst of the Nigeria's renaissance. It focuses on Nigeria's early experience with colonialism, from first contact with the British to widespread British administration.

Dipak Giri's paper *Interrogating National Identity: A Postcolonial Study of Mahesh Dattani's Final Solutions* tries to explore the problem of national identity in postcolonial India. Validation and promotion of one religion at the expense of others has given birth to the problem of communalism in postcolonial India. Putting on the mask of secularism, the nation-state India in postcolonial period has held the real face back from public. India as a community taken birth in postcolonial era has appeared more an imagined community for Hindus than a united community for other religions. The discourse of religion has made national identity more exclusionary than inclusionary. At the centre of this discourse, Hindus stand head and shoulders above other Non-Hindus. Such rise of nation out of discursive basis of power has stirred questions to many. Many postcolonial writers have come openly to challenge this. Still the way Dattani has done this in his play *Final Solutions* is an achievement in itself. Along with dealing with the theme of 'transferred resentments' of one community against another as regards question to national identity the paper also shows how the playwright has tried to draw the possible solution to end such violence and animosity through adoption of the policy of forgetting or forgiving.

Before winding up, I wish to say few words addressing to those whose aid I always seek in my life. First of all I want to thank that Omnipotent Power which is at the root of all creation. Then I want to express my special thanks and gratitude to Authorspress for bringing out such an amazing anthology. I am also thankful to my family which is guiding force to all my achievements. Finally I want to thank all my contributors only for whose valuable works this anthology has got its final shape.

April, 2018
Cooch Behar, West Bengal

Dipak Giri
dipakgiri84@yahoo.in

1

A Tryst with the Self: Migrancy, Diasporicity and Identity in Selected Short Stories of Jhumpa Lahiri

Shilpi Basak

> "I am the one
> who always goes
> away with my home
> which can only stay inside
> in my blood-my home which does not fit
> with any geography"
>
> (Sujata Bhatt, 'The One Who Always Goes Away')

Jeremy Hawthorn, while describing diaspora, critically examines the root of the word and makes following comment:

> The word 'diaspora' comes from a Greek word meaning dispersal, and was originally applied to the condition of the Jewish people living outside Palestine. With the development of post-colonialist theory the term has been extended to cover a range of different cultural and ethnic groups held together by shared cultural or religious commitment and having some sense of exile from a place or state of origin and belonging. (*A Glossary of Contemporary Literary Theory,* 78)

It is this 'sense of exile' or 'belonging' to elsewhere that largely constitutes the identity of people in diaspora. Identity as such is formed and framed by diverse issues. There are some aspects of identity that society thrusts upon a human being as soon as the person is born. Nationality, religion, language are the determining issue of identity in such cases. The outside world is supposed to know him by these tags (Indian/American, Hindu/Muslim/Christian, Bengali/English etc.). But these 'imposed' identities might be in contentious position with his/her new and evolving identity as he/she conceives it later during his/her various encounter with diverse socio-cultural situations. This is indeed emblematic of a diaspora situation. The characters in diasporic literature navigate 'between the strict tradition they have inherited and the baffling New World they must encounter everyday' (*Interpreter of Maladies*, Introductory page).They challenge the notion of a fixed always-already-there type identity and inhabit a 'in-between' subjectivity in new cultural landscape that is redrawn on the palimpsest of the previous cultural bearings.

For the present analysis I have selected the following four stories namely "When Mr. Pirzada Came to Dine", "A Real Durwan", "Mrs. Sen's", "The Third and the Final Continent". All the stories deal with the condition of Bengali immigrants in different capacities. The characters suffer from loneliness, alienation, and there is always longing for a lost world. Lahiri herself shared these kinds of emotions in her personal life. In fact her background is very important to study her writings. Asha Chobey, an Indian critic, comments: "the personal life of Jhumpa Lahiri is the very prototype of diasporic culture. Having spent more than thirty years she still feels, 'a bit of an outsider'..." (Chobey in 'The Postcolonial Web'). In an essay that appeared in a 2006 edition of *Newsweek*, aptly titled 'My Two Lives' Lahiri writes, 'When I was growing up in Rhode Island in the 1970s I felt neither Indian nor American. Like many immigrant offspring, I felt intense pressure to be two things, loyal to the old world and fluent in the new, approved of on either side of the hyphen" (Lahiri in "My Two Lives"). So the perspicacity from which Lahiri interprets the 'maladies' of diasporic identities is all the more significant if we keep in mind this biographical aspect of the author.

As the title suggests, *Interpreter of Maladies* explains emotional pain, affliction of the diasporic experience. Lahiri takes the role of an interpreter and interprets the maladies of the characters who either physically (geographically) or psychologically or in both ways are displaced from their native lands. They preserve native culture in home through attention to food, dress, and spiritual matters and by raising their children in the tradition(s) of the native lands. The lives in these stories often end with a sense of loss. In their isolation, in exile, they feel that they are missing something vital to their identities. It is their missing *something* that defines their identity.

The first story, I have chosen, is "When Mr. Pirzada Came to Dine". The story is about a Pakistani (now Bangladeshi) man who is to dine with an Indian immigrant family in USA in 1971.The whole story is told from the point of view of a ten year old girl and the readers, through the girl's eyes, experience the sense of exile, alienation and also the important yet unresolving question of identity. The narrator (the ten year old girl) belongs to a Hindu family and is an Indian Bengali immigrant in America whereas Mr. Pirzada is Muslim and Pakistani Bengali in the process of becoming a Bangladeshi (Bangladesh war of independence in 1971 was the background of the story).The contradiction of their different citizenship is juxtaposed against the linguistic and cultural oneness of the Bengali community. So tagging these characters by a single and fixed identity is not possible here. The complexities of identity and belonging become negotiations and hazards of nationality and citizenship. Lilia is caught between the tradition of her parents and American culture. Mr. Pirzada is now living in America but psychologically he is always in Dacca, his home. Lilia observes curiously:

> "Unlike the watch on his wrist, his pocket watch, he had explained to me was set to the local time of Dacca, eleven hours ahead." (*Interpreter of Maladies,* 30)

The only reason Mr. Pirzada is invited to the narrator's house was that he was Indian or as her father explains, 'Mr. Pirzada is no longer considered Indian' (after partition of India in 1947, Bangladesh was included into Pakistan and was named East Pakistan). This particular situation of complexity of identity reminds us of Amitav Ghosh' *The Shadow Lines* where we find that borderlines of nations often betray identities. Here, as also in *The Shadow Lines*, the relationship between identity and nationality is unstable and fluid both for Lilia (is she Indian/American?) and Mr. Pirzada (is he Bengali/Indian/Pakistani?).

The next story under the purview of my discussion is "A Real Durwan". It is the story about 'Boori Ma', a Bengali refugee who migrated to India from East Pakistan (now Bangladesh) during partition which created a mass migration of Bengali Hindus to India, particularly to the areas adjacent to West Bengal. During this mass migration, some people lost everything including identity. Through the character of Boori Ma, the self-appointed sweeper and a kind of 'durwan' (gatekeeper), Lahiri depicts the trauma of the partition. Boori Ma considers herself 'an outsider', 'broken inside'. We find her enumerating twice a day as she sweeps the stairwell 'the details of her plight and losses suffered since her deportation to Calcutta after partition. At that time, she mentioned, the turmoil had separated her from a husband, four daughters, a two-story brick house, a rosewood *almari*, and a number of coffer boxes whose skeleton keys she still wore, along with her life savings to the end of her sari' (*Interpreter of Maladies,* 70-71). Throughout the story Boori Ma's identity is attached to these keys that are stolen at the final stage of the story. Her past identity of a rich man's wife of East Bengal is more important to her than her present identity of a sweeper of a building of Calcutta city. She cannot forget her identity related with her homeland as she claims, "Yes, there I tasted life…there was a day when my feet touched nothing but marble. Believe me, don't believe me, such comforts you cannot even dream them" (*Interpreter of Maladies,* 71). The idea of 'imaginary home' is very much present in this story which focuses on the plight of the lower class because of forced diaspora and political struggle. In this connection, Salman Rushdie's insightful comment is significant:

> It may be that when the Indian writer who writes from outside India tries to reflect that world, he is obliged to deal in broken mirrors, some of whose fragments have been irretrievably lost.… fragmentation made trivial things seem like symbols, and the

mundane acquired numinous qualities... (*Imaginary Homelands,* 10-11)

The shards of memory acquire greater resonance in contrast with the present sense of loss. At the end of the story, a basin is stolen from the building and Boori Ma is expelled from the building out of a suspicion. This 'basin' incident is like the driving incident of the story "Mrs. Sen's" symbolizing that they had always been alienated in their new and adopted land (Calcutta in case of Boori Ma and America in case of Mrs. Sen) and her identity will always be attached to the original homeland (East Pakistan/later Bangladesh for Boori Ma and India for Mrs. Sen).

"Mrs. Sen's", the next story under my discussion, is a story which explores the life of an immigrant Indian Bengali housewife who is trying to make a little India in her house in America. It is an archetypal story of the cultural outsider. It presents the real difficulties faced by immigrant Indian lives in an alien culture without friends and family, struggling to cope with the new surroundings they cannot call their 'home'. Eliot, the eleven year old American boy (whom Mrs. Sen looked after as a baby-sitter) curiously observes, "When Mrs. Sen said the home, she meant India, not the apartment where she sat chopping vegetables" (*Interpreter of Maladies,* 116). Mrs. Sen's inability to negotiate an ethnic American identity can be understood in her simple statement about India: "Everything is there" (*Interpreter of Maladies,* 113). The main point of Mrs. Sen's alienation is that 'Mrs. Sen did not know how to drive' (*Interpreter of Maladies,* 111). Her daily activities are arranged upon the theme of escape. While she prefers delaying her driving practice (a necessity for her new life) she steadily keeps her special Indian cooking style and her interest in buying fish. Food practice here is used by Lahiri as a vehicle of one's cultural identity and resisting the continuing agency of power of new culture (here exercised symbolically through Eliot's mother who insists Mrs. Sen should learn driving soon).

In "The Third and the Final Continent", *Interpreter of Maladies*' closing story, Lahiri seems to make a transition between Mrs. Sen's cultural static and Asima's (central character of *The Namesake*) more productive cultural relocation by briefly acquainting the readers with the protagonist's wife Mala. The same immigrant themes – the initial hurdles to settle, to adjust and after sometimes to embrace the new culture – are also visible in the story narrated through a Bengali commerce graduate who moved from Calcutta to London and then to Boston. The character is modeled after Lahiri's own father. Lahiri explores the idea that identity especially for immigrants, is something that is essentially required. It gives them a sense of security. The narrator tells: "We are American citizen now, so that we can collect social security when it is time. Though we visit Calcutta every few years and bring back more drawstring pajamas and Darjeeling tea, we have decided to grow old here" (*Interpreter of Maladies,* 197).

When first came to London, he attempts to keep his cultural identity intact by keeping the most trivial of Indian tradition alive, such as eating 'egg curry'. When he was posted to America, he relied on the earlier experience in Britain (London) and converted 'ounce to grams' and compared 'price to thing in England' as a survival strategy. The narrator's ability to adjust, as Lahiri points out, is part of a strategy of human adaptation. He has discovered that the ability to feel at home – no matter what country he lives in – comes only from having a strong sense of self. The 'ambition that had first hurled him across the world' (*Interpreter of Maladies,* 197) is a part of his ability to know himself and to recognise that the strength he gains from his origin is the ideal foundation on which to build a strong identity. Though he and his wife are now American, they are still attached with South Asian food and Indian tradition. He also wants his son to retain his Indian culture. Eating rice by hand and speaking Bengali are two important symbols in this story which proves the original nationality is still important for the immigrants and their identity construction. Janine Dahinden's discussion of locality and mobility in diasporic situation specially in transnational identity formation is significant in this connection. According to Dahinden, transnational identity formations result from a combination of transnational mobility, on the one hand, and locality in the sending or/and receiving country, on the other (Dahinden, 51).

What is more significant, the story emphasizes on the moving on, the necessity of 'hybridisation' in a diaspora for survival. Unlike Mrs. Sen, Mala, the narrator's wife is successful in negotiating her identity in a diasporic situation. Lahiri herself insists on this necessity to move on and build new lives in new lands. She shares her views with Nathaniel Hawthorne when she quoted a passage from Nathaniel Hawthorne's essay "The Custom-House" and used it as the epigraph of her second short story collection *Unaccustomed Earth*:

> "Human nature will not flourish, any more than a potato, if it be planted and replanted, for too long a series of generations, in the same worn-out soil. My children have had other birthplaces, and, so far as their fortunes may be within my control, shall strike their roots into unaccustomed earth." (*Unaccustomed Earth*, Epigraph)

The idea behind is that far from being fixed, identity should be seen as a "production" which is never complete and always in flux.

Works Cited

Bauböck, Rainer and Thomas Faist (ed). *Diaspora and Transnationalism: Concepts, Theories and Methods*. Amsterdam: Amsterdam University Press, 2010. Print.

Bhatt, Sujata. *Selected Poems.* Manchester: Carcanet Press Limited, 1997. Print.

Choubey, Asha: "Food as Metaphor in Jhumpa Lahiri's Interpreter of Maladies". *The Postcolonial* Web. http://www.postcolonialweb.org/india/literature/lahiri/choubey1.html accessed on 23.09.2017

Ghosh, Amitav. *The Shadow Lines*. Delhi: Oxford U P, 1998. Print.

Hall, Stuart. "Cultural Identity and Diaspora". *Identity: Community, Culture, Difference.* Ed. Jonathan Rutherford. London: Lawrence & Wishart, 1990. Print.

Hawthorn, Jeremy. *A Glossary of Contemporary Literary Theory.* 4th ed. New Delhi: Bloomsbury, 2014. Print.

Lahiri, Jhumpa. *Interpreter of Maladies*. Flamingo: Harper Collins, 2000. Print.

Lahiri, Jhumpa. *Unaccustomed Earth*. New Delhi: Random House India, 2013. Print.

Lahiri, Jhumpa. "My Two Lives". *Newsweek*. New York: March 6, 2006. Web. http://www.newsweek.com/my-two-lives-106355 accessed on 15 Sep 2016.

Nayar, Aruti. "Jhumpa Lahiri: An Interpreter of Exile". Spectrum: 28May, 2000. Web. http://epaper.tribuneindia.com/t/756 accessed on 17 Sep 2016.

2

Things Fall Apart: An Exploration of Pre-and Post-Colonial Life in Late 19th Century Nigeria

Rabi Kanta Roy

Chinua Achebe is the father of modern African literature. Since the publication of *Things Fall Apart* in 1958, he has credited with being the key progenitor of an African literary tradition. The novel is seen as the archetypal modern African novel in English, one of the first to receive global critical acclaim. The setting of the novel is in the outskirts of Nigeria in a small fictional village, Umuofia just before the arrival of white missionaries into their land. Due to the unexpected arrival of white missionaries in Umofia, the villagers do not know how to react to the sudden cultural changes that the missionaries threaten to change with their new political structure and institution. Hence this paper is trying to focus on the effects of European colonialism on Igbo community.

Towards the end of the 19th century most European states migrated to Africa and other parts of the world where they established colonies. Nigeria was amongst other African nations that received visitors who were on a colonising mission; introducing their religion and culture that is later imposed on Igbo. The culture of the people of Umuofia (Igbo community) is immensely threatened by this change.

Achebe's primary purpose of writing the novel is because he wants to educate his readers about the value of his culture as an

African. *Things Fall Apart* provides readers with an insight of Igbo community right before the white missionaries' invasion on their land. The invasion of the colonising force threatens to change almost every aspect of Igbo community; from religion, traditional gender roles and relations, family structure to trade. Consequently, Achebe blames the white missionaries' colonial rule and invasion for the post-colonial oppressed Igbo culture; this oppression can be seen in terms of the oppressed social coherence between the individual and their society.

In the writing of *Things Fall Apart* Achebe describes the history of Igbo, he does so by describing both the perfections and imperfections of their culture and traditions that made them different from Western cultures. For example, their beliefs in the power of ancestral gods, the sacrifice of young boys, the killing of twins and oppression of women to name a few. Although the arrival of the missionaries had some benefits to Igbo, there were also a number of challenges that faced the future of Igbo.

The focus of the study is to explore Igbo community as it appears in the novel, which is before and after the arrival of white missionaries in Umofia, the effects of their arrival concerning Igbo community, consequently leading to the clash of cultures between the two parties. The novel is incorporated one critical theory, post-colonialism which is relevant for the analysis of the novel. Post-colonial criticism is mainly concerned with literature critiques from countries that are colonies of other countries (Tyson, 417). Because Achebe originates from Nigeria, a colony of British, some of the writing elements he uses in his novels such as language and style are influenced by that.

Background of the Novel

Things Fall Apart is one of the most influential novels of its time, both on a local and global scale. Most of the story takes place in the village of Umuofia, located west of the actual city of Onitsha, on the east bank of the Niger River in Nigeria. The events of the novel unfold in the 1890s. The culture depicted, that of the Igbo people, is similar to that of Achebe's birthplace of Ogidi, where Igbo-speaking people lived together in groups of independent villages ruled by titled elders. The customs described in the novel mirror those of the actual Onitsha people, who lived near Ogidi, and with whom Achebe was familiar.

When Nigeria became a colony of Britain in 1908, the country became exposed to the British political structure and its various institutions. Within the forty years of the arrival of the British, by the time Achebe was born in 1930, the missionaries were well established. He lived in the British Culture but he refused to change Igbo name Chinua to Albert. Achebe's father was among the first to be converted in Ogidi around the turn of the century. Achebe himself was an orphan raised by his grandfather. His grandfather, far from opposing Achebe's conversation to Christianity, allowed Achebe's Christian marriage to be celebrated in his compound.

Plot Summary of the Novel

The title of the novel *Things Fall Apart* comes from the opening lines of W.B. Yeats' poem "The Second Coming" (1921). The poem foresees the end of the present age and the world's approach to another phase that is completely different:

> Turning and turning in the widening gyre
> The falcon cannot hear the falconer
> Things fall apart; the centre cannot hold;
> Mere anarchy is loosed upon the world......
>
> (Yeats, 1921)

Set in pre-colonial Nigeria, the novel follows the life of Okonkwo, an Igbo ("Ibo in the novel") leader and local wrestling champion in the fictional Nigerian village of Umuofia. The work is split into three parts, with the first describing his family, personal history, and the customs and society of the Igbo, and the second and third sections introducing the influence of British colonialism and Christian missionaries on the Igbo community.

As the novel develops Okonkwo accidentally kills a man and he and his family are exiled from Umuofia. During his exile white missionaries arrive in Umuofia and change the village. When Okonkwo returns to his village he sees the major transformations that Umuofia has undergone during his exile. Unhappy with the change, Okonkwo and other villagers come together to drive the white missionaries out of their land. Their efforts are in vain as the missionaries send their messengers to abort meeting. Okonkwo kills one of the messengers and in shock at his actions the villagers let the other messengers escape. The messengers report back to the missionaries and they take off to bring Okonkwo to justice only to find him dead.

Definition of Colonialism and Post-Colonialism

Colonialism as defined OED refers to "the policy or practice of acquiring full or partial political control over another country, occupying it with settlers and exploiting it economically. In the novel, colonialism has affected people and has managed to pull them apart many directions that it eventually destroyed relationships of families, friends and tribes. Colonialism has indeed affected people to the point that the life of the protagonist is destroyed and resulted to his own death. It may be seen that European colonialism is something which is vile as it has totally destroyed the culture of Igbo community and traditions of a group of people which in turn destroyed their identity.

The term 'colonialism' is important in defining the specific form of cultural exploitation that developed with the expansion of Europe over the last 400 years. Elleke Boehmer defines 'colonialism' in her book *Colonial and Post-Colonial Literature* as "a settlement of territory, the exploitation or development of resources, and the attempt to govern the indigenous inhabitants of occupied lands." (Boehmer, 2)

Colonialism has been a recurrent feature of human history. The history of colonialism has existed since ancient times. By 1900 almost every country or region in the world had been subjugated by European colonialism at one time or another. The period after the Second World War saw an upsurge of new independence states.

India and Pakistan were granted independence in 1947. France's decolonialism was marked by wars in French, Indochina, Morocco, Tunisia, and Algeria. Belgium, Portugal, and the Netherlands all divested themselves of their overseas possessions during the 1950s, 60s and 70s. 'Colonialism' has taken different forms and has engendered diverse effects around the world.

Post-colonialism marks the end of colonialism by giving the indigenous people the necessary authority and political and cultural freedom to take their place and gain independence by overcoming political and cultural imperialism. Post-colonial discourse was the outcome of the work of several writers such as Frantz Fanon (1967), Edward Said, Bill Ashcroft (1989) and his collaborators, Gayatri Spivak, Homi Bhabha, Aijaz Ahmad (1992) and others.

"Post-colonialism", in the words of Charles E. Bressler,' "is an approach to literary analysis that concerns itself particularly with literature written in English in formerly colonised countries" (Bressler 265). It usually excludes literature that represents either British or American viewpoints, and concentrates on writings from colonised cultures in Australia, New Zealand, Africa, South America, and other places and societies that were once dominated by European cultural, political and philosophical tradition.

The hyphenated term "Post-colonialism" marks a historical period as is suggested by phrases like 'after colonialism', 'after independence', 'after the end of empire' whereas the term 'Post-colonialism' referring to all the characteristics of a society or culture from the time of the colonisation to the present.

As a historical period, Post-colonialism stands for the Post-Second world War decolonising phase. Although the colonial country achieved political freedom, the colonial values do not disappear with the independence of a country. It seems that Post-colonial theory (Gandhi) emerged from the colonised peoples' frustrations, their direct and personal cultural clashes with the conquering culture, and their fears, hopes and dreams about their future and their own identities. How the colonised respond to changes in the language, curricular matters in education, race differences, and a host of other discourses, including the act of writing become the context and the theories of Post-colonialism...

Post-colonialism expresses the opposite idea of colonialism. Hence Post-colonialism literature is a consequence of colonialism. Through literature we understand the primary focus of Achebe's *Things Fall Apart,* a novel written by an individual who grew up under colonial rule in response to the effects of colonialism on his cultures. Achebe writes back at the writings of European writers and the misrepresentation of African in their writings. A colonised individual is usually forced to follow the culture of their colony regardless if they are against it or not. Post-colonial writers usually write about how their rich native cultures were destroyed under the power of imperialism.

Pre-and Post-Colonial Life

The Igbo people are the genuine example of the primitive culture where natural and democratic society was in function. It is the well set culture with much richness. The root of cultures is quite the same in different parts of the world. The basic concept of African cultures is respectable and life sustaining: "The Igbo (or Ibo) people form one of the largest ethnic groups in Africa, with about 15 million living Nigeria and another million living outside. Their farming communities are broadly situated between the Niger River in the west and the cross River in the east, stretching from delta swampland near the southern coast through tropical rain forest to open grasslands to the north (Ohadike, i)."

The Igbo myths point to the origins of agriculture, the antiquity of the family and the importance of iron working in shaping the Igbo community. The agricultural system was based on shifting cultivation, a type of rotating cultivation where the same fields were planted for several years in succession and then were left fallow to regain their fertility. In *Things Fall Apart* Okonkwo's father is portrayed as too lazy to clear forest land; he prays to the spirits to grant him better harvest but is rebuked for his own lack of initiative (Ohadike, iv).

A striking feature of Igbo society was the lack of centralised political structures. The existence of democracy was the great achievement and proof of the high culture. The Igbo lived in autonomous villages and towns, rules by their elder. Relationships were based on blood ties, and each person traced his or her descent to three groups: uno, or house; umunna, or lineage and obodo, village or town (Ohadike, iv). A town or compact village was sometimes named after its founder, or after a striking geographical feature that best described its location.

The Igbo communities were known as 'extremely democratic', yet they had no centralised governments for running the community. The Igbo subscribed to the principal of direct participation in government which is a much democratic concept. Their entire social and political structure revolved around the idea of "cross-cutting ties." As seen in *Things Fall Apart,* the traditional Igbo communities did indeed fall apart in the twentieth century when the Europeans destroyed their cross-cutting ties in the process of colonial rule.

It was a very important centre of power in the Igbo society with much authority and control in a democratic depth. Matters affecting lineage members were discussed at the meeting of its elders, with the assistance of the adult members of the lineage as seen in *Things Fall Apart.* An age-group association were known as ogbo or otu and composed of men or women who were of about the same age. The age-group system promoted respect and comradeship among the people and acted as a powerful and effective way of social as well as political set up.

The Igbo people emphasized personal achievement but succession to titles was not by birth. Every Igbo man began his life as an apprentice as we see in the case of Okonkwo in *Things Fall Apart.* Okonkwo struggles severely in his cultivation though he was the greatest wrestler of the nine villages.

The Igbo women had their own clubs, age-group association, and title associations that complemented those of men. The controlled certain spheres of community life showing the balance in the masculine and feminine existence. Women were perceived to possess superior spiritual well-being and headed many of the traditional cults and shrines. In Achebe's *Things Fall Apart* the oracle is served by a priestess. Women also gained status by amassing wealth through trading, farming, or weaving, and were treated as wealthy persons.

From political point of view, the Igbos had no king. Their "kings" were priests (Eze). In the novel there is no king as it is shown by the following answer to the missionaries: "They asked who the king of the village was, but the villagers told them there was no king. "We have men of high title and the chief priest and the elders," they said. So, when they first arrived in Mbanta, the missionaries expected to find a king.

In Igbo society, there were some secret societies for men and women exclusively and some for both the sexes. In chapter ten of *Things Fall Apart* the egwugwu (masked ancestors) decide over the legal village cases. They take action against the Christian church with much wisdom and did not shed any blood. But it is the colonisers who took bloody revenge on the colonised people by totally wiping out villages for misunderstanding between an intruder Christian man and some aggressive Igbo people which resulted in killing of the Christian man.

There is a realistic effect with the structures of kinship and particularly marriage. In real life, in Africa, marriage was a fundamental aspect of the survival of the societies and followed a certain number of principles. Polygamy was common. In the novel, marriage is essentially seal according to a precise ritual of real world. The theme of polygamy recurs in the novel.

The white missionaries arrive in Umuofia. They serve as a ray of hope to the people that Igbo religion gives no favour to. For example, it is common and acceptable practice in Igbo culture that twins are killed, boys are sacrificed or dead infants are mutilated etc. (Achebe, xxxvi). Some villagers are excited to go along with the white men's idea seeing that it is the only way to escape from their own religion. Okonkwo's son Nwoye is among the first converts to

Christianity (Achebe, 107). The decision came after the sacrifice of Ikemefuna who was almost a brother to Nwoye. Nwoye was totally against the decision made by Igbo to kill his brother, hence he protests against this act by joining the church and choosing to attend school. Okonkwo ends up disowning his son, Nwoye after he abandons the Igbo religion. Another convert to Christianity is a pregnant mother. She converts to Christianity to protect her unborn child or children.

Achebe is successful in making readers aware that although the effect of European colonialism challenges the culture of Igbo, the benefits of it can also be seen. Igbo society stands to benefit from the school and from other smaller things such as bicycles that the white men come with. Forcing Igbo people to abandon their own way of life to follow theirs seems to be the only factor that makes the white missionaries bad people in history.

Conclusion

Achebe's novel shatters the stereotypical European portraits about the native Africans. By unfolding the devastating effects of colonialism on the life of the Igbo people in *Things Fall Apart* Chinua Achebe has successfully made a comprehensible demarcation between the pre-colonial and the post-colonial life of the Igboland in Nigeria. By setting these two periods opposite to each other Achebe demonstrates the value and authenticity of the Igbo traditions in a more unambiguous manner. Thus this paper is an attempt to show an insight of pre and Post-colonialism on Igbo community in late 19th century Nigeria. It is argued that the interaction between the whites and the Igbo people had both negative and positive consequences. It is evident in Achebe's novel that the Europeans greatly influenced the lifestyle of Igbo community.

Works Cited

Achebe, Chinua. *Things Fall Apart.* Oxford: Heinemann Educational publishers, 1996. Print.

____ . "Chinua Achebe." Interview by Brandford Morrow. *Conjunctions 17* (Fall 1991). Print.

Ashcroft, Bill; Griffiths, Gareth, & Tiffin, Helen. *The Post-Colonial Studies Reader*, London: Taylor & Francis, 2003.Print.

Bressler CE, *Literary Criticism: An Introduction to Theory & Practice*, New Jersey: Prentice Hall, 1999. Print.

Boehmer E. *Colonial and Post-Colonial Literature,* Oxford & New York: Oxford University Press, 1995. Print.

"Colonialism." *Oxford English Dictionary* (www.oed.com).

Finneran, Richard J. Ed. *The Collected Poems of W.B. Yeats*. New York: Scribner, 1996. Print.

Gandhi L. *Post-Colonial Theory: A Critical Introduction*, Delhi: 1999. Print.

Ohadike DC. *Igbo Culture and History*, London: Heinemann, 2000. Print.

Tyson, Louis. *Critical Theory Today: A User-Friendly Guide.* New York: Routledge, 2006. Print.

3

A House of My Own: *A House for Mr. Biswas*

Dr. Shachi Sood and **Dr. Saleem Wani**

Naipaul's first major novel *A House for Mr. Biswas* belongs with such classics of New literatures as Patrick White's *Voss* and Chinua Achebe's *Things Fall Apart* in which through portrayal of an individual the complexities and aspirations of the colonised self is represented. Like these two novels, it is imaginative, fictional recreation of the past. The main characters, places and events are largely based on Naipaul's reminiscence of his early life in Trinidad. The novel is an individual's search for authentic selfhood which is symbolised in his desire to turn his state of unhousement into enhousement. Biswas's desperate desire to have a house of his own is an allegorical representation of the colonial man's desires to locate his place at a strange and alien world, "To his son's question 'Who are you'. Mr. Biswas replies, 'I am just somebody. Nobody at all. I am just a man you know." (Mason, 46)

The novel is in the tradition of James Joyce's Portrait of the Artist as a Young Man because Naipaul's alter-ego Anand gives us a glimpse of what it was to grow up as a young man in Trinidad. *A House for Mr. Biswas* is different from the earlier novels of Naipaul in some aspects like first, in the novel exhaustive portrayal of an East Indian family along with the acclimatisation of an individual in Trinidad society and his attainment of a social distinctiveness is given. Secondly, even though it is the most personal of Naipaul's novel yet it is not limited to a personal social context but talks about the predicament of colonial man in a post-colonial world. In this sense Biswas is the colonial everyman.

A House for Mr. Biswas is located solidly in the geography and history of Trinidad and Tobago during the period from 1931-1948. The details of a world ridden by orthodox customs and rituals are delineated. Child labour, rigid caste relations and child bribes were the norms in the world:

> It is an economically under developed world where
> Colonialism has made many children old before they
> Can enjoy their childhood (Mr. Biswas himself appears
> Never to have a childhood in that he is never called
> Anything but Mr. Biswas.) Dearth of food is an everyday
> Fact of life, life expectancy is short and ambition is not a
> Part of natural order. (Cudjoe, 52)

A House for Mr. Biswas provides a social history of the community brought in the mid-nineteenth century to Trinidad replace the freed black slaves. The Indian were indentured laborers on contracts with few right, the British later refused to pay for their return. In Trinidad the Indians reformed their societies, even restoring caste distinctions and purchased land for farming, but they remained isolated from the dominant White and Black communities, had no education in English and no legal rights e.g. Hindu marriages, were for many decades unrecognised by law. During Naipaul's childhood improvised homeless Indians who spoke only Hindi were still expecting to return some day to Mother India.

When talk of independence came to Trinidad the Hindu Indians felt insecure, fearing being left by the British under the dominance of the brown and the black communities which had organised themselves politically and which concentrated in the cities having gained access to English language education, staffed the police service and civil service and influenced the government. The British labor party wanted decolonisation and favored Black intellectuals like Eric Williams, who had studied in England, to lead the nation. But for Trinidadian Indian the rhetoric of decolonisation was filled with Black Nationalism, pan-Africanism, Judea-Christian notions of black racial deliverance and Marxist models of single party state. In such a situation the Hindu Indian was the outsider, the marginal, the opposition to those who felt destined to inherit the apparatus of the state at independence.

Eric Williams who led Trinidad to self-government and independence was a brilliant, ruthless politician who demanded discipline and who treated violently those whom he considered enemies: opposition political leaders were ruined and forced into exile. Those within the ruling party who opposed its corruption and waste were destroyed. Williams built his party around rhetoric of Black Nationalism while cooperating with the local white business community. He found a place for the Indian Moslems but treated Hindu Indians as enemies and regarded their opposition to national independence as treason. Elections were characterised by violence and by Indian claims the results were rigged. Agriculture, the area of the economy dominated by Indians shared in the government; even now tensions run high between blacks and Indians in Trinidad.

Naipaul hated the narrow, circumscribed, brutal life which surrounded him in Trinidad with its limited possibilities, small range of professions, notorious political corruption and racial and religious conflicts. Traditional Indian culture was decaying as its rituals did not fit with the society in Trinidad. The Indians among whom he was raised lived in a social order of their own, uninvolved with other races. The Trinidadians of African descent appeared to have no traditional culture of their own and modeled themselves on English. The local Whites had produced nothing of lasting value, were drunkards, uneducated and privileged. They had the best jobs. There was a bond between the descendants of former slaves and slave owners from which the Indians were excluded and which resulted in the Blacks replacing with the Whites as the dominant group as Trinidad moved towards self-government. Naipaul wanted to escape and had his own fantasies of being one of the early Aryan horsemen who conquered India and created its great Sanskrit culture.

The novel starts with an expression, acclamation of sorts, on the life of Mohun Biswas. The first name Mohun means considerably, "beloved", the name that has been assigned to Lord Krishna by the milkmaids. The Prologue also talks about the complicacies of life, such as dream of a profession and a house of his own, esteemed objects like Biswas's yellow typewriter, his failures and his achievements and then his life's story from birth to death. The novel divides that story into two parts with six and seven sections respectively. The plot has symbolic significance and provides an effective backdrop of chaos against which Mr. Biswas sets out on his quest for form. The sections included in Part I and Part II concentrate on the two halves of the hero's life one predominately rural and the other more urban. Part I of the novel visits his ancestral origins and childhood days which reflect his dependence on his uncle Bhandat and later on the Tulsi's family (his in-laws) to his distracted departure for Port of Spain and the commencement of his career as a reporter for the Trindad sentinel.

Part II talks about his career at the sentinel, his alteration of jobs and residencies. It also reflects his son's increasing expectations contrasting with his own declining ambition, his deteriorating health and discharge from the sentinel and finally his death of a heart attack at the age of forty-six. The novel's chapter divisions suggests that Biswas's life is largely shaped by basic necessities-food, shelter, security and identity which are a contrast pressure on him and his family reversing his intention and undermining his dreams.

The protagonist has a picturesque existence moving from place to place changing jobs and housed frequently. At Tulsi store in Awacas he meets Shama, a Tulsi daughter, whom he married mainly because of the pressure of the domineering Mrs. Tulsi and started living at Hanuman house with the other Tulsi's sons and daughters and then families. But soon conflicts arise between Biswas and Tulsis which force him to leave and work as a shopkeeper at Tulsi store in a village called Chase. After six years Biswas abandons the indebted shop and reluctantly takes a job as a driver on the Tulsi sugar estate in Green Vale. Though he is an overseer her but has to live a humiliating life with the workers in the estate barracks. In order to escape his depressing living quarters and his identity as the "son of a labourer", he hires a carpenter to build him a house away from the worker's house. When Biswas falls ill and Seth, his brother in law and manager at Tulsi's family business takes him to Hanuman House to recuperate, the angry workers burn down his house. Biswas with a wife and two children to support finds himself houseless and jobless. After having recovered from his ill health he leaves his family to look for a job in the city, Port of Spain.

In the Part two of the novel Biswas switches to a profession and moves into a house of his own. At the onset he finds work as a sign writer at the Trinidad sentinel and afterward gets an opportunity to be a reporter for the newspaper. As a writer, Biswas started writing a short story, "Escape" which he failed to complete. He soon become frustrated with this monotonous job, he quits the job and gets a higher paying one at the social welfare department. He involved himself more enthusiastically in his son Anand's education and future than his own professional and literary ambitions. He is enormously overjoyed when Anand win a scholarship to a college and then to a University in England. Biswas realises his lifelong ambition by purchasing a house on Sikkim street. But soon he discovers that he has been tricked out of his dream of a house of his own by an unscrupulous agent. His health gradually deteriorates and he gets a heart attack which leaves him unable to work and he is laid off. Shortly before he dies:

> He imagines a gallant, half-moking, un-self-pitying
> Headline for his obituary – "ROVING REPORTER
> PASSES ON" – but the actual notice reads, "JOUR-
> -NALIST DIES SUDDENLY". The difference
> Between the two headlines the one fanciful. The
> Other matter-of-fact-encapsulates Biswas's life
> History: fantasy rejected or revised by history.
> His dreams and history modification of them sum
> Up the struggles of his life and concentrate the
> various forces shaping him, his community and society.
>
> (Weiss, 51)

The unsettled period of Naipaul's own childhood, moving houses, living among relatives, is reflected in Biswas's story as, probably are fears for the future of the Indian's in Trinidad and the insecurities of his early period as a writer in London. Houses, gardens and family gatherings are often symbols in Naipaul's novels because they represent order, society, civilisation, achievement or at least their potential or ideal even when actually disillusioning. The father's obstinacy is reflected in Biswas's rejection of the Tulsi's and his satire of Hindu practices such as parentally arranged marriages and the tradition of not educating the female child. Seepersad Naipaul like Biswas actually remained an outsider, even within his own family, "my father had always been on the other side. The family with all its pundits was the defenders of the orthodox Hindu faith. My father wasn't." (Weiss, 62)

Mr. Biswas is not just a representation of Naipaul's father he becomes a symbol of the displaced colonial self. By equating him with Rama and Lear, both of whom suffer some sort of exile and displacement from their kingdoms, Naipaul has invested Biswas's personal struggle with universal implications. The leitmotif of the novel is the protagonist's search for order amidst disorder and chaos. Naipaul uses imagery of darkness, unhousement and decay to convey the alienation and misery experienced by Biswas. Like a picaro he moves from house to house, place to place and job to job. His desire to own a house and have a settled job is symbolic of his desire to reclaim his roots. Right from the outset Mr. Biswas seems suffering from all pervasive sense of insecurity. His birth is dominated by inauspicious signs, as he is born with six fingers. The pundit predicts that he will have "an unlucky sneeze" and "will eat up his father". The boy who is later ironically called Mohan. The beloved, is set apart at the moment of his birth, by the title "Mr." which he keeps throughout his book. The purpose of giving the comic title, "Mr." is not to make him a ridiculous figure, but to provide a constant reminder of his struggle to attain some human dignity in a world which is often denying it to him:

> Malnutrition gave him the shallowest of chests…it never
> Bothered him that he didn't go to school. Life was unpleasant

> Only because the pundit had forbidden him to go near ponds
> And rivers. (Naipaul, 22)

Mr. Biswas's life is flooded with calamities and misfortunes. Two important incidents of his life that make the high point in the plot and setting off the series of disruptions in Biswas's life are his father's death by drowning, when his father tries to save Biswas and his marriage to Shama, the Tulsi daughter which is in fact the most catastrophic event in his life. In the Tulsi tradition, Mr. Biswas goes to live with his wife's family, and he is trapped in their suffocating world. He joins the ranks of the Tulsi son-in-law whose names were forgotten and they became Tulsis. Mr. Biswas is now completely imprisoned. The Tulsis symbolise the disorder that Mr. Biswas is constantly fighting to escape. Their abode Hanuman House is the major battle ground where Mr. Biswas wages a war to free himself from the tyranny of the mighty Tulsis. The house is named after Hanuman, the Indian deity of strength and power but the statue of Hanuman on the top of the house is depicted as sinister and alien to Biswas. The image focuses on the displacement of the Indian milieu in an alien society which is represented not only by the unity but the fragmented nature of the Tulsi family. For Biswas the atmosphere inside Hanuman house is an oppressive and alien as the society outside it. The description of Tulsi household permeates with images of impenetrable darkness, reflecting the Tulsi frame of mind and Biswas's own fear of and resistance to that darkness.

When he goes to work in the Tulsi estate he is threatened not only by the workers but also by the natural world. A terrible storm occurs. Winged ants invade the house, bite Anand and soon die. A column of fire ants appear and soon capture and cart off the winged ants. Anand hears human voices outside the house which he and his father think are those of dismissed workers planning to harm them. The wind and torrential rain worsen, the roof shakes, some of the corrugated sheets are torn off or flap dangerously. The house seems likely to collapse. There is thunder, lightning, the wind blows out the lamp and "when the lightning went out the room was part of the black void." (Naipaul, 292) Anand hears human voices outside the house which he and his father think are those of dismissed workers planning to harm them. The wind and the torrential rain worsen the roof shakes, some of the corrugated sheets are torn off or flap dangerously. The house seems likely to collapse. There is danger, lightning the wind blows out the lamp and "when the lightning went out the room was part of the black void". (Naipaul, 292) Anand screams and screams as the wind sweeps through the now floorless, wall less house until he sees a labourer carrying hurricane lamp and a cutlass looking for a lost calf. The lamp illuminates a 'wet chaos'; but Anand and Biswas are now saved, although the latter has temporarily lost his mind and does not know where he is and what has happened.

The Biblical symbol of the flood echo the beginning of the time before creation, an unmaking of the protection, comforts and order offered by civilisation and society. In the "Green Vale" chapter the protections of society are removed and Biswas and Anand are isolated, helpless against the violence of others and the natural world. They are reduced to the condition of the insects that are defenseless against the attack of organised group of other insects. Nature is uncaring, dangerous; life is short; creatures naturally at war with each other and protected only by being part of a community. Biswas's fear of harm and death is also a fear of extinction and annihilation. The void is in his mind, a kind of insanity in which his selfhood and individuality are lost. The stripping away of the physical comforts and protection of civilisation results in a loss of rationality. He is metamorphosed into something primitive, sub-human. Although supposedly a rationalist he chants a mantra for protection. The chaos in Biswas's life has been transmitted into his son.

Like many of Naipaul's central characters, Biswas is also an existential rebel, an outsider, who refused to conform. The first part of the novel shows such rebellion as futile because Biswas is without the means of self-support. Biswas can only taunt and insult those upon whom he is dependent. Unlike Biswas's rebellion his wife Shama remains closely attached to the Tulsi family and accepts pressure to conform. Tulsi house is hierarchical feudal society with Mrs. Tulsi and his two sons the royalty. There are some suitable roles for those who conform such as Hari who becomes family priest and pundit. Everyone except the mother and her two sons are treated as dependents.

In the later part of the novel Naipaul presents Biswas as an antihero in his refusal to conform. His resilience, his ability to bounce back is remarkable. In spite of numerous odds against him he never ceased to love, romance and freedom and a life when he and not the Tulsis would decide his future. A house becomes the symbol of everything that has been denied to him by life. The house is the single integrating metaphor that provides unity to the multitudes of characters, events and location. Even the doll's house which Mr. Biswas buys for his daughter Savi, stands for order and security. The Tulsis at once recognise the symbolic implication of the doll's house and consider it as a threat and an embodiment of Mr. Biswas's rebellion. They destroy the doll house immediately as they cannot tolerate the assertion of individualism on the part of Mr. Biswas.

The images of decay are replaced by images of hope and brightness. The butterfly orchid that Mr. Biswas had planted was "flowering again", the son was ready to move out to a bright future. In the first half of the novel, Mr. Biswas strives to cope up with his milieu and almost loses his sanity in the process but finally succeeds in coming out of his chaos and enters a new setting. The anarchy surrounding Mr. Biswas acquires new perspective in the second half, which ends in his final triumph over his hostile environment.

Works Cited

Cudjoe, Reginald. Selwyn. *V.S. Naipaul: A Materialistic Reading.* Amherst: University of Massachussetts Press. 1988.52. Print

Mason, Nondita. *The Fiction of V.S. Naipual.* Calcutta: The World Press Pvt. Ltd. 1986. 46. Print.

Naipaul, V.S. *A House for Mr. Biswas.* London: Penguin. 1969. Print.

Weiss, Timothy F. *On the Margins: The Art of Exile in V.S. Naipaul.* Amherst: University of Massachussetts. 1992. 51.Print.

4

The Impact of Binaries in Constituting Social Conflicts: A Reading of *A Fine Balance* by Rohinton Mistry

Mahendran U.

Binaries in general are twofold. But to be specific, the first one within the two, is taken to be superior and influential. To exemplify, man and women, rich and the poor, the educated and illiterate, able and disabled, and others, have been operational in exaggerating the former at the cast of the later. But the deconstructive and postcolonial theoreticians have offered significant analytical tools, which have been utilised to reverse the order of those has hitherto been considered as an unassailable ultimate. The invalidation of the 'double-binds', has not only reduced the important accorded to the primary one, the so-called inherent meaning has been subverted. The contradiction could not be entertained, as it carried preconceived notion, effectively supplied into the pair to demystify the second of the two. Ironically, the 'logo centric' analysis has not put an end to the realistic presence of the binary opposites completely. The novel standing for textual production, do contain several instance of discriminatory aspects, which is to be viewed from the perspective of collective conscious that of the society. In other words, novel, which is intended to record the compelling reality, must have to accommodate binary in its unaltered form.

The role of binary is brought into action through Ishvar, an elderly and sensible figure found in the fiction. He informs Maneck, whom Ishvar and Om have encountered on their journey to the city, that he is not prepared to prolong his stay in this unimpressive urban condition. "We have also come for a short time only. To earn some money, then go back to our village. What is the use of such a big city? Noise and crowds, no place to live, water scarce, garbage everywhere Terrible" (Mistry, 5). This analysis is a typical example for the age-old distinction of nature verses culture. Here, it is culture, which is getting destabilised with a hope to elevate the lifestyle exist in village. As far as water and other natural amenities are concerned, it is village, which would stay at the top. Nonetheless, when it comes to economical upliftment, the order will have to be reinstated. The rural would be pushed to the edge of the pair, and the urban scenario will assume significant position. Even within the binary, the signified has been restricted to the level of impermanency due to an indeterminate social background. Maneck on the other hand, reveals that he is longing to get back to his own place after completing his higher education, because of his closest association with his home, which is picturesquely surrounded by the mountain region.

After realising that all three have been advised to come to a same place, they decide to reach out together. Dina Dalal, who is going to employ the tailors, conduct a formal interview. Finally, they express their consent to work for her. Dina is unhappy to have found Maneck Kohlah, who happens to be the son of her closest sophisticated friend in the company of the tailors. She does not want him to have any sought of relationship with them. She instructs him as, "You must be careful who you talk to. Never know what kind of crooks you might run into" (Mistry, 6). The judgment of Dina proves to be self-opinionated. She firmly believes that the tailors should have been dishonest. She bluntly comes to such conclusion based on their Physical appearance. The threadbare clothes, in which they are found, could have made her to postulate this kind of inadmissible suggestion to Maneck. If this discrimination is looked at in a larger context, it is this psychic conception, which does play a vital role in constituting classes and sections in the society. It is highly evident when Dina cautions Maneck to behave in a way which is expected from the person belonging to superior class. "No. and I should tell right now – I don't like your chatting so much with them. They are my employees; you are Aban Kohlah's son. A distance has to be kept" (Mistry, 187). Such sharp statement should have been nothing but a preconceived attitude towards embedded class structure in the society.

An intensified biased approach is getting reflected in the words of Dina when she offers a piece of advice to Maneck. Once again, it is to prevent him from the company of the tailors, specifically from the younger one of them. It cannot be considered that Dina is desirous of breaking their friendship to make Omprakash work more for her. The premeditated psyche of Dina emerges to align her with the society which is irrevocably rooted in the class structure. "I was ashamed for you, to see you behaving like a loafer. Like a roadside mavali. From Omprakash I cannot expect better. But you, from a good Parsi family. And I left you to watch after them, I trusted you" (Mistry, 197). Dina evaluates the characters of both Omprakash and Maneck based on the family reputation, rather than what they are in reality. She is not prepared to give a thought over such perception at all. In fact, it is Omprakash and Ishvar who work right through the day for her livelihood. They ensure that she is a punctual and disciplined contractor. But they are taken to be untrustworthy, mainly because they belong to the lower strata in the society.

In reality, Dina is getting orders from Mrs. Gupta. Dina has been assured of continuous contract, if she is able to complete the work by employing the skilled tailors. Consequently, the working-class is found to be hierarchical. Dina Dalal could have promoted herself to the position of supervisor. But she has been subservient to the manager of the exports named Revoir, who is none other than Mrs. Gupta. The manager lets out to Dina that perfection is utmost as for as the assignment is concerned. Moreover, she informs her as, "I told you before, I prefer to deal with private contractors. Union loafers want to work less and get more money. That's the curse of this country – laciness" (Mistry, 47). Mrs. Gupta's remark is nothing but presumptive in a stunning manner. That regardless assumption has made her to approach the union based workers in such low esteem. Her utter disgust is absolutely aimed at elevating personal expectations, rather than being considerate to the needs of employees, irrespective of the division to which they belong. The split among workers as union oriented and private is a wishful binary generated by the capitalist.

The self-centered attitude can be realised when Mrs. Gupta conveys her extreme satisfaction over the declaration of the internal emergency. According to her, the emergency has brought an end to all the troubles faced by the capitalist in the form of protest, agitations and strikes. They all have been arrested and lodged in prison to prevent internal disturbance. "The Prime Minister's declaration yesterday of the internal emergency had incarcerated most of the parliamentary opposition, along with thousands of trade unionists, students and socialworkers. Isn't that good news?" (Mistry, 47). The statement by Mrs. Gupta does open up other binaries as well. The emergency period, which was in vogue from 26th June 1975 until 18th January 1977, had created a political binary. Those who did not extend their support to the emergency were considered as spiteful threat to the internal peace of the country. The protesters and the union workers got manhandled in the name of maintaining discipline across the country. It had resulted in favoring those who were influential and the other who were not blessed with such specialties. The poor and the weaker section of the society were the ultimate sufferers at the hands of the officials and party men.

There are several instance of how those impoverished people would have been targeted during the emergency. In actuality, the poor were pushed to the condition of binary which is twice in proportion. First, they are being conditioned as poverty-stricken. Secondly, they get disillusioned and displaced due to the ruthless programmes implemented during the emergency. The people, who live in slums, are asked to produce the Family Planning Certificate to be able to acquire ration card. When Ishvar and Omprakash go to a government office to get it, they will be told authoritatively as follows, "If you let me arrange for your vasectomy, your application can be approved instantly" (Mistry, 118). The tailors would be shocked at the option laid out for procuring ration card. Though the tailors would plead him saying that they have already undergone the operation, immediately he would demand for a family planning certificate (FPC). The rations officer would go a step further and tell Ishvar and Omprakash that the sterilisation can be done again, even it is performed already. The doctor, whom he is in touch with, will do it once again as an additional Favor. "Lots of people do it twice. Brings more benefits. Two transistor radios" (Mistry, 118). It shows very clearly that the poverty of the people is being treated as an advantage by the government which has become dictatorial.

Such inconsiderate implementations have been the major reasons for the split of the powerful and the powerless in the political arena. The government would repeat it time and again that it has been working for the upliftment of the poor. But in reality, it is the poor, who get victimised, and would be driven to the position of passive recipient. They neither can protest nor can resist by asserting the rights ensured in the constitution. Here in this particular novel, in the name of beautification programme, all those innocent people, who are the inhabitants of hutment colony, would forcefully be evacuated. Without any prior intimation what so ever, their dwellings would be demolished in a merciless manner. First the officials would enter into the colony as though, they have come to inspect and bring possible change to the place. Later, the bulldozers would be rushed in, and destroying work would commence in a fracture of second. Ishvar and Omprakash come cheerfully with the hope of offering a special supper to Maneck. But to their horror, Rajaram would make them aware of what did take place. "The men, the once who said they were safety inspectors. They tricked us. Sent by the government, they said, to check the colony. At first the people were pleased, the authorities were taking some interest. Maybe improvements were coming-water, latrine, lights, like they kept promising at the voting time. So we did as they told us" (Mistry, 199). Later, when all would be out of there huts, the gigantic machines would enter and level down all the habitations. Here it is government which seems to capitalise on the poverty of the slum dwellers. They get uprooted by the government which should have protected and ensured that they are unperturbed with sufficient facilities. The multiple entanglements experienced by the people of hutment colony are the major reason for such unstoppable humiliation. Being rendered as powerless and moneyless, they have no choice but to get accustomed to what life in other stage might pose. The persistency of such binary is intolerable, primarily because, it distances them so far from the mainstream that none is able to feel the disillusionment as it could have been processed in their metabolism.

Having been driven to the level of homeless, Ishvar and Omprakash, sleep at the entrance of a pharmacy by paying little amount to the security guard. In one such night, they witness Sergeant Kesar, accompanied by the facilitator who has demanded money for the ration card which is denied to them for not possessing family planning certificate. Under the pretext of beautification programme, they forcefully gather up beggars and the other uncared people in a truck to be taken out of the city. "Looks like they are waking all the beggars. They are beating them, pushing them into a truck" (Mistry, 217). It is carried out not to arrange for a better place for all of them. Instead, they are all sold out to a contractor by bribing the facilitator and Sergeant Kesar. Including the lunatics, the blind and the children are loaded up. "Those blind ones are fine. Blindness is no problem, they can do things with their hands. Children also, many little works for them" (Mistry, 218). Though the facilitator conveys his disappointment over the counting that of the beggar who is found to be crippled on the grounds that he and few others will be unfit for a construction work, the police do not take his murmur into consideration.

The predicament of the beggars and the other physically weaker people explained above would reveal how the binary is perpetrated in the social hierarchy. The police, who are physically strong, are deployed in the task of washing out the beggars from the city. Again the absolute power is exercised to batter the most affected one. The atrocity goes to the peak when the police compel Ishvar and Omprakash to get into the truck due to the shortage in the count which should have been ninety-six. Though they deny that they are not beggars but serving as tailors, the police don't pay attention at all. They will be told that sleeping on streets is illegal. When the tailors try to explain the reason for sleeping in such place, Sergeant Kesar would twist it as yet another breach of law. "Police-sahab, we are sleeping here only because your men came with machines and destroyed our Jhopadpatti. What? You lived in a Jhopadpatti? Two wrongs don't make a right. You could get double punishment" (Mistry, 219). The power being sanctioned to the government wing which is bestowed with enormous muzzle power, nothing but such repressive tendency would only be geared up.

The emergency would turn out to be biased to the fullest possible when Nawaz, the unfortunate tailor get arrested on the false charges. The man who owes money to Nawaz would make use of the emergency, and get him imprisoned. It is done deliberately with a sheer motive to exhibit the political influence upon the working class. The faultless Nawaz, will have to surrender himself without any kind of resistance, because it is law which has been used to justify the illegal accusation. It would be obvious when Ishvar and Om be intimated about the emergency as follows, "With the emergency, everything is upside-down. Black can be made white, day turned into night. With the right influence and a little cash, sending people to jail is very easy. There's even a new law called MISA to simplify the whole procedure." (Rohinton Mistry, 202). The intensity is such that whoever might have posed as serious threat to the powerful individual, they could have been targeted. The binary of this sought is more painful. The reason is that the economically weaker section must have been taken into task, with the conscientious act that they are politically voiceless.

The unjust fate underwent by Omprakash will have to be taken into account in order to understand the communal bias. This particular novel, being written in line with the chronological happenings of India, contains some hard-hitting facts with regard to social discrimination as well. Omprakash and his family would be burnt alive, just because they have emerged economically stable in their village. The upper cast people have become extremely intolerant of the progress that Narayan, the dead father of Omprakash, has made as a tailor. He has constructed an enviable house with a tailoring shop. Some years ago, Narayan's father Dukhi has completely stopped to execute his work in the village as a lower cast laborer. All have added fuel to the jealousy fire which has been burning in the form of Thakur Dharamsi, the influential upper-class man in the village. According to him, it is Dukhi who is to be blamed first. It is he who has transferred the cobblers into tailors. "What the ages had put together, Dukhi had dared to break asunder; He had turned cobblers into tailors, distorting society's timeless balance. Crossing the line of cast had to be punished with the utmost severity" (Mistry, 99). Thakur Dharamsi considers that Dukhi has broken the age-old sacred tradition, strictly adhered in this village. As for as determining binary in the village is concerned, the professional based discrimination is yet another crucial one. People are limited to a specific lifestyle in keeping with the work that they carry on generation after generation. The word "balance" stands for something it does not contain. It sharply reminds of powerful imbalance which is operated out in the society to favor a section of people with vested interest.

Conspicuously, Narayan has kept fighting for the equal rights for the lower class to which he does belong. He is not able to digest the fact that untouchability is found very much alive even after the independence. Once he would argue with his father Dukhi and express his innate desire. "More than twenty years have passed since independence. How much longer? I want to be able to drink from the village well, worship in the temple, walk where I like" (Mistry, 96). Such binaries are kept alive to maintain social hierarchy. Especially they can be found in terms of cast distinction and communal segregation. These painful regulations have effectively been imbibed in the psyche of the society. After that, those informed behaviors would be there to compete with one another to establish respective rights over the general wealth. To be frank, those common properties do attain enormous focus, because they function as an exact manifestation of that binary which is getting constituted. Moreover, Narayan is terribly upset over the approach of the upper cast. He would convey his utter disappointment to his father that they treat the lower cast people just like the animals. The ill-treatment projected in any form could only be considered as binary in the crudest condition.

Narayan's rightful demand to cast his vote by signing on the sheet, eventually results in his brutal death at the hands of communal custodians. Thakur and his men torture, and finally hang Narayan and two others to death. "The still, silent bodies were taken down from the tree. When they began to stir, the ropes were transferred from their ankles to their necks, and the three were hanged. The bodies were displayed in the village square" (Mistry, 98). Even the legally granted provisions are vehemently disapproved by the biased men. For them, the inadmissible modification brought out in any form could not be entertained. They realised that such change would amount to the precarious condition, to the firm ground on which they have stood so far and discharged absolute power over the rest. It is this binaric psychic resonance which has been major cause in inflecting fatal end to Narayan and his companions. The behavior of inhumane bigotry being practiced by Thakur and his senseless subordinates is of course, a perfect embodiment of socialised binary.

Later on, when the voting gets over, Thakur Dharamsi lets his men hunt down the lower cast people. Irrespective of Men and women, or aged and children, all are wounded, attacked and murdered. He wants to bring back the oldest tradition of making the lower-class highly respectful. In other words, Thakur is convinced to erect an unbridgeable gap as it has existed earlier. He firmly believes that it is possible only through merciless intimidation. The class which Thakur Dharamsi represents is not prepared to give up the superiority being enjoyed for years together. This particular unjustifiable tendency drives Thakur to commit yet another horrific crime. He locks up Dukhi and his family members inside a room and burns them alive! "The house was set alight. The first flames licked at the bound flesh. The dry winds, furiously fanning the fire, showed the only spark of mercy during this night. The blaze swiftly enfolded all six of them" (Mistry, 99). This hideous act of Thakur has gone on to sacrifice innocent lives to sustain their communal agenda, which is so much intertwined with keeping alive the ever divisive binary as an infectious force.

Works Cited

Chandra, Bipan. *India since Independence.* UK: Penguin Publishers PVT LTD, 2008. Print.

Cudden, J.A. *The Penguin Dictionary of Literary Terms and Literary Theory*. London: Penguin publication LTD, 1998. PDF file.

Eagleton, Terry. *Literary Theory An Introduction.* UK: Blackwel Pub Ltd, 2008. PDF file.

Mills, Sara. *Discourse, the New Critical Idiom*. London: Routledge, 1997. PDF file.

Mistry, Rohinton. *A Fine Balance*. London: Faber & Faber LTD, 2006. Print.

5

Depiction of Religion as an Oppressive Weapon in Chimamanda Ngozi Adichie's *Purple Hibiscus*

Dr. Romina Rashid and **Asma Zahoor**

Introduction

Literature and life have since ages been connected to each other such that the experiences of life easily find a way in the literary works of any age. Life in its entire multiplicity is far from being a simple phenomenon; its complexity owing to the varied dimensions it is composed of makes it an appropriate subject matter for literature. The culture, traditions, society, politics etc. all being an indispensable part of life are therefore also a part and parcel of literature. In the words of Mary Modupe Kolawole, "from the beginning, literature…was often a recreation of cultural histories with political and ideological undertones" (2).

Literature written in any age is shaped by the ideology that prevails during that time. This ideology is determined by the agencies in power which are in turn designated by the economic base according to Marxist thought. The prevalence of any ideology requires certain agencies which Althussar has divided into two separate groups i.e. Ideological State Apparatus (ISA) and Repressive State Apparatus (RSA). As far as the latter is concerned, it includes the ways which subconsciously work on the minds of people such that people don't get the slightest idea of being influenced. This apparatus makes use of the agencies like educational institutes, social and political structures, media, religion etc.

Religion is one of the major influences in an individual's life. In the novel, the religion has been misinterpreted and misused as an agency creating violence and dominating people in spite of their dissent which takes the form of nothing but silence. Here religion acts as a neocolonial force which paralyses the mindset of people to the point of dysfunction. The neocolonial victims like Eugene completely lose their own sense of right and wrong and rely wholly and solely on the understanding of a higher authority which in the novel is Father Benedict whom he considers superior than his Igbo traditionalists. This concept of the psychological impact of colonisation has been laid down by Fanon in *Black Skin White Masks* where he says that the internalisation of the superior status of coloniser doesn't end even after the colonisation. Instead the victims continue to appropriate themselves with the colonisers till they are rejected not only by the masters but by their own people. In the novel, the same thing happens to Eugene who because of his extremism is finally killed by his own wife after she fails to endure his further aggression.

Religion and Literature

Religion from the remote past has had an important bearing on Literature because both emerge from the same fundamental sources. Through religion, man gets connected to the Ultimate Being who provides him power to explore the substance lying behind phenomena; to attain answer to the questions like 'where', 'how' and 'when' of life. Literature on the other hand also seeks to represent the same fundamental relationship between life and its source; it tends to justify the existence and reconcile the opposing forces so as to derive comfort and consolation for the humanity in general. Because if this eternal link, religion has always been in accompaniment of literature, acting as a guiding principle. Ancient Greek Literature is fraught with the religious themes of Divine Providence, eternity and universality, reward and punishment etc. e.g. "Homeric poems are pervaded with the religious atmosphere of wonder, of obedience to the eternal, and of the recognition of the interest of the gods in human affairs" (Thwing). Likewise, though in a lesser impressive manner, the poems of Virgil bathe in religious mystery and submission.

British Literature also, since its inception, has shown no lesser connection to religion. In fact the literature of the medieval period was based on the religious themes. In addition to the Mystery Plays and Miracle Plays, the great poets took religion as the central point from which their thoughts took a flight e.g. Chaucer in *Canterbury Tales* foregrounds a religious setting in the form of a religious pilgrimage which provides a constant background against which the characters are worked out. Milton on the other side bases his magnum opus, *Paradise Lost*, entirely on the religious battle that took place between God and Satan. Even in the present day, religion doesn't cease to be an overly worked theme in literature because life itself continues to be dictated by its principles. The present paper would therefore look into this theme but from a different perspective i.e. a comparative study of two religious characters who though uphold the similar faith have markedly distinct personalities.

Religion in Essence

Religion refers to a set of beliefs, a staunch faith in the Supernatural which a person accepts as the sole source of energy, guiding us to live in a particular way. Religion makes a constant appeal to life which it believes is governed by the orderly use of reason. It emphasises the strength of emotions of love, fear, curiosity, reverence etc. and the imperative of conscience and self-controlled will (Thwing). In the novel such ideas about religion are held by Father Amadi who, rather than being a staunch religious bigot like Eugene, is quite liberal in his attitude towards religion. However his liberality does not purport misrepresentation of religion. "Amadi, like everything else around Ifeoma and her children in Nsukka is authentically Christian. Despite his down-to-earth approach to life and his creative relationship with others, he is nonetheless ever mindful of his vocation to priesthood" (Ogwude). Therefore, he becomes a point of greater attraction because of his individualised understanding of Catholic doctrines with which more people are able to associate than otherwise. This is corroborated by the words of Ifeoma who says that Father "is so popular with everybody on campus already. He has invitations to eat in everybody's house". Amaka responds by saying, "I think he connects with our family the most" (PH, 67). Agreeing with this view of Amadi, Ogaga Okuyade writes:

> Through Father Amadi she [Kambili] discovers a new brand of Catholicism, which is not mechanical and dictatorial but lithe, which is a direct contrast to the one her father and Father Benedict practice, one which makes room for dissent. (Okuyade, 2009)

Father Amadi is a storehouse of love and passion, simultaneously a man of righteousness who will not allow his love to take an undesirable form. He uses this device of love to help Kambili break that cocoon in which Eugene had compelled her to live without giving her a chance to cherish the life God bestowed on her. But Amadi on the other hand becomes a reason that Kambili smiles. He breaks through her programmed psychic networking and cracks her frozen sense of comportment while utilising religion to achieve his goal (Okuyade) when he says to her:

> Do you love Jesus?" Father Amadi asked, standing up. I was startled. "Yes. Yes, I love Jesus". "Then show me. Try and catch me, show me you love Jesus." He had hardly finished speaking before he dashed off and I saw the blue flash of his tank. I did not stop to think; I stood up and ran after him. (Adichie, 176)

For Amadi, religion is to be imbibed in essence rather than in the outward practices. If a person doesn't serve humanity and create comfort for them, his faith is maligned no matter with how much of strictness and dedication he follows the religious rituals. Owing to this mentality, he doesn't mind singing Igbo songs during the Mass or for that matter using Igbo language in the Mass. For him, one language is not superior to another and using Igbo language would in no way compromise with the solemnity of the Mass. This very mindset also allows him to wear the clothes which would have been otherwise considered ungodly and sinful for a priest, as expressed by Kambili when she says that Amadi "look[ed] even more unpriestly than before, in khaki shorts that stopped just below his knees" (74). Though he wore shorts at certain times, he didn't demean the dignity of his priestly robe which he used during the religious congregations when he "wore his soutane, long-sleeved and loose-fitting, with a loose black rope slant[ing] around his waist" (80). This shows that neither the language nor the dress according to Amadi determined the intensity of an individual's faith.

In addition to fulfilling his duty to the church he is at the forefront when it comes to helping people especially belonging to his own community. Adichie highlights this aspect of his personality not once but many times in the text. When Ifeoma runs out of petrol and has to visit Abba to bring her ailing father to her house in Nsukka, it is Father Amadi who furnishes her the petrol from the reserve stock of chaplaincy because he can't stand the sorrow and dejection of his people. He says, "We have some emergency fuel reserves in the chaplaincy… I am sure I could get you a gallon. *Ekwuzina*, don't sound that way" (74). Amadi doesn't maintain a façade of respectability and alienation when it comes to establish affectionate cords with people of any age especially with children. His sober and fun loving nature allows Chima to pounce on him whenever Amadi visits while Amaka talks with such a frankness which Kambili could have never imagined with Father Benedict or even her own father Eugene. Likewise with the boys, he is one of them, playing football with all the seal and enthusiasm that Kambili found lacking in other priests. She says, "With his upper body bare, his shoulders were a broad square…My eyes were on the football field, on Father Amadi's running legs, on the flying white-and-black football, on the many legs of the boys, which all looked like one leg" (87). Thus kambili found in Amadi a real human in flesh and blood, with all the human considerations, which is the basic condition for one to be a priest. Amadi therefore doesn't use his religion as a shield against the societal forces neither he makes it an instrument of personal gain. His religion enables him unite people and create a world full of love and respect.

Religion as a Tool of Oppression

Religion enlightens us to spread love and oneness among people based on universal brotherhood, sympathy, mercy and compassion. However, in the novel *Purple Hibiscus,* these attributes of religion are thrown to wind as far as the character of Eugene is concerned. Outwardly, he is a staunch religious fanatic but when it comes to his own household, he is a patriarch, letting loose his tyranny over all the members. He coerces his family into following a rigid code of conduct to the extent that his children, Kambili and Jaja, become almost robotic. This regimental outlook is the result of Father Benedict's influence on him which materialises in the form of oppression that he does in the name of his Catholicism. Describing this aspect of Eugene's life, Okuyade says, "Eugene on the basis of his staunch religiosity which he has inherited from Father Benedict creates a world that lacks ventilation, which guarantees a steady relationship with outside when the inside becomes too suffocating" (Okuyade, 2010). He upholds the decadent doctrines of Catholic Christianity which in the name of inculturation are disintegrating even today. His lack of adjustment with his ancestry and acceptance of the White culture pitches him against his own traditional values (Ganyi).

Eugene's character is a composite of paradoxes. On one hand, he fights against the corruption in the political system but on the other his entire life is based on the corrupt practices of a misunderstood religion which drives him to adopt harsh measures against his family if they fail to meet his religious standards. Adichie presents an episode when Kambili due to illness breaks her Eucharist Fast almost before ten minutes of the Mass and all the members are severely beaten up by Eugene, exhibiting a totally unethical and unreligious attitude:

> He unbuckled his belt slowly...belt made of layers of brown leather... It landed on Jaja first, across his shoulder. Then Mama raised her hands as it landed on her upper arm... I put the bowl

> down just as the belt landed on my back... Papa was like a Fulani nomad…as he swung his belt at Mama, Jaja, and me, muttering that the devil would not win. We did not move more than two steps away from the leather belt that swished through the air. (Adichie, 52)

Though Eugene aspires for the freedom of his people, he colonises his family to the extent of committing brutalities on them. On one hand he distributes his wealth among the poor and needy but on the other, his own father lives with the meager resources which barely make his both ends meet. Sadiya Abubakar commenting on this aspect of Eugene says:

> It is quite surprising that Eugene, a man who has dedicated his life to fight for his people's political freedom from the threats of newly emerged government is a wife beater. His wife…seems to be very calm…silently accepting his torture which he inflicts in the guise of religious ideology (Abubakr).

Eugene …a fanatical catholic strikes fear in the hearts of his wife and children… stresses it on them that all traditional customs are devilish and unchristian, warning them against engaging in tradition-related activities and even discouraging them from developing a close relationship with his father. This he does because his father is a traditionalist (Yerima Dina). He assumes a savage behavior against everyone in the family who accept it on the excuse of religion. Thus Eugene uses religion as a tool to suppress his family such that they strangulate all their wishes and desires which he labels as ungodly and sinful.

Eugene seems to have lost all humanity as he pours boiling hot water on Kambili's feet for having shared a house with her unreligious grandfather, beating her to the level of landing her in hospital for admiring her Papa Nnukuwu's painting and altogether banishing his father from entering his house. His behavior turns even more ridiculous on his father's death. He doesn't attend the funeral though he sends the money so that the funeral could be grand. He believes that his father would straightaway land in hell being a 'heathen'. Eugene doesn't leave a single instance of inflicting torture on his family; he beats his wife to the point of inducing miscarriages not once but twice just because she keeps her wishes above his so called Godly faith.

Conclusion

From the arguments presented in above sections it is concluded that though Amadi doesn't appear to be a staunch religious person, the impact of his teachings is more than those of Father Benedict owing to the love and respect he has for others. On the contrary, Father Benedict seems to have compartmentalised the religion so that rather than appealing to the people, it suffocates them and so is finally resented. Eugene for not creating a balance in his life meets a tragic end where he is slowly poisoned by his wife whom he tortured in every possible way. Amadi on the other hand continues to preach his religion in many parts of the world and gains love and respect of all.

Works Cited

Abubakr, Sadiya. "Traumatic Experiences of Nigerian Women: An Archetypal representation in Adichie's Purple Hibiscus." *IRA – International Journal of Management and Social Science*, vol. 4, no. 3, 2016

Adichie, Chimamanda Ngozi. *Purple Hibiscus*. Sydney, HarperCollins Publishers (Australia) Pty. Ltd, 2000.

Dina, Yerima. "Conflict, Doubleness and Self-Realization in Adichie and Habila." *Research Journal of English Language and Literature (RJELAL)*, vol. 3, no. 4, 2015.

Fanon, Frantz. *Black Skin White Masks*. 1st ed., Arcway Road, London, Pluto Press, 1986.

Ganyi, Francis. "Tragic Heroes and Unholy Alliances: A Reading of Adichie's *Purple Hibiscus* and Mariama's *So Long A Letter." Global Journal of Arts Humanities and Social Sciences,* vol.1, no. 2, June 2013.

Kolawole, Mary Modupe. "Text, Textuality and Contextuality-Paradigms Lost and Paradigms Regained in Literary Theory." *Inaugural Lecture Series* 175. 28 Aug. 2017, Ile-Ife Nigeria, Oduduwa Hall, Obafemi Awolowo University.

Ogwude, Sophia O. "History and ideology in Chimamanda Adichie's fiction." *Tydskrif Vir Letterkunde*, vol. 48, no. 1, 2011.

Okunyade, Ogaga. "Changing Borders and Creating Voices:" *The Journal of Pan African Studies*, vol. 2, no. 9, Mar. 2009.

____. "Trying to Survive: Growth and Transformation in African female narratives." *California Linguistic Notes*, xxxv, no. 1, 2010.

Thwing, Charles F. "Religion and Literature." *Christian Classics Ethereal Library*, 6 Mar. 2004, www.ccel.org/s/schaff/encyc/encyc09/htm/iv.vii.cxxxix.htm. Accessed 27 Aug. 2017.

6

From Migration to Madness: Female Migration in Doris Lessing's *The Grass is Singing* and Margaret Atwood's *Alias Grace*

Gouri Kapoor

Maintenance of native identity and the values associated with it is one of the major challenges that migrants confront. Whether internal or external, migration entails adjustment and conciliation to the new culture. Given the manner in which social norms function, a higher demand is made on women for the upkeep of traditional values in most cultures. Often the literal home space – conventionally deemed 'feminine' – is the one where resistance is offered to the unfamiliar culture when immigrants find themselves contending with the pressure to adapt exerted by the majority group. The future of the minority cultural group under threat is fortified and its past sheltered in that particular space through the task of preservation assigned to women under the traditional "division of labour" scheme. As a result, migration usually has a much stronger impact on the cultural identity of a woman than that of man and home comes to be defined by values that are found absent in the outside world. Since women are the ones who are seen as repositories of the values that the immediate social environment lacks, attempts are often made to diminish immigrant women's contact with the outside culture to prevent their "corruption". In such circumstances, an equivalence exists between the native country, its culture, and the home.

Owing to their rootedness in the home and the cultural values it represents, women generally find it harder to deal with the anxiety that an interaction with an alien culture brings in its wake. The social categories of race, ethnicity, class and gender often intersect to make migration a complex, onerous occurrence, more so for the female immigrant. Migration need not always have a negative effect on women's self-identity and can also be interpreted as an opportunity for refashioning of the self along lines that their native culture may never permit. Such an exercise can provide the means of liberation from the dominant gender and sexual discourses oppressing them. Yet most women are unable to take advantage of it because their entrenchment within the native culture pre-empts an easy assimilation of the new culture. This sometimes results in a psychological conflict regarding the cultural identity they need to project in their everyday life. Lessing's *The Grass is Singing* and Atwood's *Alias Grace* present a picture of this psychological conflict, the former perhaps in its most brutal form.

One's view of oneself relies heavily on the *point of view* from which a subject looks at himself/herself. This point of view is often provided by the subject's cultural location and social milieu in which he or she lives, and it finds a microcosmic expression in the space of home. Home, in this manner, comes to act as a metaphor for the national identity, since it has a bearing on one's cultural positioning. It is also through this cascading that the idea of home becomes central to the process of self-formation and identity. Homi Bhabha appears to discuss the concept of the 'unhomely' and its importance for all post-colonial literatures keeping in mind this metaphorical connection in his essay titled *The World and The Home.*

The 'unhomely', as Bhabha puts it, is a moment when it dawns upon a subject that the boundaries between the public and the private are actually imaginary constructs. Instead of being an insular "safe haven" against the outside, her home was always under the influence of social forces that characterise the outside; it was always located *in* the world. To put this in Bhabha's own words:

> To be unhomed is not to be homeless, nor can the "unhomely" be easily accommodated in that familiar division of social life into private and the public spheres. The unhomely moment creeps up on you stealthily as your own shadow and suddenly you find yourself . . . "taking the measure of your dwelling" in a state of "incredulous terror." (Bhabha, 141)

The 'unhomely' is then an awareness of the liminality that threatens one's sense of identity based on the certitudes that are part of one's native culture. It implies a setback arising out of non-recognition of the fact that one's values are not absolute or fail-safe. Bhabha may have used the concept as a postcolonial universal, but the complexities that are a result of the intersection of race, class, sex/gender, nationality and/or ethnicity give the experience of the 'unhomely' a wide spectrum. Its different manifestations thus need to be discursively established, one of them which could be the madness that is seen displayed by the female protagonists of *The Grass is Singing* and *Alias Grace*.

Many feminist thinkers like Gilbert and Gubar, Susan Bordo and Jane M. Ussher have observed and discussed at length how psychological diseases like hysteria, anorexia nervosa, agoraphobia and claustrophobia are often a manifestation of the lack of ease felt by women in patriarchal societies. Instead of looking at these diseases purely from a psychoanalytical, medical perspective, they try to highlight their cultural signification and how it is often the overbearing societal norms that lead to the decline of the female subject's mental health. In case of the protagonists of the novels under discussion, their madness also has deep social underpinnings. The paper argues that their dis-ease is not only indicative of their discomfort with male-domination, but also with being an outsider to the culture they come to inhabit due to migration. Both of them were compelled to migrate because of the men in their lives; migration in their case was more of a compromise than a volitional act. Due to this reason, they fail to cope up with the pressures of everyday living in a cultural environment which makes them feel like outcasts. The unhinging and the 'unhoming' moment are one and the same for them.

The experience of migration does not involve a simple movement from one geographical location to another, but rather a traversing of a completely new psychological landscape. This is especially true when it comes to discussing the changes wrought upon the lives of women by migration. Traditionally, migration has been viewed as a largely male enterprise where women's migration occurs as a dependent and therefore contingent. As Kevin Kenny points out, women were a minority among the early cases of migration. This is because there were many restrictions on their movements in most countries unless they were married. Apart from the Irish in the late 19th century, there weren't many young, single women who migrated to other countries on their own during those times. As a result, little attention has been paid historically to women's migratory and diasporic experiences which are generally deemed to be no different from that of men. In recent times, however, the growth of feminist thought has ensured that the approach usually adopted to study the role of gender in migration is revised. Substantial attention is now being paid to women's specific experience of migration across disciplines in social sciences, including literary criticism. It is through such moments of scholarship – when social phenomenon like migration is explained through its existence in literature and its gendered aspect is also paid due attention to – that the link between literature and society becomes most evident and the potential value of the former is realised in its fullness.

The plot of Lessing's first novel *The Grass is Singing* revolves around its female protagonist Mary who is compelled to leave behind her comfortable life in a South African town, "one of those sleepy little towns scattered like raisins in a dry cake over the body of South Africa," (*Grass* 41) because of the social pressure to marry. The white colonial society that she was a part of disapproved of her existence as a thirty-year-old single woman. Giving way to social customs, she unconsciously begins to search for a prospective partner and ends up being with Dick Turner. He, on his part, agrees to wed her so that he could fulfill what he deems to be his social destiny –take a wife and then have children. Even though the attraction between the two was never very strong, Mary moves to Dick's farm in the country hoping that they could perhaps make the union work. This internal migration, however, only ends up ruining their relationship further as it brings Mary into contact with cultural forces she had never encountered during her life in the town.

While she lived in the town, Mary had a busy social life. She was "a rare phenomenon: a woman of thirty without love troubles, headaches, backaches, sleeplessness or neurosis. She did not know how rare she was." (*Grass,* 45) Having been the only surviving child out of three to her parents, she had the opportunity to have a good education, even though her parents were never very rich. Although she had spent some part of her childhood in the country with her parents, Mary's self was really a product of the town as she had spent a better part of her life in the latter; she had thoroughly internalised the ways and manner of its world. Working as a personal secretary to her employer by the time she was thirty, Lessing tells us how Mary had no real understanding of a life of deprivation and discrimination prior to her move to the country in the following words:

> It had never occurred to her to think, for instance, that she, the daughter of a petty railway official and a woman whose life had been so unhappy because of economic pressure that she had literally pined to death, was living in much the same way as the daughters of the wealthiest in South Africa, could do as she pleased – could marry, if she wished, anyone she wanted. These things did not enter her head. 'Class' is not a South African word; and its equivalent, 'race' meant to her the office boy in the firm where she worked, other women's servants, and the amorphous mass of natives in the streets, whom she hardly noticed. . . .They were outside her orbit. (*Grass,* 41-2)

The painful explication of her naiveté by Lessing in this passage foreshadows Mary's eventual doom. Her non-engagement with the terms of the racial binary made her inept to understand the gravity of the social tension created by it. Race as a concept never occupied her mental space because her physical space made no requirement on her to concede black presence. Her environment, however, changes once she moves to her husband's farm in the country where the blacks could no longer be rendered invisible. The quantity of the labour they performed for the whites and their sheer number in the country made it difficult. Furthermore, her internalisation of the cultural values of the urban, white community prevents her from coping with the new realities surrounding her and she thus finds herself increasingly abandoned in the new environment.

The poverty of the Turners made it impossible for them to build a healthy social interaction with their white neighbours, making Mary extremely depressed. Dick, who "disliked the town" (*Grass,* 53), was able to expend his socialising energies while working on his farm. Lack of profits from his labour did not deter him or lessen the joy that he found in his work. A different professional line, where he could be more successful in his endeavours, is not an option he wishes to avail. There was, however, no such outlet for Mary who was used to the ways of the town where she could even afford to go to watch movies "five nights a week." (44). She had assumed country life would bring her "close to nature"; what she learns is that she no longer had much access to the society and means of entertainment she had once taken for granted.

The gender system Mary's home culture approved of and the one that she had unquestioningly accepted insisted on the man being the primary bread winner, even if the woman could do it better. Even after she had taken over Dick's work during his illness, she goes back to her passive life which limited her involvement to taking care of the household. The couple's sufferings arising out of a lack of economic resources would have been alleviated by her active assistance to her husband in the farm work, but she chooses to self-incarcerate herself at home that further deprive her of the will to live. Mary's tragedy is thus precipitated by her own immature participation in the maintenance of an oppressive gender system. She continues to be in the role of a dependent despite having proven herself, and displays through this attitude a socially sanctioned learned helplessness.

The movement from the city to the country also prompts Mary to confront her racism while living the hard life on the farm. She thinks of blacks as "native mongrels" (134) and "Filthy savages," (135), but they in their turn too "resented her, a woman, supervising them." (136) These are indicative of how Mary's explicit racism was responded to with equal negativity by the black male population on the farm through their microagressive behaviour towards her. At one instance in the novel, she whips Moses, the native who ultimately murders her out of jealousy, because he dares to oppose her order while working in the field under her supervision during Dick's illness. Yet given the fact that for her, "the word 'Home' spoken nostalgically, meant England, although both her parents were South Africans and had never been to England," (37) the problem runs far deeper than the surface behaviour reflects. As a child, Mary could only look "covertly at the little Greek girl whom she was not allowed to play with, because her mother said her parents were dagoes." (38) Discrimination was thus ingrained in her. The colour bar was an active part of the British culture, which found its way into Mary's life not just through her parents but also through the British magazines and the novels she reads in her life. The racial ideas governing her thoughts and actions were commonly shared by the white population in Apartheid South Africa. One of the ways through which it succeeded in keeping its hold over the majority black population was cultural domination.

Mary's post-marriage migration brings her out of her comfort zone for the very first time, and when she tries to go back to it, she finds she was no longer welcome in her previous, all-white company. As her relationship with Dick increasingly deteriorates over years, she finds herself getting attracted to their black servant Moses despite her racism. Her loneliness and his kindness – combined with her rejection by the hypocritical white community due to poverty – increasingly makes Mary Turner realise the fallacy of the rhetoric of white superiority and racial discrimination. Her unconscious internalisation of the same, however, would make her disavow that realisation, ultimately resulting in her 'unhomeliness' and a complete mental breakdown.

In Atwood's historical fiction *Alias Grace*, migration results in the loss of the protagonist's childhood and proves to be a difficult experience both physically and psychologically. A young Grace Marks was made to migrate to Canada from a village in North Ireland along with her family due to paucity of money at home. The father's alcoholism and economic unproductiveness compels her Aunt Pauline and Uncle Roy, her husband, to arrange for their voyage to Canada. It was a clever manoeuvre on their part to have the Marks family off their backs, as "Many were doing it, and there was free land to be had in the Canadas . . ." (*Alias,* 127)

The journey on the ship that was to take them to their destination proves to be one marred by deprivation and disease, as the following extracts indicate:

> . . . all the passengers were stuffed together, with no walls between, and most as sick as dogs . . . hardly any air got in, and so the hold became fouler and fouler and the stench was enough to turn your stomach inside out.
>
> . . . there were no proper ways to relieve yourself. There were buckets provided, but in plain view of all . . . there were gropings in the dark, and curses, and buckets being overturned by mistake, and even if the bucket remained upright, what didn't go into it went onto the floor. . . . (*Alias,* 134)

The only good that Grace saw emerging out of the journey was the setting aside of the sectarian differences by the passengers on the ship, who were "Catholic and Protestant mixed, with some English and Scots. . ." (135) The grotesque reality of the journey combines with a personal tragedy for Grace when her mother dies due to an unknown illness of the abdomen on the ship and could not even be given a proper burial. The distress of migration gives in to trauma for her at this moment, which she expresses in the following words to Dr. Jordan years later:

> I did not cry. I felt as if it was me and not my mother that had died; and I sat as if paralysed, and did not know what to do next. (*Alias,* 139)

The memory of maternal loss could be recounted objectively because of the emotional distance that the intervening time period had introduced between the event and the moment of recollection, during which Grace had witnessed several other deaths and emotionally challenging circumstances. The opening bracket for these later memories however was those of the journey towards Canada, which gave the latter experiences a more ominous colouring and also advanced her 'unhoming'.

Migration pronounces further deprivation of family support for Grace when she gets separated from the rest of her family due to her work as a housemaid at Mrs. Parkinson's. Canada in the 19th century was indeed being seen as a promised land by the poor Irish who migrated to several parts of North America both before and after the famine of 1847. Since the conditions at home were not conducive, a lot many Irish women in the 19th century often migrated to Canada without being chaperoned by a male family member as well with the hope of finding a better life. Their experiences of migration, however, did not always attest their expectation, which is also visible in Grace Marks story, both the historical and fictional one.

The Irish domestic servants in 19th century Canadian society were looked at suspiciously as their morals were often thought to be questionable. As Marlene Goldman in an essay on *Alias Grace* observes, Irish women had acquired the notoriety of being insane and criminal by the time Grace arrives in Canada. A negative image of Irish servants was already in wide circulation in the society that made their employers vary of trusting them.

Such cultural stereotypes about the Irish added another layer of difficulty to Grace's post-migration life in Canada. Women's everyday interactions with each other were also governed by these cultural stereotypes – a fact reflected in the inquiry about Grace's being a Catholic or a Protestant. The question made by the English housekeeper Mrs. Honey prior to her hiring at Mrs Parkinson's and its attendant fears relate to the fact that most Irish people migrating to Canada were Catholic, who she believed to be "superstitious and rebellious Papists who were ruining the country." (*Alias,* 148) The country alluded to here is not Canada, but England, which served as the idea of home for most initial settlers. Canada, on the other hand, was to the settler imagination the untamed land that they needed to cast in the image of the mother country. Very often, as Atwood writes in *Survival*, the settlers found themselves confronted by natural forces to which they would succumb and thus begin to see themselves as victim of their circumstances. In *Alias Grace*, it is not nature that acts as the oppressor, but rather the arbitrary yet naturalised social attitudes that are pointed out as the culprits.

In the 19th century British Canadian society, women had access to very few "respectable" vocations and thus made the activity of finding work a struggle. For Irish female immigrants like Grace, there were plenty of employment opportunities available as domestic servants, but at a meager salary. It was the fortuitous help of her landlady that gets her hired at Mrs. Parkinson's as a maid. In addition to economic exploitation, the threat of sexual harassment also loomed large over the heads of Irish female immigrants employed as domestic help. At Mr. Kinnear's, Grace often appears to be dealing with this threat, and even later, when she is in the asylum and the prison. Grace's mental illness – her hysteria and multiple personality disorder – in fact seems to get triggered by her growing realisation that like her fellow Irish Mary Whitney (whom she befriends while working at Mrs. Parkinson's and who dies due to a lack of proper medical care during an abortion procedure as it was illegal), she too would be used by a gentleman and then left by him to perish. She feared she too would have nowhere to go or seek help since she was no longer at home. The safety that the sense of belonging to a land and its people brings with it was absent for her in Canada. Her understanding of her altered reality following Mary Whitney's death is the 'unhomely' moment for Grace, the first appearance of her madness, as is evident from the following:

> They said I lay like that for ten hours . . . and that when I did wake up I did not seem to know where I was, or what had happened; and I kept asking where Grace had gone. And when they told me that I myself was Grace, I would not believe them,

> but cried, and tried to run out of the house, because I said that *Grace was lost*, and had gone into the lake, and *I needed to search for her*[italics mine]. . . . (*Alias,* 208)

The crisis of identity that triggers madness in Grace is similar to that of Mary's in *The Grass is Singing* in the sense that they both realise that the values acquired by them in the physical and psychological space they had always identified as home were fallible when confronted by the values of another culture. They both suffer from cognitive dissonance due to this, and hence lose their mental balance.

After Mary Whitney's death, Grace was disinterested in continuing her work at the Parkinson household, and leaves it to go work for Mr. Kinnear subsequent to her meeting with Nancy Montgomery. Although an Irish domestic servant like Grace, Nancy had managed to acquire a position of power in Kinnear household through her illicit sexual relationship with the owner. The 'textual' Grace – it then seems – murders Nancy Montgomery in her madness because despite identifying with her, she feared Nancy was violating the norms of the society much like Mary Whitney. The murder was a punishment meted out to her by Grace for wanting to gain upward social mobility. By persecuting one of its members who a part of her perceived as already guilty, she was trying to prevent further ostracisation of the group. Nancy Montgomery is thus turned into a sort of a scapegoat for the Irish community and the supposed ills that they were spreading in Canada by the textual Grace. The exact role of real-life Grace Marks in the Thomas Kinnear and Nancy Montgomery murders, however, still remains unclear and thus open to speculation.

In *Alias Grace*, Atwood has shown through Grace Marks a female character that is desired by men because of her ethnic difference from other women in their cultural environment. Based on this difference, she is given a negatively differential treatment. Her class position and her criminal status complicate matters for her furthermore, as the men around tend to view her as more sexual. This reveals as to how cultural stereotypes about Irish women and particularly female convicts result in discriminatory practices. Atwood, through such instances in the text, seems to be supporting the idea that womanhood is characterised not just by sex and gender but also by other socio-cultural factors like race, class and nationality. As Judith Butler suggests, any homogenised used of the term 'woman' implies suppressing the differences that mark a significant shift in attitude of the cultural 'Other'. These differences that are suppressed do play an important role in determining the manner in and the extent to which a woman experiences oppression and thus, can not to be ignored. Grace's loton this front improves after she migrates to America, where her criminal history was unknown to anyone, having married Jamie Walsh. Nevertheless, there were many other Irish female immigrants like Grace for whom there was no escape from the ignominy of arrest. They were arrested for reasons as varied as vagrancy, insanity and larceny, to name just a few.

To conclude, the psychoscape of the migrant comprises of two places at the same time – the homeland and the hostland. It is the tussle for primacy between the two which results in his/her identity crisis; the individual often has to make a choice and negotiate a way around it. In case of a female migrant, she finds it all the harder to choose between the two as both are, more often than not, creations of patriarchy. If nations are imagined communities (to use Benedict Anderson's phrase), then it is mostly men who possess the power to imagine them. It should then hardly be surprising that sometimes the only response to this conflict that a female migrant can have is madness, a state which absolves her from taking responsibility of making a choice in the first place. The madness exhibited by the protagonists of *The Grass is Singing* and *Alias Grace* is that response.

Works Cited

Aghazadeh, Sima. "Sexual-Political Colonialism and Failure of Individuation in Doris Lessing's The Grass is Singing". *Journal of International Women's Studies.* 12.1 (2011): 107-21.Web. 14 Nov 2017. http://vc.bridgew.edu/jiws/vol12/iss1/9

Atwood, Margaret. *Alias Grace.* London: Virago Press, 1997. Print.

____ *Survival: A Thematic Guide to Canadian Literature.* Toronto: McClelland & Stuart Inc., 1996. Print.

Bhabha, Homi K. "The World and the Home". *Third World and Post-Colonial Issues.* 141-153. Duke University Press Stable, 1992.Web.

Bordo, Susan. *Unbearable Weight: Feminism, Western Culture, and the Body.* Berkeley: U of California, 1993. Print.

Gilbert, Sandra M. & Gubar, Susan. *The Madwoman in the Attic: The Woman Writer and the Nineteenth-Century Literary Imagination.* New Haven and London: Yale University Press, 2000. Print.

Goldman, Marlene. "Memory, Diaspora, Hysteria: Margaret Atwood's Alias Grace". *Memory and Migration: Multidisciplinary Approaches to Memory Studies.* Eds. Julia Creet and Andreas Kitzmann. University of Toronto Press, 2011.210–232.Web.

Kenny, Kevin. *Diaspora: A Very Short Introduction.* Oxford: Oxford UP, 2013. Print.

Lessing, Doris. *The Grass is Singing.* London: Heinmann, 1950. Print.

Loomba, Ania. *Colonialism/Postcolonialism.* 2nd ed. London: Routledge, 2005. Print.

Mclean, Lorna R., and Marilyn Barber. "In Search of Comfort and Independence: Irish Immigrant Domestic Servants Encounter the Courts, Jails, and Asylums in Nineteenth-Century Ontario". *Sisters or Strangers?: Immigrant, Ethnic, and Racialised Women in Canadian History.* Eds. Marlene Epp, Franca Iacovetta and Frances Swyripa. Buffalo: University of Toronto Press, 2004. Print.

Menjivar, Cecilia. "Migration and Refugees". *A Companion to Gender Studies.* Eds. Philomena Essed, David Theo Goldberg and Audrey Kobayashi. West Sussex: Wiley-Blackwell, 2009. Print.

Stearns, Peter N. "Immigration as culture contact". *Gender in World History.* 2nd ed. New York and Oxon: Routledge, 2006. Print.

Sue, Derald Wing. *Microaggressions in Everyday Life: Race, Gender, and Sexual Orientation.* New Jersey: John Wiley & Sons, 2010. Print.

Ussher, Jane M. *Women's Madness: Misogyny or Mental Illness?* Amherst: U of Massachusetts, 1992. Print.

Young, Iris Marion. "House and Home: Feminist Variations on a Theme." *On Female Body Experience: "Throwing like a Girl" and Other Essays.* New York: Oxford UP, 2005. 123-54. Print.

7

When the Subaltern React and Create a Space of Their Own: Re-locating Identity in Arvind Adiga's *The White Tiger*

Samiksha Sharma

Subaltern are the people who are considered static, ignorant and incapable to speak for themselves. Subaltern is formed from two Latin words; 'sub' and 'alter', former means 'under' and latter means 'other', thus subaltern refers to a person or a group of inferior rank based on race, class, gender or ethnicity. Antonio Gramsci, an Italian Marxist theorist first used the term 'subaltern' in his article "Notes on Italian History" which was later published in his book *Prison Notebooks.* Subaltern critic, Julian Wolfreys defined subalternity as "the groups that are marginalised, oppressed and exploited on the cultural, political and religious grounds" (Wolfrey, 84). Subaltern Studies has its root in post-colonial theory; as it originated from the concept of self and the other. The self is a governing body and acts supreme and the rest comes under the umbrella of the other. The self tries to subdue the other and push them beyond the margin by relegating them as an outcast from the mainstream. In South Asian countries, colonial regime has ended but the after effects are still prevalent among the natives. Aftermaths of Colonialism are more dangerous, as the visible form of oppression has ended but the more internal form of suppression has submerged upon the lower strata of society. The lower strata of society participated in the Freedom Movement with the hope for better future and more opportunities. After independence, New masters (the elite class) appeared and replaced the colonial masters and the situation of lower strata remained the same. They were made to believe that their position is justified and following orders and serving the elite class would be beneficial for them. These people who have no historical roots, no identity of their own form the subaltern group. In Indian context, members of working class, rural peasantry, subjugated women and the untouchables who suffer silently under the hegemonic domination of elite class form the subaltern group.

In 1980's, emerged a group of scholars from India, Britain and Australia known as 'Subaltern Studies Group' with a prospect to liberate the powerless by challenging the authority of powerful. The group is headed by Ranjit Guha and joined by eminent scholars like Dipesh Chakraborty, Gyan Pandey, Eric Stokes, David Arnold, Partha Chatterjee, Gayatri Spivak, Shahid Amin, Sudipta Kaviraj and others. The subaltern critics shift their focus towards the lost historical narratives of subaltern people particularly of South Asian ethnicity. Ranjit Guha in his *Elementary Aspects of Peasants Insurgency in Colonial India* attempted to unveil the reality of peasant life which was not recorded by elite class historiographers. Dipesh Chakraborty, member of 'Subaltern Study Group' established a relation between post-colonialism and subalternity in his book *Provincialising Europe: Post-colonial Thought and Historical Difference.* An eminent critic, Gayatri Chakraborty Spivak came with a theory of subalternity in her essay "Can the Subaltern Speak?" which formulated that "the subaltern has no history and cannot speak, the subaltern as female is even more deeply in shadow" (Spivak, 287). Literary writers also followed the trend of subaltern critics and started writing fiction to uplift the suppressed voices of society. Amitav Ghosh expressed his concern for the downtrodden people in the novels like *The Circle of Reaso*n, *The Calcutta Chromosome* and *The Hungry Tide.* Rohinton Mistry, a Canadian writer of Indian descent projected the plight of untouchables in Modern India through his novel *A Fine Balance.*

Aravind Adiga showed an abiding interest in the narratives of the voiceless people living in Modern India and represented them in an integrated manner in his novel *The White Tiger* (2008) which won the Man Booker Prize for the year 2008. In this novel, Adiga projected Balram as a pivotal character who was born inferior and wanted to transcend his inferior status. Adiga highlighted the evil face of poverty, exploitation and alienation through the story of a common man. The protagonist of the novel, Balram narrated his story in the form of a letter to the Premier of China, Wen Jiabao who is about to visit India. Balram described himself as a son of a poor rickshaw puller who lived a life of misery and servitude. The novel is a crude satire on the division between the powerful and the powerless while rendering on the complex concepts of poverty. On one instance, Balram's father exclaimed "My whole life, I have been treated like a donkey. All I want is that one son of mine – at least one – should live like a man" (Adiga, 26). The words of Balram's father throws light on the condition of poor and downtrodden people, living in the darker India far from the brightness of progress. Balram's father lived an unhappy life and spent his last days waiting for the doctor inside an ill-equipped hospital of Laxmangarh. This incident reflects on the crippled health facilities provided by system to the poor people of rural areas. The reality of corrupt political system is also exposed in the novel when Balram visited a government agent and he marked his age eighteen years merely to make his vote countable.

Balram attended school for few years, where the school teacher consumes all the funds reserved for the needs of the poor students. Once, an inspector visited the school and called Balram "the white tiger" and this incident fills Balram with a sense of pride. Balram observed his surroundings minutely and he learned about the life as a keen listener. Balram says, "There are just two castes: Men with Big Bellies, and Men with Small Bellies. And only two destinies: eat or get eaten up" (Adiga, 54). Large population of India is still crushed and mashed under the feet of rich people, who use the poor to quench their selfish motives and thus deprive them of basic human rights. Adiga uses Balram as his mouth-piece to criticise the corrupt social and political system of India which sidelined the needs and problems of marginalised people.

Adiga used the word "Rooster Coop" (147) for the subaltern people of India. As Rooster in a coop silently watch his companions being slaughtered and he knows that his turn is also near but the Rooster never rebels or try to escape the cage. Likewise, poor people watch silently that their rights are being crushed by greedy ruling class but they show no resistance, meekly accept their fate and summon to the desires of governing bodies. Moreover, if someone tries to escape this domination, members of his own community target him as disloyal and crush the hope for better tomorrow. The life of the marginalised people is a complex riddle; they are themselves not aware of their remitted past and trapped present. Adiga described the journey of Balram from "Rooster Coop" status to high status by using the metaphor of "the Darkness" (150) and "the Light" (150). "The Darkness" is the poverty stricken rural India whereas "the Light" reflects on the luxurious life style of elite people. From the very beginning, Balram tries to navigate from "the Darkness" to "the Light" and seeks to differentiate himself from the invisible status.

Balram was forced to drop his school to earn money for the marriage of his cousin. He worked at a tea stall and showed great interest in the profession of a driver. One of the driver named Vijay appeared to him successful, someone who has left behind the status of marginalised and achieved a uniform in his life. Adiga projected the power hegemony existing in the rural areas of India and critised the dominance of landlords over the peasant of villages. Through the character of Balram, Adiga exclaimed that "a handful of men in this country have trained the remaining 99.9 percent . . . to exist in perpetual servitude" (103). Balram refers to the four landlords of Laxmangarh as Four Animals; the Stork, the Wild Boar, the Buffalo and the Raven who control the village. The bestial comparisons of human beings reflect on the hatred among the villagers for the landlords who eschew the poor for economical gains. After learning to drive, Balram sets out to find a job and knocked at the door of the Stork who hired him as a driver. Later, Balram shifted to Delhi as a personal driver of the Stork's son, Ashok and started driving the luxurious Honda City which Balram considers as a prestige and feels proud of the achievement. On one instance, Ashok and his wife Pinky Madam visited a mall for shopping and Balram was standing down as chauffers were not allowed to enter the mall. Meanwhile, a poor man tried to enter the mall and guards prohibited him to enter because of his low class attire, the man started crying, "Am I not a human being too?"(125). The words of the poor man instigate us to think about the plight of low class people who are not even treated as human beings and denied the basic human rights. Thus, we can qualify that poverty has a de-humanising effect which render the low class people (subaltern) devoid of dignity and respect. In the words of Gayatri Chakraborty, subaltern is not allowed speak; even if subaltern tries to speak nobody pays attention.

Balram wanted to escape the life of destitution and tried to segregate himself from his own family and adopted the life style of the rich people. His world was shattered when Pinky Madam killed a child during her rash drive and Balram was persuaded to accept the blame on himself. Balram was shock-stricken and he realised his position as a slave who is bound to follow the orders. Thus, Adiga highlighted the corruption in judicial system which hardly enquires to find the truth and target the poor folks as scape goats. Adiga exposed the roots of corruption in Modern India where the rich people easily escape to pay the taxes by bribing the politician and as a result, the social gap between the rich and poor is increasing which hinders the spirit of democracy. When Ashok filled his red bag from various ATM's and was heading towards the Minister's lodging to bribe him, Balram felt a deep sense that this money belongs to him; the same money could be used to improve the lives of poor people if paid in the form of tax. Finally, Balram reacted and reached the end of social mobility by killing his master, Ashok and stealing the money from the bag. He left the city and headed towards Bangalore. Balram has learnt how to survive in this corrupt world, he bribed the police and established himself as an entrepreneur at taxi services.

In his journey of upward mobility, Balram adopted the vicious means to escape the "Rooster Coop" status and re-located himself in "the Light" by destroying his roots. We can say that it was the journey from rags to riches at the cost of lost morality and lost affections. The novel *The White Tiger* challenges the 'Harato Alger myth' which suggests that through hard work, perseverance and dedication, young men aspire for upward mobility. Haratio was a famous American writer of nineteenth century who wrote stories about the aspiring young men who beat poverty with hard work. *The White Tiger* altogether negates the 'Haratio Alger myth' and represents protagonist as an anti-hero who adopts vicious means to get success. Question arises here, whether upward movement is possible only by adopting unfair and corrupt means. Is corruption the solution to poverty? When the subaltern reacts and tries to establish his own space and identity in "the Light" – whether there exists any way to achieve it through fair means? Poor has to sacrifice his morality and family to transcend the life of "Rooster Coop". Subaltern is born to suffer in one way or another – perpetrators can be different and forms of suffering can be different – if not poverty then guilt or haunting memories of the past. Balram fulfilled the dream of his father and experienced the life of a man. He justified the murder as an act of rebellion; the reaction of a subaltern, when he found no way to uplift his lower status.

The novel *The White Tiger* raised the question of domination and subordination. Through the character of Balram, Adiga provided a space for silenced, subaltern and voiceless people who are overlooked as unrecorded in the history. Firstly, the poor and downtrodden (subaltern) cannot speak, if someone becomes conscious of the fact and tries to rebel, he is not allowed to rebel, as members of his own community cause hindrance. Secondly, under the corrupt social and political system, it is hard to live a virtuous life. Thirdly, for a subaltern to move upwards, one has to sacrifice his emotional attachments and ignore the welfare of one's own family. The guilt of being a rogue and an abscond renders him mad and engulfs his peace of mind. Adiga in his novel *The White Tiger* tried to portray the realistic picture of contemporary India where subaltern people are living in the state of destitution; being marginalised and suppressed, nobody pays heed to them and they live an invisible life in this visible world.

Works Cited

Adiga, Aravind. *The White Tiger.* Haper Collins, 2008. Print.

Spivak, Gayatri Chakravorty. "Can the Subaltern Speak?" *Marxism and the Interpretation of Culture.* Edited by Cary Nelson and Lawrence Grossberge. University of Illinois Press, 1988, pp. 271-313. Print.

Wolfrey, Julian. *Critical Keywords in Literary and Cultural Theory.* Macmillan, 2004. Print.

8

An Attempt to Study Familial and Marital Discourse in *Family Matters* by Rohinton Mistry

Shweta Verma

The concept of history fiction interface is successively practiced by Rohinton Misty in nearly all of his novels. Unlike his earlier works like *A Fine Balance, Such a Long Journey, Family Matters* too is left untouched from receiving critical accolades. As Linda L Richards rightly remarks: "his most recent novel *Family Matters* is brilliant. It manages to be warm and familiar while – for North American readers – at any rate fragrantly exotic" (Dodiya, 81). Thereby shifting his perspective from foregrounding the heterogeneity of identity within a Parsi community and the dynamic nature and their obsessive love for their rich culture and tradition in his hard-to-be-suppressed novel *Family Matters* Mistry simultaneously deals with familial matters and the fact that family does matter. Though it's been set against the backdrop of communalist politics and corruption but it does not hesitates to foretell that how the public world impinges in the private space of a person. A man's obsession for his culture, traditions, society, beliefs and practices indicates his attempt towards achieving economic status and financial security. Can the society also be responsible for the familial and marital discord as it happens in the *Family Matters?* The concept of familial ties cannot be refuted though family is considered as a refuge from the real world but it still is a part of it. For it is believed that values aren't dictated by any particular law, profession or society but rather these are those principles and ethics which tend to define the individual as a human being thereby establishing his relationship with the broader aspects of life and not just emphasize upon the negative emotions. Cultural background, race, religion, ethnicity belongs to the individual. Marital satisfaction which is usually believed as an individual's perception of the quality of his or her married life can be achieved only if people forget the binaries and gives up their orthodoxical beliefs. For a person who has achieved martial satisfaction in his life appears to come out as a totally different person from the one who has not. Taking into consideration the protagonist of the novel Nariman Vakeel a seventy-nine years old Parsi widower and the patriarch of a small discordant family who is beset by Parkinson's disease residing in once-elegant apartment Chateau Felicity with his step children Jal and Coomy.

Nariman Vakeel for whom his marriage is a complete failure can achieve some sought of satisfaction only through the nostalgic memories which are free and his only. How much importance does a person gives to the hollow skeptical norms and tradition than to a person of flesh and blood is very well depicted through professor Nariman Vakeel's nostalgic memories as he remembers, "his father said she might be a wonderful person as gracious and charming as the queen of England but she was still unsuitable for his son because she was not a 'Zoroastrain' case closed" (Mistry, 132).

The Parsis always felt that their community is failing day by day and in order to overcome their communal perspective they developed a hostility against inter-caste marriage and practices and condemns severely to such practices. Marzaban Vakeel, father of Nariman Vakeel presents his hostile perspective in somewhat same fashion when he says,

> such a monumental waste of time and energy the lawsuit had been he thought as he remembered the religious controversy that had fuelled the feud. A priest had performed a navjote ceremony for a son of a Parsi mother and a non-Parsi father – an absolute taboo for the conservative factions. The event had ignited one of those periods of debate and polemics and bickering that infected

> the reformists and the orthodox from time to time like the flux (Mistry, 132).

Furthering his critical perspective on the notion of inter-caste marriage Nariman's father goes on to criticize the priest by saying,

> that for the misguided dustoor in question, the sacred investiture ceremony of sudra and rusti had no more significance than trying an ordinary string around one's waist, given the cavalier way he was bestowing it on all and sundry that it was renegades like him who would destroy this three thousand years old religion that Zoroastrianism had survived many setbacks in its venerable history but what the Arab armies had failed to achieve in AD 652 priests like him would accomplish the purity of this unique and ancient Persian community the very plinth foundation of its survival was being compromised. Ignorance may be bliss he wrote however the ignorance of mischief making priests was anything but it was poison for the Parsi community (Mistry, 132).

Since it is believed that a person's degree of global autonomy is not fully determined by how autonomous or non autonomous in relation are his or her personal choices. A person can be permitted to all in a so called self-directed fashion only when there are others too who exert a governing influence over his or her choice. But here we find that Nariman is no self-determining man. For he tends to face numerous interferences throughout his life either through social, psychological or physical means be it cohesion, manipulation weakness of will or bodily impulse. Due to the familial and societal pressure he decides to marry "Yasmin Contractor, a widow with two children" (Mistry, 15). For she was apt in each and every manner as they say "everything has been considered: personality, family background, cooking and housekeeping skills. Yes the widow is our number-one choice. She will make you a good wife" (Mistry, 16) but somewhere in his mind he knew that the marriage won't survive and he considered himself responsible for the psychological and hysterical condition of Lucy which led towards her death. Thereby being flabbergasted by Lily's decision of doing domestic drudgery at Mr. Arjani's house when he asks Lucy of it, "He asked her if she was doing it for the money. He would help her, no need to humiliate her would find her an office job. Smiling she shook her head, don't you understand why I am here? You are on the third floor, and I am on the ground floor and it comforts me" (Mistry, 134). Neither could Nariman concentrate upon his married life with Yasmin nor could he forget the past events which took place in his life. For even after his marriage to Yasmin Lucy decided to be a part of his life which effects Nariman's relationship with Yasmin drastically. Its long lasting effect is very well visible on the familial discord and ties. After he returned from his work "he found Jal and Coomy beside their mother, trying to console her. They would not look at him. They no longer came to wish him good night before going to bed" (Mistry, 135). The discord was clearly visible in his relationship to Yasmin, "She said he will regret the day he was born if he didn't heed her warning .She had had enough she was going to stand up for her rights if not as wife then at least as mother (Mistry, 136).

Cultural and societal restraints can separate persons but what about the feeling the emotions which one shares with the other. As Nariman confesses when he finds his wife going to meet Lucy on the pavement and hence in order to prevent her from holding Lucy responsible for he says, "But I do feel responsible he said for the past eleven years he had gone out with her but also for driving her in part to this act of desperation" (Mistry, 137). If one goes on to analyse the drastic results of familial and peer pressure upon Nariman Vakeel the dominating restraints of societal pressure one can say that they bore no fruitful results as such. For the void which took place between Nariman and Yasmin was also responsible for the discord which was going to take place between him and his step children. Jal and Coomy rather than considering their step father as a responsibility in his old age and illness they considered him more of a burden in. For in some way or the other they held him responsible for their mother's death. Lucy being reminded from her very girlhood that for a girl like her love of father served as a sunshine and fresh water devoid of which one could not expect a daughter to bloom but a stepfather was considered useless on this part. Hence one can also say that whatever a child hears or sees leaves a very deep impact upon a child's delicate mind. And thereby gives birth to bitter feeling in a relationship. Their very first encounter with Nariman Vakeel as New Pappa for, "the word stung like a pebble each time it was hurled to his face .He made light of it at first, laughing it off: "that's all – just New Pappa? Why not a longer title? How about Brand New Improved Pappa?" (Mistry, 9).

Nariman Vakeel's marriage was just a bond for financial stability and nothing more than that but the love he bestowed upon Roxana his very own daughter made his relationship with his step children more stressed and strained. Once when Nariman asks Coomy that has she informed Roxana about his illness she replies very rudely to him, "What do you think said Coomy? Have I had one free moment since you went and broke your bones? I apologise if your lordship is not happy with the service" (Mistry, 79). Her careless attitude towards Nariman when he asks for his teeth, "I forgot my teeth said Nariman letting his dentures protrude to remind her. She fetched the glass from the bathroom and held it under her mouth .That water has not been changed he sucked the teeth back in. I'll change it tomorrow, I'm exhausted .he released his dentures into the stale water (Mistry, 71-72).

Where on one hand Coomy is fastidious in caring for her stepfather but at the other moment she is cruel too. Her gesture is mean spirited and deviously hatched when she plans to get rid of her father's responsibilities,

> Coomy put her fingers across her lips an idea was gathering shape inside her head. Whenever Pappa met Roxie's family he's in a good mood. He and Yezad are always laughing and enjoying so he should be with them for the bright and cheerful atmosphere doctor prescribed (Mistry, 85).

To Nariman Vakeel however emigration is an enormous mistake. In his very own words he realises "Emigration is an enormous mistake. The biggest anyone can make in his life. The loss of home leaves a hole that never fills" (Dodiya, 84). For the problem of displacement was not only his sole problem but rather it becomes a reason for the upcoming queries and voids which were going to take place in the life of his daughter Roxana and Yezad her husband. It is believed that the contrasting pulls and pressure of modernity brings a change not only over the community alone but also in the institution of family as well. The effect of the guilt, compassion, and familial obligation verses desire for independence and the building of human relationship "begin to appear soon in the lives of the characters thereby giving birth to conflicts" (Dodiya, 84). Thereby shifting the emphasis from the wellbeing of his family to the sense of individualism and self-fulfillment. It can be admitted in the words of Yezad, while he was having his dinner, "Yezad thoughts kept turning to the days ahead. The morning stress the overcrowding the smelly front room – all of it would continue. And providing for more than one person, when every rupee was budgeted meant a shortfall of twenty-five percent in Roxana's food envelopes. Not to mention things like soap and washing and dhobi" (Mistry, 187).

How a warm witty man became saddled with vicious temper and smoldering disappointments is very clearly visible in the words of Yejad: "He walked as she gave her his mouthwash. Nariman gargled and a thread of saliva hung from his lips stretched to the limit it broke clinging to his chin. Yezad looked away to keep his mind on his breakfast" (Mistry, 146). His resenting attitude towards Nariman Vakeel's thereby turns him into a sadist for he refuses to give Nariman Vakeel the bottle he needs to urinate and hence prevents his son's from helping their grandfather he goes on to say, "First they should learn about fun and happiness and enjoy their youth. Lots of time to learn about sickness and dying" (Mistry, 88). His strange attitude towards the unexpected guest Nariman Vakeel becomes bitterer when he comes to know that Jal and Coomy are in a no mood to take him back as it is revealed in the words of Coomy, "I can't have him back, please don't force me. I haven't even found to replace Phoola, the sweeping and swapping is breaking my back" (Mistry, 172).

While on the other hand when Yezad and Roxana become clearly aware of their clever mind they decide that "if they play this game so will we. They kick him into our house we find a way to kick him back into theirs" (Mistry, 195). Where on one hand family is considered as a site of primary loyalties filiations as it has rightly been said by Edward Said while on the other hand it functions as a locus of tangled and unresolved issues. While we can expect family to be a comforting space but one should not forget the fact that it can also stifle with the blanket of over protectiveness .The foresaid sinister example of strict parental control can be found out not only in case of Nariman Vakeel who was forced to marry against his wishes and hence ruined his life, for something similar occurs in the relationship of Yezad and his older son Murad later.

Deeper study of novel clues one towards the underlying and suppressed practices of culture tradition, and beliefs which on no point are a substitute to nostalgia, alienation and seclusion which Nariman Vakeel has been suffering at the hands of his step children and how the forthcoming generation becomes a prey to that too. For though Yezad cherished the honesty he received from the Parsi community and specially from his father for whose "ingratitude" for an exemplary display of courage and honesty in the course of duty. When his father was presented with a commemorative clock which Yezad continued to cherish and hence prevents Murad from winding it but later on we tend to find that he himself is seen compromising with his Parsi honesty belief and. His visit to Villete the Matka Queen as she was called,

> "Well? He demanded.
>
> Ville smiled my dear one is the opening".
>
> She saw the relief in his face and wanted to give him a way out. It's not too late to cancel your closing if you don't trust my dream (Mistry, 263).

Though he was very well aware of the fact that gambling was illegal and his wife too was strictly against it. Moral complexity in the novel tends to give a new twist to Mistry's novel. The concept of goodness is well understood by the faith of Zorostrainsim. As in the novel the requirement to be met by the Zorostrainsim faith munashni, guvashini, kurashni meaning god thought, good words, good deeds. But do the characters orient themselves to these believes which have been prescribed in their Zorostrainsim faith and to what extent. For in Zorostrainsim good and bad is something which is quite separate from one another. Where on one hand good being a positive value which has been emanated from the wise lord, on the other hand the latter being the aftermath of the intrusion Ahriman into the Ahuru realm. Still in the words of the Yezad and his family one can very clearly see that the notion of truth is adulterated and evil is something which is imminent in mankind. The manner in which Coomy behaves with her step father instead of considering him as a responsibility she considers him more of a burden and thereby finds a way of getting rid of him. For she used to behave like a hysterical headmistress, crafting rules to govern each and every aspect of her stepfather's life. As Mistry narrates,

> She should have been a headmistress enacting rules for hapless girls, making them miserable. Instead her she was, plaguing him with rules to govern every aspect of his shrunken life. Besides the prohibition of against locked doors, he was required to announce his intention to use the WC. In the morning he was not to get out of the bed till she came to get him, bath was possible only twice a week when she undertook its choreography, with Jal enlisted as stage manager to stand by and ensure his safety. There were more rules regarding his meals, his clothes, his dentures, his use of the radiogram, and in charitable moments Nariman accepted what they never tired of speaking: that it was all for his own good. (Dodiya, 86)

On finding out that the lock of the bathroom door close Coomy yells at him, "Coomy took over, how many times have I told you Pappa? Don't lock the door! if you fall or faint inside how will we get you out? Follow the rules!" (Mistry, 2). When he comes out of the bathroom door she once gain yells at him "you will drive me crazy said Coomy my heart is going dhuk dhuk wondering if you collapsed or something" (Mistry, 2) When Nariman Vakeel comes back home after his morning walk on the day of his birthday with abrasions on his elbows and a limp Coomy comments, "tomorrow you'll complete seventy-nine years, and still you don't act responsibly. No appreciation for Jal and me or the things we do for you" (Mistry, 7) Feeling irritated by the new responsibility which comes upon Coomy's shoulder of taking care of her father Coomy replies, "I don't want to be disgusted with Pappa while he lies helping in bed said Coomy but I can't help hating him" (Mistry, 7).

One can say that it can be a subconscious act of her revenge for the way her father had treated her mother. Culture, man and society are the interlinked as well the intangible aspects whether it is the case of Nariman Vakeel or Jehanghir. Past repeats itself once again in the novel.

After the death of Nariman Vakeel we find that Chenoy family moves through their first process of displacement into the house of Jal and Coomy though it no more belongs to Coomy for she is dead. Chenoy's family has started an independent life with minimal familial interferences and responsibilities for Nariman Vakeel dies too after his second displacement at his own house. But to what extent has the person become independent in their virtues, values and principles we can't judge approximately but can surely make an estimate of it. A massive change has taken place in the life of Yezad. He is no more the same person who was loved and aspired by his family members. For he blames himself for those uncontrollable acts which were destined and hence finds solace in religion and spirituality. After shedding the responsibility of his family for now he believes that because it's the right path which is the standard procedure in an orthodox household. For when his wife says, "orthodox households I know all about, Yezad my mother's family followed those same practices but you and I have never lived like that" (Mistry 350) to which he says, "I was ignorant before. Now I have studied the religion attended the lectures of learned men" (Mistry 350) for now he finds religion and spiritualism as a solution to each and everything. From the words of Murad we come to know about Yezad as a totally different person who had set up a cabinet framed pictures of:

> Zarathustra and the Udava fire temple along with a silver model of the Asho Farohvas, photographs of the ancient remnants of

> the Persian Empire the ruins at persepolis palaces fire altars and royal tombs of the Archaemenian and Sassanian dynasties. The arrangement of items is in a rough semicircle that keeps growing. His latest acquisition is a miniature afargaan plastic with a tiny electric fire. (Mistry, 461-62)

Rather than being a father and caretaker of the family he speaks and practices more like a theologist and a priest. For when Yezad enters his prayer space after having a haircut he yells at him and thereafter remarks to his wife, your son is a wit and a half and he isn't he? Don't use Zoroaster that's a Greek perversion of our prophet's name say Zaarathustra. And before you mock me read the scriptures: Vendidad fargard XVI explains the distance (Mistry, 463)

In the words of Jehanghir,

> for the last few year ever since we left Pleasant Villa Daddy has been reading nothing but religious books as though making up for lost time. In addition to the holy cabinet my parents' bedroom has filled up with volumes about Parsi history and Zorvastrianism various translations of the Zend-Avesta, interpretations of the galḥas commentaries books by Zaehner, Spiegal, Darukhanawala, Dabu, Boyce, Dhalla, Hinnells, Karaka and many many more. Some of them used to be in a book case that belonged to grandpa's father. His name is inscribed in them on bookplates: Marazban Vakeel. (Mistry, 463).

Emphasizing upon his father's nature Jehanghir comments:

> my father has emerged from the bedroom and is doing his kusti by the cabinet. His expression is always very intense when he prays. He finishes tying the notes and silssils with his prayer book before the electric afargaan in the wooden chair no one else is allowed to use. He sits as though he is carrying a secret burden whose weight is thrusting him .He frowns a lot, his face contorting in pain. He doesn't just close his eyes he clenches the eyelids shut, the cheeks rising, the brows pressing downwards to squeeze out whatever it is that haunts him. His avesta recitations – the various yachts, gehsnyaishes depending on the hours – all like a rebutta a protest. He is locked in a struggle. For now days

> he hardly smiles let alone laughs. And he never whistles, never joins in with songs on radio. (Mistry, 465)

For now he is more of a spiritualist who finds seclusion, in scriptures and temples. For him now the family, children he once loved so heartily and dearly matters him no more. He spends most of the time either in the temple or:

> the league of orthodox Parsis and the association for Zarathustruamn education meet once a week. He returns from their sessions to tell us in detail about the agenda considered and the action taken, the petitions circulated and injunctions filed the campaigns to be waged against films or publications that have given offence. (Mistry, 466)

But a person doesn't understand that it is the feelings, emotions and love which tend to function the necessity of time and not those dead scriptures and beliefs and virtues. For Nariman Vakeel's father never made an effort to understand his feelings his needs and he as a whole. His accusation, his allegations against marrying an inter caste were as baseless and void as those of Mr Arjani, he calls, "Mr Arjani a prime example of the substandard mind whose cogitations were clearly worthless unable to grasp the simplest tenets of the religion and the supreme significance of the naryole" (Mistry, 215)

He writes, Mr Arjani's views he wrote did not deserve the dignity of debate for we find Yezad Chenoy behaving in the somewhat similar fashion when it comes upon his own son Murad, On catching his son with a girl, he says,

> I would not give a parjaat girl the satisfaction of seeing me argue with my son. At least he had the shame to leave the moment he saw me. But just wait till he's home" (Mistry 481) Rather than changing the mindset and blindly believing the practices which he thinks are sufficient enough to widen the gap which has been vacated between him and his son. Rather than behaving as a father who should speak to him he more on tends to behave like a theologist and says all the non-Zarathusti images must go in a Zarathusti home, they interfere with the vibrations of Avesta prayers. It's no wonder there is so much quarrel and fighting in

> this house. Once the pictures are gone, my prayers will be more officious understanding will come to Murad. (Mistry, 491)

After analysing novel in detail one can conclude that in his fully-fledged text Mystry not only emphasizes upon the protagonist though he has done so much but also successively proved that like all his other text this work too reaches out to the world through its pan universal nature. A compassionate piece which is wise in its ways for it acts as a mirror to the society who can relate themselves to the characters thereby associating with their problems.

Works Cited

Dodiya, Jaydipsinh. *Perspectives on the Novels of Rohinton Mistry*. New Delhi: Sarup and Sons, 2006. Print.

Mistry, Rohinton. *Family Matters*. London: Faber and Faber, 2002. Print.

9

Social Deprivation and Identity Issues in Aravind Adiga's *White Tiger*

Tabish Wani and **Rumana Nisar**

The White Tiger is framed as a narrative letter written over seven nights to the Chinese premier, wen Jiaboa, it is a tale of servitude, revolt and murder. The novel employs first person narrator, Balram Halwai, whose unique, sarcastic voice carries the reader through his life in "new India". Balram writes the letter in response to a statement he heard on the radio – "Mr Jiaboa is on a mission: he wants to know the truth about Bangalore". Balram is an expert on the truth about the harsh realities and hidden cruelties of India. The novel presents the contrast between India's rise as a global economy and the plight of the marginality class of society living in devastating rural and urban poverty through, Balram, the narrator and the protagonist. Balram, a son of rickshaw puller – an intelligent and promised child is forced to leave the school at an early age and work on a small tea shop and also break coal in order to support his family and learn driving to earn more money. Stork, a rich landlord hires him as a chauffeur to drive a car of Mr Ashok and his wife.

Adiga portrayed the different images of India: India of Light and India of Dark. But his focus is on the latter – and tries to give it a literary voice. The life of underclass darkens was corrupt and defunctioned education system was operating there. In Laxamangraph there is a typical school teacher called "Big Paan" and spit man (29) goes to sleep by noon, and drinks toddy in school.

Supply of free food to the school goes to the teacher who gives legitimate excuse for it." he hadn't been paid his salary in six months (33) Trucks full of uniform that government had sent to school is not issued to the children, but a week later they turned up for sale in the neighboring village ". (33) The whole education system is governed by the "crowd of thugs and idiots" (35) which Adiga calls "jungle". (35)

Balram's father is hit by poverty and tough manual work. His body tells the history of his life and sufferings. Balram reports:

> A rich man's body is like a premium cotton pillows, White, soft and blank ours are different. My father's spine was a knotted rope, the kind that woman use in village to pull water from Wells, the clavicle curved around his neck in high relief like a dog's collar, cuts and nicks and scars like little whip marks in his flesh, ran down his chest and waist, reaching down below his hipbones into his buttocks. The story of a poor man's life is written on his body, in a sharp pen. (26-27)

Medical services are shown are shown as an object of political mockery and social stigma. The Great Socialist inaugurated lohia universal free hospital in view of election result. There is no doctor in the hospital, doctors seldom visit the hospital, and even the rooms are not safe, Balram reports:

> Cat has tested blood. A Couple of Muslim Men has spread a newspaper on the ground and were sitting on it one of them had an open wound on his leg. He invited us to sit with him and his friend. Kishan and I lowered father onto the newspaper sheets. We waited there......the Muslim men kept adding newspapers to the ground, and the line of diseased eyes, raw wounds and delirious mouth kept growing. (45)

The post of doctors is auctioned and doctor gets the job offering bribe and touching the feet of great Socialist. "You can keep the rest of your government salary and go work in some private hospital for the rest of week. Forget the village because according to the ledger you have been there – you have treated my wounded leg, you have healed that girls jaundice "(50).

Balram narrates the worst part of being a driver:

> ... you have hours to yourself while waiting for your employer. You can spend this time chit-chatting and scratching your grion. You can read murder and rape magazines. You can develop the chauffeur's habit – it's a kind of yoga, really – of putting a finger in your nose and letting your mind go blank for hours. You can sneak a bottle of Indian liquor into the car – boredom makes drunks of so many honest drivers. (149)

Balram faced identity issues also. He was first called as "munna". This name "munna" was not accepted by school teacher so he was given the name Balram by the school teacher. Balram reports:

> He (teacher) passed his hand through his hair and said we'll call you Ram –
>
> Wait don't we have a Ram in this class? I don't want any confusion it'll be
>
> Balram. You know who Balram was, don't you??
>
> 'No, sir'
>
> 'He was the sidekick of God Krishna. Know what my name is?
>
> 'No, sir'
>
> He laughed, Krishna. (13-14)

When inspector visited the school, he pointed out Balram's unique nature in learning his lessons well:

> The inspector pointed his cane straight at me you, young man, are an intelligent,
>
> honest, vivacious fellow in this crowd of thugs and idiots. In any jungle, what
>
> Is the rarest of animals – the creation that comes only once in a generation "?
>
> I thought about it and said,
>
> 'The white tiger'
>
> That's what you are in this jungle. (55)

He starts his life as an entrepreneur. He takes his name as Ashok Sharma, the white tiger of Bangalore, he became a successful Entrepreneur but is not sure how long his identity losts. He writes to the premier:

> .... I'll get bored of it sooner or later. I'm a first – gear man, Mr. Premier. In the end, I'll have to sell this start up to some other moron – entrepreneur, I mean
>
> – And head into a new line. I'm thinking of real estate next you see, I'm always a man who sees' tomorrow 'when others see today." (319)

Balram considers himself "half baked" as he was deprived of schooling like most children of his age group in India. The key metaphor in the novel is of the Rooster coop – Balram is caged like the chicken in the Rooster coop. He, being a white tiger, has to break out of the cage of freedom.

Go to old Delhi and look at the way they keep chickens there I'm the market. Hundreds of pale hens and brightly coloured rooster, stuffed tight into wire. They see the organs of their brothers lying around them. They know they're next. Yet they do not rebel. They do not try to get out of the coop. The very same thing is done with human beings in this country (173-4).

Finally, Balram is identified as just a man – resembling like any other man. After murder is done, he flees to Bangalore. Wall posters, displaying his face are seen at the rail stations one illiterate man showed that posters and asked what the person in the poster did. Balram thought he was being watched and that illiterate man found him out.

> But suddenly he asked:
>
> You know who the fellow in the poster looks like??
>
> "Who? I asked
>
> 'He grinned,'
>
> 'Me'

I looked at his face and the photo

"It's true, 'I said, slapping him on the back.

I told you: it could be the face of half the man of India. (295)

This speaks of the universal self that Balram identifies in Him.

Works Cited

Adiga, Aravind. *The White Tiger*. New Delhi: Harper Collins Publisher India with India Today Group, 2008. Print.

Pratima Roy, "Issue of identity in Aravind Adiga's *White Tiger* – International," *Journal of English Language*, literature and translation studies.

10

An Ecofeminist Study of Margaret Atwood's *The Handmaid's Tale*

Ragini Kapoor

The term Ecofeminism was first used by French radical feminist Francoise d' Eaubonne (1920-2005), in 1974, to synthesize two movements previously thought of as separate – Ecology and Feminism. D'Eaubonne saw clear interconnections between the domination of women and that of nature, and she hoped to rescue the planet from destructive effects by her activism. Ecofeminism is a philosophy and a movement, born from the union of feminist and ecological thinking, and the belief that the social mentality which leads to the domination and oppression of women, is directly connected to the social mentality that leads to the abuse of the environment.

The most prominent idea running through the thoughts of all activists of ecofeminism is the linkage between the denigration of nature and the oppression of women. This is the basic argument of ecofeminism to which all ecofeminists ascribe. This basic argument stems from the idea that there is a link between the oppression of women and the oppression of nature. It is a worldview in which domination is seen to be a key axis of organisation, the enactment of which is explicitly embodied within the organising principles of Western culture. The same thought is echoed by Ynestra King who takes it a notch higher by declaring ecofeminism as "a holistic way of thinking" where issues like violence against women, military violence, and degradation of the planet are connected. In fact, it is very interesting to note how the prominent Eco feminists are so vocal about spelling out a number of items to be enlisted on the feminist agenda such as equal rights, quality of work, child care, reproductive choice, and domestic violence, and then interconnecting it to the environmental agenda. This sentiment is echoed by the following assertion of Val Plumwood that "Ecological feminism is essentially a response to a set of big problems thrown up by the two great social currents of the latter part of the last century, feminism and the environmental movement" (Adams and Warren, 10).

Ecofeminism is viewed primarily in terms of the creation of a new form of collective identity. Noel Sturgeon makes the same point when she says, 'Rather than understand ecofeminism as a new form of identity politics, I want to challenge the notion that movements produce fixed identities. Instead, I want to demonstrate the shifting and strategic qualities of various forms of identity politics...I want to show the way these identities appear and disappear, shift and change, when viewed in movement contexts' (Adams, 5). She emphasizes that it is this understanding of a social movement that is part and parcel of her exploration of ecofeminism as a movement and as a theory. Ecofeminism is a response to the perception that both women and nature have been devalued in Western culture and that both can be elevated and liberated through direct political action. The earth is being dominated by the complex social patterns called capitalist patriarchy – in which men labour in the marketplace and women labour in the home. The support a homemaker provides her husband in enabling him to carry out work outside the home with ease, is ignored and never ever considered worth for a mention, and, likewise, the fact of human dependence on the earth for our very sustenance is disregarded. Rather than being seen to contribute essential aspects of living, both women and nature are regarded as mere "resources", background to the more "worthy" furthering of human "culture" and "civilisation".

Before coming to *The Handmaid's Tale* by Margaret Atwood and then vis-a-vis to her interpretation of ecofeminism in it, it is important to sum up by saying that ecofeminism is a biocenteric environmental movement with cultural and social concerns. It seeks to replace patriarchal and hierarchical notions of power and domination in any form. The commonality between women's liberation and the liberation of nature is not difficult to perceive as both seek to free themselves from the capitalist patriarchal world that creates dichotomies or binaries of superior/inferior, exploiter/exploited, consumption/production, active/passive, and so on. Feminists have long criticised this dichotomy particularly the structural division of man and nature which is seen as analogous to that of man and woman. The eco-feminist movement/theory/ practice/activism all vouch for the concept of freedom and emancipation; and preserving and nurturing natural cycles of regeneration. It is a movement that celebrates the logic of emancipation and enlightenment, i.e., spiritual consciousness.

Margaret Atwood's works reflect her profound respect for the natural world, a commitment to Canadian culture and her firm belief in the rights of the individual. In her novels she explores the possible ties of combating patriarchal structures of power and domination that refuses a woman's equal claims as an individual in society. She advocates human rights of women and gives a clarion call for the destruction of gender-based injustices. Her novels raise a voice for the protection of Canadian environment, organic living, and the deep rooted relation and bonding between nature and humans. Her works illuminate the complex themes ranging from political and feminist to nationalist and psychological, her stories take a flight from gothic to science fiction; her texts speak of power-politics and for equity and equality; her tales are not just memories or archetypal fairy tales but are deeply embedded historiographic narratives; her works are a fine blend of linear structure, simple techniques and technical complexities. The work of this eloquent writer is captivating and intellectually engaging, and she takes the reader into marked as well as unobserved territories of contemporary life, life realisation, and a unified vision. There is a fusion of multidimensionality in the creative writings of Atwood as she transcends barriers of beauty, conventionality, time and space, yet deviates from social concerns which are pertinent to her personally and politically.

In a 1972 interview with Graeme Gibson, Atwood draws a parallel between the psyches of her heroines and Canada: What I'm really into...is the great Canadian victim complex. If you define yourself as innocent then nothing is ever your fault – it is always somebody else doing it to you, and until you stop defining yourself as a victim that will always be true. It will always be somebody else's fault, and you will always be the object of that rather than somebody who has any choice or takes responsibility for their life. And that is not only the Canadian stance towards the world, but the usual female one. Look what a mess I am and it's all their fault. And Canadians do that too (Nischik, 216).

Atwood draws a parallel between the psyches of her heroines and Canada, but rather than encouraging the great Canadian victim complex, she would much rather see her female protagonists shed off their "victim-image" and instead "surface" with a new awareness of being survivors with a distinct identity of their own. Coming of age during the feminist revolution of the 1970s, Atwood echoes the sentiments of women's rights in all of her books, asking tough questions about where we're going and where we've been. Atwood never shies away from hard-hitting political statements like unfettered, unguided nationalism, the penchant for violence in the Americans and anti-abortion demonstrators in her work. She serves as a constant and strident voice in the ongoing political and social movements of the day, speaking out against anything that does not push society towards tolerance and understanding.

The Handmaid's Tale, a tale of a new captivity, presents itself as an interpolation of the untold story about the "beasts" of history, whose imperialistic legacy is re-enacted, in Gilead, a regime reverting to, and actually exceeding, the prejudice of the original Puritans. Existing as an outgrowth of a utopian attempt to purify American culture and obliterate liberal tendencies identified with the wilderness, the Gileadean regime views females – who are associated with the "Mother" Earth – as "dark" and "native" forces threatening traditional patriarchal male (Dodson, 69). The novel focuses on one handmaid, Offred (she is given the name of the man whose children she is expected to bear). Offred becomes a handmaid after an attempt to escape with her daughter and husband from Gilead. Their attempt fails and her daughter is given away to a needy woman in the upper circles. Offred does not know whether her husband is alive or dead, whether he has escaped or has been captured. Offred is in the service of the General and his wife, Serena Joy. Serena Joy hates the fact that she is unable to bear children and hates Offred for taking her husbands' seed. The deal is that if Offred does not become pregnant promptly, Serena Joy would undoubtedly take revenge by sending her away possibly to the toxic colonies. Offred does not become pregnant, but she does develop an unexpected relationship with the General. He plays games of Scrabble with her (all forms of writing are officially denied to handmaids) and gives her gifts of cosmetics and old fashion magazines. One night he dresses her in a cocktail dress and takes her to an illegal night club where Offred runs into an old female friend, now a prostitute in the club. Serena Joy, desperate for children, finally arranges for Offred to sleep with the chauffeur. The two are happy together; she thinks she is pregnant. Soon after, Serena Joy finds the cocktail dress the General had given to Offred. She knows her husband is to blame, but accuses Offred anyway and sends for the police to take her away to certain death. When the van arrives to take her away, however, it is driven by rebels who carry Offred to safety.

In the novel's fictional epilogue the events of the novel occur shortly after the beginning of what is called "the Gilead period". The epilogue itself is a transcription of a Symposium on Gileadean Studies written sometime in the distant future, and according to the symposium's "keynote speaker", Professor Pieixoto, Professor Knotly Wace discovers Offred's narrative recorded onto "thirty" supposedly unnumbered "cassette tapes", places these tapes in a probable order and transcribes them, calling them collectively "the handmaid's tale" – a reference to *The Canterbury Tales* of Geoffrey Chaucer. Offred's narrative is disjointed in a grim, internal stream of consciousness style, out of order, and unfinished, ending abruptly when she indicates that she is about to be escorted away in a van to an unknown fate. In the Republic of Gilead there are seven main categories of "legitimate" women, who make up mainstream society, and two main categories of "illegitimate" women, who exist outside of mainstream society.

In the legitimate category, "Wives" are at the top social level permitted to women. They are married to the higher-ranking functionaries. Wives always wear blue dresses, presumably as a reference to the traditional depictions of the Virgin Mary. After the death of her husband, a Wife becomes a "Widow" and must dress in black. Second in the hierarchy come the "daughters" who are the natural or adopted children of the ruling class. They wear white until marriage. The narrator's daughter has been adopted by an infertile Wife and Commander. Next are the "handmaids" who are the fertile women whose social function is to bear children for the Wives. They dress in a red, including red shoes and red gloves. The only exception to the "all red rule" is the white wings they wear. Handmaids are produced by re-educating fertile women who have broken the gender and social laws. Owing to the need for fertile handmaids the number of gender-crimes, gradually increases in Gilead. The Republic of Gilead justifies the nature of the handmaids through the biblical stories of Jacob's wives (Gen. 30:1-3) and Abraham (Gen. 16:1-6).

"Econowives" are women who have married relatively low-ranking men, meaning any man who does not belong to the ruling elite. They are expected to perform all the female functions: domestic duties, companionship, and child-bearing. Their dress is multicoloured red, blue, and green to reflect these multiple roles. The division of labour between women engenders some resentment between categories. Marthas, Wives, and Econowives perceive Handmaids as sluttish, and Econowives resent their freedom from domestic work. The narrator mourns that none of the various groups are able to empathise with the others; women are taught to hate and fear other women. In the illegitimate category there are two distinctions. The first are "Unwomen" who are sterile women, widows, feminists, lesbians, nuns, and politically dissident women, all women who are incapable of social integration within the Republic's strict gender divisions. They are exiled to "the colonies", areas of both agricultural production and deadly pollution, as are handmaids who fail to produce a child after three two-year assignments.

The second category is of the "Jezebels" who are prostitutes and entertainers, available only to the Commanders and their guests; some are lesbians and attractive, educated women unable to adjust to handmaid status. They have been sterilised, which is illegal for other women. They operate in unofficially state-sanctioned brothels, and they seem to exist unbeknownst to most other women. Jezebels, whose title comes from the Biblical character, dress in the remnants of sexualised costumes from "the time before" viz. cheerleaders' costumes, school uniforms, and Playboy Bunny costumes. While Jezebels have some degree of freedom in that they can wear makeup, drink alcohol, and socialise with men, they are still tightly controlled by aunts. Once their usefulness for sex is over, they are sent to the colonies.

The Handmaid' s Tale, from the ecofeminists' point of view is blasphemous to the extent that it takes oppression of women to a very crass and a very dehumanising abyss. Human sexuality in Gilead is regulated by the notion that sexual intercourse is fundamentally degrading to women. Men are understood to desire sexual pleasure constantly, but are obliged to abstain from all but marital sex for religio-social reasons. The social regulations are enforced by law, with corporal punishment inflicted for lesser offences and capital punishment for greater ones. "The Ceremony" is a non-marital sexual act sanctioned solely for the purpose of reproduction, based on a Biblical passage described below. This Gileadean enactment has the Handmaid lying supine upon the Wife during the sex act itself. The handmaid is to lie between the Wife's legs as if they are one person. In this way, the wife has to invite the handmaid to share her power by inviting her to lie in her own personal space, which is considered both humiliating and offensive by many wives. Offred describes the ceremony: "My red skirt is hitched up to my waist, though no higher. Below it the Commander is fucking. What he is fucking is the lower part of my body. I do not say making love, because this is not what he's doing. Copulating too would be inaccurate, because it would imply two people and only one is involved. Nor does rape cover it: nothing is going on here that I haven't signed up for" (Atwood, Handmaid, 104-5).

Once a handmaid is pregnant, she is venerated by her peers and the wives. After the baby is born, if it is not an "unbaby" or a "shredder" (i.e., babies born with some birth defect or are born physically deformed), it is given to the Wife of her Commander, and she is reassigned to another household. She has the guarantee that she will never be declared an "unwoman". This novel indicates that pre-Gileadean society was not favourable for women. This society was a late twentieth century version of the United States as Atwood envisioned it developing at the time of its writing (1985). In this society, women feared physical and sexual violence, and despite long-running feminist campaigns, they had not achieved equality. Feminist campaigners like Offred's mother and Moira were persecuted by the state. Radical feminism had teamed up with social conservatives in campaigns against pornography. In addition, mass commercialisation had reached a nadir of "fast-food" and "home delivery" sexuality. Women outside of prostitution in "the former times" were subject to a socially constructed vision of romantic love that encouraged serial monogamy in favour of men's social and sexual interests.

Atwood, by highlighting the background of violence in a colonial empire-building culture, forces us into an intertextual rereading of both American history and the American literature as Offred's tale is read. Just as the seventeenth century Puritans did, the Protestant reformers who created Gilead violently ousted, hanged, or enslaved – and ultimately silenced – those dissenting against their religious and racial ideology. To rewrite the story of Puritanism in the novel, and to tell the truth about its dystopian legacy of intolerance and violence, Atwood focuses upon the stories within the American tradition that emphasize slavery (Dodson, 68).

The Handmaid's Tale shows that the future of ecological imbalance results in the oppression of women. It is a feminist dystopia set in the twenty-first century in the USA, which is now the Republic of Gilead, where, 'Still births, miscarriages, and genetic deformities were widespread and on the increase, and this trend has been linked to the various nuclear plant accidents, shutdowns...chemical and biological warfare stockpiles, and toxic-waste disposable sites...chemical insecticides, herbicides, and other sprays' (Atwood, Handmaid, 317).

In this frighteningly possible science fiction novel, Atwood creates a feminine dystopia and for some time it will be viewed as a test of the imaginative power of feminist paranoia. The ecofeminists' point of view has been extended not only to the women who are in trouble in the Christian nation but also the "children of Flam" are being relocated from their cities to their new homeland in North Dakota. Jews have been packed aboard ships supposedly headed for Israel. It is open season on Catholics, Quakers, former abortionists, and "gender traitors" (male homosexuals), all of whom are likely to be hung up from hooks on the wall that runs along the city of Gilead. But women are in a particularly tight spot. Some combinations of plague and toxic waste have decimated the human gene pool, so that women who may still have the potential to bear children have been pressed into service as full-time breeders, or "handmaids". A handmaid's job is to service a "Commander" and, indirectly, his usually sterile, ageing wife, in a lewd little *menage a' trois* justified by the scriptural arrangement between the childless Rachel and her maid Bilhah. Though victims of racial differences have been categorised and displaced from Gilead's dominant culture, fertile Caucasian females remain within it, used as objects at the discretion of powerful males. Women with working wombs are branded as different from males and from other females. The surface similarities between the female protagonists of slave narratives and the handmaids of Gilead are underlined by the legal role of the patriarchal white male in reproduction – 'As in slavery, despite the woman's labor, the white slave-holders, like the men in Gilead, retain legal property rights over the product of the woman's body' (Kauffman, 234).

Inspired by women's struggles for the protection of nature as a condition for human survival, this paper has gone beyond a statement of women as special victims of the environmental crisis. Gender-politics constitute a major thrust and an overriding preoccupation in Margaret Atwood's novels wherein she questions sex and gender roles and protests against patriarchal structures of power and dominion that subsume and expropriate the woman's identity. Atwood problematises the feminine search for a distinctive identity within a feminist framework and postulates a contextual discourse on feminine identity that explores and exposes the male will to power, and reiterates the need to recognise and resist hegemonic and homogenising patriarchal power structures.

A close analysis of Margaret Atwood's novels reveals that they are all ecofeminist texts. Atwood, with great insight, portrays the bondage of all her protagonists to various patriarchal structures along with their quest for dignity and freedom and their re-alignment with nature in their struggle for survival. All her protagonists are in their respective ways threatened by the extremes of patriarchy and by the various inadequacies they feel in themselves because of it. In the end, and again in their very different ways and out of their very different dilemmas, all of them find within themselves an ability to survive, not just to go on living, but to change and to move into new areas of life, in tune with the natural rhythms of the world. As an ecofeminist woman writer, Margaret Atwood is also concerned with women's fate and their position in this world. She explores sympathetically and critically the plight of women in twentieth century, and thus creates a vivid world inhabited by women relentlessly searching for true understanding of the self.

Understanding diversity among women and understanding the complex changing world within which women are variously located is the need of the hour. Equality is valuable only when it encourages rather than destroys differences. In the final analysis, it can be seen that Atwood's protagonists have a universal dimension. They can be seen not only as victims of an imperialistic and patriarchal society, but their anguish and suffering can be visualised as an alienation from nature. Their re-attachment with environment shows a relative progression towards inner freedom and a fully satisfying spiritual development in the lives of all her protagonists.

Works Cited

Adams, Carol J. (ed.). *Ecofeminism and the Sacred.* New York: Continuum. 1993. Print.

____., Karen J. Warren. *Feminism and the Environment: A Selected Bibliography.* American Philosophical Association Newsletter on Feminism and Philosophy 90, no. 3 (1991): 148-57. Print.

Atwood, Margaret. *The Handmaid's Tale.* London: Vintage, Random House. 1996. Print.

Dodson, Danita J. *We Lived in the Blank White Spaces: Rewriting the Paradigm of Denial in Atwood's The Handmaid's Tale.* Utopian Studies. Volume: 8. Issue: 2, 1997. Print.

Kauffman, Linda. *Special Delivery: Twenty-First Epistolarity in The Handmaid's Tale, Writing the Female Voice: Essays on Epistolary Literature,* ed. Elizabeth Goldsmith. Boston: Northeastern UP, 1989: 221-44. Print.

Nischik, Reingard M. (ed.). *Margaret Atwood: Works & Impact.* (2000, rpt.). Toronto: Anansi Press. 2002. Print.

Nordquist, Joan. *Ecofeminist Theory: A Bibliography (Social Theory: A Bibliographic Series, No. 36).* Santa Cruz, Calif.: Reference and Research Services. 1994. Print.

11

Rootlessness and Quest for Identity in Bharati Mukherjee's *Wife*

Surabhi K.

Bharati Mukherjee is one of the famous writers of Indian writers in English. Most of her works deal with nostalgia for homeland, multiculturalism, experiences of cultural shock and loneliness of being a diaspora. The author herself being an expatriate could easily connect herself to the plights of a diaspora. She has migrated from India to Canada and then to America and written numerous novels and two collections of short stories. Her experience of crossing the boundaries and her displaced self is reflected in many of her characters. She says in an interview,

> We immigrants have fascinating tales to relate. Many of us have lived in newly independent or emerging countries which are plagued by civil and religious conflicts. We have experienced rapid changes in the history of the nations in which we lived. When we uproot ourselves from those countries and come here, either by choice or out of necessity, we suddenly must absorb 200 years of American history and learn to adapt to American society. Our lives are remarkable, often heroic. (Mukherjee, 653-654)

Wife is her second novel written in 1975. The protagonist Dimple Dasgupta lives in Calcutta and fantasizes about her marriage. She dreams of marrying a neurosurgeon whereas her father seeks for her a suitable engineer in matrimonial advertisements. Her father chooses Amit Basu as her husband who is an engineer and would be soon emigrating from Canada to U.S.

Dimple believes that marriage would free her, fill her with passion and she waited for real life to begin. She has always wanted to marry a young man with mustaches, dressed in spotless white, peering into opened skulls and hoped that marriage would bring her freedom, cocktail parties on carpeted lawns, and fund-raising dinners for noble charities. She has always wished to live in an apartment in *Chowringhee,* her hair done by Chinese girls and to trip to *New Market* for nylon saris. Being born in Indian family and inculcating all traditional values she imagines herself like Sita, the ideal wife of Hindu legends. She wished to have all material comforts in her new marriage. With the dreams within and days passing, she gets married to Amit only to find all her dreams shattered. She fails to find anything attractive, neither her relationship nor her in laws or the place she lives in. The pregnancy also makes her feel everything out of place which she fanatically aborts. Soon the news of migration gives her some hope but she soon finds this dream too unreal. The alien land completely spoils her life with an extra marital affair, not fitting in to the food or land. She is now physically and psychologically displaced and in frenzy kills her husband to free herself from all the confusions and disillusionment.

Dimple and the Dislocated Self

William Safran in 1991 has put forward some defining attributes of Diaspora. He terms it as qualifying markers of being a diaspora. According to him one should disperse from a 'centre' to a foreign periphery to be a diaspora, they should have a collective memory and myth of homeland when in the hostland, and they should suffer from sense of alienation. He opines that the diasporas should believe their ancestral homeland as their ideal homeland and hopes for an eventual return to their native land. There is a commitment for their own soil and a continued identification of the self with the homeland. These attributes of being a stranger in a foreign land and a dream for eventual return to the native land is seen in most of Bharati Mukherjee's novels.

Dimple, the protagonist in *Wife* suffers from identity crisis from the very beginning. She is always concerned about her outer looks for not being fair and having smaller breasts. She tries to make herself more appealing for her future husband; trying to whiten her complexion, increase her bust through isometrics and completing her graduation. She is also irritated when her mother-in-law prefers to call her by a traditional name Nandini, instead of Dimple. She struggles with her identity in all stages of her life. When she gets pregnant, she regrets for carrying a baby as she wouldn't want to carry anything of her past when she has to move abroad and start a new life. She considers the baby to be "tyrannical and vile" thing that was induced in to her body. She urges to create her own new self, a new identity leaving every old thing back there. Her act of getting rid of the baby can be seen as her act of freedom and all constraints of marriage and womanhood that she is now into.

> The truth is that Dimple is insecure about her identity; moreover, her own embryonic and stinted mental growth makes her perceive her own child as a threat to her life. Her abortion and vomiting sessions make her an independent agent who is in partial control of her body. But this rebellion does not have the making of a victorious rebellion as this is the reaction of a misinformed, insecure female subject. This insecurity stems from the sexual and social subjugation of woman in the hierarchical patriarchal set up, where even the unborn child is guarded as the family's 'communal property'. She believes that America would provide her the chance to self-fashion herself to anything she wants. (Rao and Khushu-Lahiri, 138-139)

Now with the news of going to a new land, Dimple hopes for a better future. She soon finds out that her marriage is a failure and both the partners cease to understand each other. She had made up her mind of suffering from cross culture in America in the beginning but she had never thought the pain could be so drastic and beyond endurance. She is more Indian in America and is often reminded of her "Indianness." She has left behind everything to begin a new life as an expatriate but couldn't leave her native culture and traditions. She finds herself alien in a land of strangers. She couldn't even mingle with her own community people. She feels out of home whenever she finds westernised food and hates American accent. She finds it difficult to assimilate when she realises about cultures which do not go with each other and that people don't celebrate *Durga Pujah*[1]. She is afraid to operate elevators and is confined to her four walls of apartment. She sleeps whole day and hardly cooks anything. Even Amit couldn't provide her solace or make her comfortable whenever she was lonely. Thus she seeks the company of Meena Sen, watching T.V and reading newspaper. This easily took her to the American world of violence where people murder and divorce for petty reasons. She realised that talking about murders in America was like talking about the weather in India. She thinks of her own land where everything was so peaceful. Dimple in the news land is afraid of gadgets, elevators and policemen whom she remembers were friendly to others.

Form the author's own experiences of being an expatriate, she says:

> There was a pattern of discrimination. I was refused service in stores. I would have to board a bus last when I had been the first person on line. I was followed by detectives in department stores who assumed I was a shoplifter or treated like a prostitute in hotels. I was even physically roughed up in a Toronto subway station. I found myself constantly fighting battles against racial prejudice. Toronto made me into a civil rights activist. I wrote essays about the devastating personal effects of racism. For many years I didn't find the strength to turn my back on Canada and do what I really wanted to do: write fiction. (Mukherjee, 652)

Soon Dimple is influenced by her Indian American friend Ina Mullick, whose American ways life awes her. She is now completely in to the unreal world of soap operas and T.V where everything is fictitious. Now she in another dinner party at Meena's place, tries to prepare a salad which is most American looking salad and attempts to use foreign ingredients to assimilate to her new place 'America'.

The extra-marital affairs, a major theme of the soap operas in the American culture influenced her to fall for Milt Glasser. She soon depends on him for emotional support and identity. She is

---

1 *Durga Pujah*, also called *Durgotsava* and *Navaratri*, is an annual Hindu or Bengali Hindu festival in Indian that reveres the goddess *Durga*.

hardly guilty about her relationship with her new lover which itself shows her drift from her own self and culture to a new culture of modernisation. But soon after the relationship goes more deep, she is afflicted by a sense of guilt for cheating her husband, her culture and losing her identity. She starts to live like a shadow without any feelings, alienated, trapped and out of mind. In state of abnormality she stabs her husband to death overcome by guilt and disgust. This act of frenzy symbolises freedom from her husband and indeed from the foreign land, both of from which she is alienated. The act of killing itself is seen to be foreign, which she would have never done if she was in Calcutta.

Stuart Hall's ideas about conceptions of cultural identity is important here: he argues that identity is the product of multiple representations, each of which are formed by unique contexts, and that these cultural identities can be thought of in two distinct ways: first, that there is "one true self" residing as a common spirit among all members of the same ethnicity, and second, that cultural identity is not a question of "are" but rather of "becoming" (Sathian, 27).

Conclusion

The novel portrays the predicament of an Indian wife, who feels marginalised, finding herself out of place in an alien land. The protagonist sudden changed life from a same city of Calcutta and an unsupported husband paves way to her psychological struggles. The initial plight makes her caged and uninterested to life and marital life; and her gradual assimilation to the host country impacts her so much to the extent of completely becoming an alien.

Bharati Mukherjee deals with the complexities of life thrown between two cultures. In the novel *Wife*, the protagonist fails to assimilate with the new land, its cultures and ways of life. Alienation and Rootlessness, identity crisis forms the major themes of the novel. The plights are to the extreme for the women migrators who go to the host land. They feel deprived when they are not supported by their husbands and are subjugated. She always lives in the memory of homeland and a hope for eventual return with family as in the case of Ashima in Jhumpa Lahiri's *Namesake*.

Multiculturalism, cross cultures, food and identity crisis all makes them a complete stranger in the new land. All the trauma of being a diaspora led the protagonist in to cultural shock, drastically affecting her mind. The novel is very well successful in bringing about the traumatic experiences in the process of migration. The writer's women protagonists like. Dimple, Tara, Vinita, Angela, Nafeesa were brutally affected by psychological conflicts caused in the process of being an expatriate. But her other women characters like Jasmine, Hannah, Panna, etc... have emerged as successful immigrants.

> ... American opulence is in stark contradiction to the Indian scarcity symbolised by Dimple. Ina can successfully transform herself, because she can transcend the boundaries of the domestic domain. Thus, Mukherjee undoubtedly upholds the kitchen as a place of refuge from cultural shock; nonetheless, she implies that the true progress of a female immigrant subject takes place when she transcends that comforting albeit constricting zone and moves out into the world outside (Rao and Khushu-Lahiri, 141)

Works Cited

Carb and Mukherjee. "An Interview with Bharati Mukherjee." *The Massachusetts Review.* Vol. 29, no. 4, 1988. pp.645-654. https://www.jstor.org/stable/pdf/25090039.pdf?refreqid=excelsior%3Acac750011303b7490c6491c4c85198bf. Web. 28 July 2017.

Joshi and Barche. "Bharati Mukherjee's *Wife* – A Tragedy of Unfullfilled Dreams." *International Journal on Studies in English Language and Literature (IJSELL),* Vol. 2, no. 9, 2014, pp.118-121. https://www.arcjournals.org/pdfs/ijsell/v2-i9/15.pdf. Web. 28 July 2017.

Krishnan. "Cultural Construct and the Female Identity: Bharati Mukherjee's *Wife.*" *The International Fiction Review,* Vol. 25, no. 1 & 2. 1998. https://journals.lib.unb.ca/index.php/IFR/article/view/75 99/8656. Web. 28 July 2017.

Mukerjee, Bharati. *Wife.* New Delhi: Penguin Books (India), 1980. Print.

Rao and Khushu-Lahiri. "Indian Wife in American Kitchen: A Study of Wife". *Bharati Mukerjee: Critical Perspectives.* Ed. Somdatta Mandal. New Delhi: Pencraft Books; 2010. 134-143. Print.

Sathian, Sanjena. "Gender and Nation in the South Asian Diaspora: Transnational Cultural Spaces in Bollywood Cinema." *Columbia Undergraduate Journal of South Asian Studies,* vol. 2, no. 1, 2013, pp.22-41. http://www.columbia.edu/cu/cujsas/SATHIAN.pdf . Web. 20 May 2017.

12

A Postcolonial Overview of Arundhati Roy's *The Ministry of Utmost Happiness*

Supriya Mandal

The novel *The Ministry of Utmost Happiness* appears with so many contemporary issues and its answers. The novel is like a magic-realism which combines history and realism in perfect balance. It was dappled with so many subjects, Kashmir insurgency, Hindu-Muslim pogrom in Gujarat in 2002, the humiliated and battered life of transgender and the brutal experience of Dalit. The novel is a story of a transgender woman, Anjum who used to be Aftab and the love story of a Kashmiri militant Musa and an ultra-modern girl, Tilo. The author questions repeatedly either we are in postcolonial state or we are colonised by our own people. The experience and the reminiscences of her characters reveal the truth. Anjum was forced to live in a graveyard because the so called *Duniya* was not fit for her. She was scratched, stoned, humiliated and exploited like a tree. The 'cultural ideology' of so called *Duniya* fails to explain her. She was beyond explanation, beyond language, beyond gender identity. Jahanara Begum knew " ...all things, not just living things but all things – carpets, clothes, books, pens, musical instruments – had a gender. Everything was either masculine or feminine, man or woman. Every-thing except her baby" (8). A person cannot live in a vacuum, s/he needs a cultural identity. But Anjum has no identity. Not only she but all the *'hijras'* go through this crisis. They have no schooling, no education, they are only forced to confine themselves in 'balcony' to see the school going 'normal' children. Roy portrays Anjum's experience but this is the experience of the whole transgender community. In our society women are 'double colonised', trapped by both patriarchy and colonialism but the transgender are trapped by tripartite system of colonialism. They have no legal rights, no jobs, they have to live by begging or by miser amount of Government and NGO's allowances or by '*badtameezi* – bad behaviour'. Through the portrayal of Anjum's anxiety the novelist sketches the anxiety of all transgenders. Roy expresses Anjum's mental anxiety through her narration –

> She is a woman trapped in man's body... She, who never knew which box to tick, which queue to stand in, which public toilet to enter (Kings or Queens? Lords or Ladies? Sirs or Hers)...She, augmented by her ambiguities... (p. 122).

Roy assails back Hindu mythology where the transgender are regarded as "forgotten ones". In Ramayana when Ram, Sita and Laxman were going to forest for fourteen years, the citizenry decided to go with them, and reached the outskirts of Ayodhya where the forest began. Then Ram addressing to the people said – 'I want all you men and women to go home and wait for me until I return' (p. 51).The transgenders were also there but Shree Ram only addressed the men and women to go back but he forgot to mention the transgenders. They waited fourteen years at the edge of forest. So they are taken as 'forgotten ones' not only in past but in the present also.

The novelist through her spokesperson, Dr. Azad Bharatiya, gives a hint of Foucault's 'Panoptical' view and 'Governmentality' prevailing in our society, Panopticism, is a social theory, named after the Panopticon, coined by Jeremy Bentham and it was developed by French theorist Michel Foucault in his book *Discipline and Punish*. Here constant observation acts as a control mechanism. In the novel, we see that Dr. Azad Bharatiya is fasting against the issues – the Capitalist Empire, US Capitalism, Indian American State Terrorism etc. For this particular reason, he has been put under twenty-four hours surveillance by the American Government. The American Government have installed their camera in the traffic light also. Thus power becomes more effective through the mechanisms of observation or watchful eye to control or modify behaviour, and to track people who aren't confined. Thus people are surrendering to the unseen power that endeavours to control people from afar.

Roy through her strong narrative presents the contemporary political upheaval. She presents the factual history through Anjum's reminiscence of her experience in Gujarat riot and the 'Flyover Story', at the time of India's first Emergency, declared by the then Government. By the declaration of emergency, fundamental rights were suspended, newspapers had been censored, police atrocities were shrouded over the country. In the name of population control, people were forcefully sterilised. The Government's enactment of new law – Maintenance of Internal Security Act gave permission to arrest anybody on mere suspicion. The jail was crowded over by the opposition leaders without any trial. The Democracy and Indian Constitution became puppet in the hands of political leaders. Anjum depicted the 'Flyover Story' to Zainab but in reality this incident was much bitterer. Their driver was arrested and rigorously tortured by the police. They (the transgenders) were forcefully instructed to "...run all the way home if they did not want to be arrested for prostitution and obscenity" (35). The author ironically asks if this is 'democracy or demon crazy' where the transgenders have no right and respect as human being, where common people were tortured in the name of controlling intolerance. In 1984, the then prime minister Mrs. Indira Gandhi was assassinated by her Sikh bodyguards. The whole Sikh community was ruthlessly tortured by her supporters. The whole community had to pay for the wrong doing of a few men.

Roy's '*The Ministry of Utmost Happiness*' is a critique of Indian political ideology. She unknots the hidden discourse of Indian politics. Some political parties are preaching about 'Secularism', some about 'Hinduism', some in the favour of 'Minority', some on the issues of 'Dalit' and at the same time they are preaching about India's unity. The author questions if we are united why the political leaders have different populism that cause riot. People are mesmerised by their overarching totalitarian views of democracy, liberty, equality and fraternity. But, is there any fraternity among Hindu-Muslim-Christian-Sikh, any equality among human beings? She hates the jingoistic nationalism of Bharatia Janata Party that causes Gujarat riot in 2002. Anjum, the victim of the riot, was a shattered survival. The brutality of the riot made her away from the so called '*Duniya*'. When in Akshardham 66 pilgrims were burnt alive by the Muslims, Gujarat ka Lalla never tried to appease the Hindu chauvinism but he unofficially announced that "every action would be met with an equal and opposite reaction" (45). So the 'reaction' was the terrible *'Godhara'* incident. The miscreant's devil dance destroyed everything. The overtly nationalist Hindu right wing mobs with "steel talons and bloodied beaks – all squawking together: "*Mussalman ka ek hi sthan! Qubristan ya Pakistan*!" ("Only one place for the Mussalman! The Graveyard or Pakistan") (62). The massacres were everywhere, at homes, business places, shops, and hospitals. The police were also the part of the mob. They did not lodge any missing dairy during the riot period. Zakir Mian had been brutally murdered but Anjum was saved for the traditional belief. The only one thing can appease them, then 'prospect of bad luck' (62) "*nahi yaar, mat maro, Hijron ka maarna apshagun hota hai.*" ("Don't kill her, brother, killing Hijras brings bad luck") (62). They 'folded men and unfolded women' (62) but they left Anjum "alive. Un-killed. Un-hurt. Neither folded nor unfolded. She alone. So that they might be blessed with good fortune" (63). The Muslims shaved their beard and tied red thread in their hands to pass themselves as Hindu in riot's time. After returning from Gujarat, Anjum always chanted Gayatri Mantra, even she helped Zainab to recite it because she was afraid that "Gujarat could come to Delhi any day" (48). People are not safe in any part of country. Notwithstanding the massacre, "*Gurjat ka Lalla*" won the election and people said that he would be usurping the throne of Central Government also.

Anjum understands the core issues of life. The hyper nationalism makes India a grave. Anjum is afraid that Gujarat can come anywhere any day. Saddam Hussain opines that actually it will not come but it exists. The whole India is like a Gujarat. Some time they (political leaders) disown farmers from their field and hand over their fields to the coalminer, sometime they displace the people from riverside and make there dams without any rehabilitation, and evict the slam dweller from the city, –

> Skyscrapers and steel factories sprang up where forest used to be, rivers were bottled and sold in supermarkets, fish were tinned, mountain mined and turned into a shining missiles. Massive dams lit up the cities like Christmas trees. (98)

Jantar Mantar was the place for political elites who cry for 'corruption free India', 'caste free India', 'classless India,' so and so forth. Roy attacks the cunning politicians and pseudo social workers. They make people believe that they are only struggling for the cause of the poor. But in reality they only do to come to the limelight. She criticised Anna Hazare, 'a tubby old Gandhian, former-soldier-turned-village-social-worker' who fast for the 'dream of a corruption free India'. She belittled his idea by categorising it as 'dream' but this dream would remain unfulfilled because "His dream of a society free of corruption was like a happy meadow in which everybody, including the most corrupt, could graze for a while" (102). The most corrupted businessmen, politicians funded for his struggle. The author punctured the exaggeration of his struggle. The old man was sly enough to understand that it would not be fruitful to stick to only one subject like corruption, he connected pseudo nationalistic ideology and announced that "he was leading India's Second Freedom Struggle" (102) to get attention. He supported the 'Hindu chauvinism' and when Muslims were dissatisfied, he arranged for a visit by Muslim film star who sat beside him. When Dalit were burst into fury, the committee arranged a sweeper girl who is dressed well and that girl serves his drinking water to 'underline the message of Unity in Diversity'. For the nationalists he cried, *"Doodh maangogey to kheer dengey! Kashmir maangogey to chiir dengey!"* ("Ask for milk, we'll give you cream! Ask for Kashmir we'll rip you open seam to seam") (103).The politically supreme class of people need to congregate citizenry with common interests, and they are positively able to play it with nationalism. In this way, ethnic politics is appreciated and ratiocinated and it advertises that they are building this state not for their own private interest but for their ethnic group. And their totalitarian speech mesmerised people. There were so many struggles. A Gandhian activist made fast on behalf of thousand farmers and indigenous tribal of West Bengal. But she was not covered by media like the sly 'old man'. Besides the old man's 'anti-corruption movement', there were Manipuri Nationalists asking for the withdrawal of the Armed Forces Special Powers Act. Tibetan refugees were calling for free Tibet. The Association of Mothers of the Disappeared, whose sons were missing, came with their banner,

> The story of Kashmir
> DEAD=68,000
> DISAPPEARED=10,000
> Is this Democracy or Demon Crazy? (115)

No TV camera captured their banner. The idea of freedom for Kashmir and the protest of Kashmiri women became audacious to them. They were heckled by the TV channel and the police outcry, – "Muslim terrorists do not deserve Human Rights!"(115). The Bhopal Union Carbide Gas victims protested for justice for a long time. The company had changed its name, now DAW Chemicals. The author questions through her spokesperson, Dr. Azad Bharatia:

> But these poor people who were destroyed by them, can they buy new lungs, new eyes? They have to manage with their same old organs, which were poisoned so many years ego. But nobody cares, (130).

There is no one to heed at their demand, no one to listen them. That's why Saddam Hussain wants to take revenge but revenge against revenge, the war against war go on. But when it will end?

This novel is the perfect remonstration against India's ingrained caste system that is always exhilarated by the political parties. The lower caste people are degraded not only by the upper caste Hindu but also by the police, the preserver of law. The author depicted the heinous experience of Saddam Hussain. The police atrocities and humiliation forced him to renounce his religion. He was a Dalit but later he inclined towards Islam. He was nourishing a revengeful mentality for the lynching of his father by the Hindu mob. He himself changed his name as 'Saddam Hussain' because he was encouraged by the courageous/boastful death of Saddam *Hussein*, the President of Iraq. His father and father's friends were lynched by the mob in front of the police station. The reigning government always preach that people should obey and make belief on law and order of the country. But where is law and order? Here the police want their 'cut' and if they are dissatisfied, they will hand over the seemingly accused to mob. The little Saddam, his father and his father's friends were returning from collecting the carcasses of cow, they stopped at Dulina police station to pay the 'cut' to Sehrawat, Station House Officer. The officer demanded more on that day but they had not much money. The officer locked them on the charge of 'cow slaughtering'. They (police) spread the rumour that they were 'cow killer'. The mobs who were invigorated by the Hindu ideology of '*Gau Rakhsha'*, butchered the men on the basis of rumour. Saddam was too small to understand the circumstance. He was also mingled with the crowed, "I was part of the mob that killed my father" (89). Saddam was terrified by the sight, "Everybody watched. Nobody stopped them (89). The blood of his father was flowing "as if it were rainwater, how the road looked like a street in the old city on the day of Bakr-Eid" (89) The government make the 'Holy Cow' national emblem and the '*Gau Rakshak Bahini*' get enough power to utilise their atrocities. The people who ate beef were beaten to death by the mob. Their brutality was evident when Anjum told the inhabitants of Graveyard to drive away the old cows (to shun the allegation of cow slaughtering) because "If they (cows) die here – not if, when they die – they'll say you killed them and that will be the end of all of you...You have to be very careful"(402). Saddam expressed his fearful attitude that "If they want to kill you they will kill you whether you are careful or not, whether you have killed a cow or not, whether you have even set eyes on a cow or not." (402)

The novel portrays the racial conflict and humiliation in the life of S. Murugesan, a soldier. He died from an explosion. He was from lower caste and always treated with humiliation by his fellow soldiers. Even after his death, the high caste did not allow his body to pass their house. So, the Government who made a documentary film on him for their grand narration about the valour of army and their sacrifice for the sake of country became futile. It did not make him able to get respect. Even when his statue was erected at the beginning of the village, some higher caste people did not like "an Untouchable Man's statue put up at the entrance" (318). Few days later the statue was amputated and beheaded. How ridiculous it is that a soldier who served his country and lost his life for the sake of country are dishonoured and disgraced only because he belongs to a low caste! The 'grand narration' about the sacrifice of a soldier and his greatness do not succeed in getting any respect for him.

The postcolonial literature not only discloses the view of politics and the hidden discourse of dominant ideology but also it helps people to make resistance against exploitation. The upper caste people always need lower caste peoples' help to make them clean and pure but they never acknowledge their contribution. In return they are humiliated. Saddam Hussain forsook his idea of revenge when his people stood against exploitation and humiliation. The reincarnation of the incident like Saddam's father made them aware about the exploitation. Five Dalits were humiliated when they were returning from collecting carcasses of dead cows. They protested and denied to work for upper caste Hindus. The rejuvenation of Dalit charmed Saddam and he renounced his idea of revenge, "my people have risen up! They are fighting! What is one Sehrawat for us now? Nothing!" (407).

Arundhati Roy is a fierce criticiser of military insurgency in Kashmir. For her powerful criticism she was also accused of the charge of sedition. But she criticises not only military but also the pedant Maulanas and Maulabis. She rebukes the Kashmiri idea of 'jihad' as an 'inbuilt idiocy'. This idea percolated into Kashmir from Pakistan and Afghanistan. The Moulanas use religion to spread intolerance. They want to build an Islamic state. They shut down the cinema hall, liquor shop as 'un-Islamic'. The boy Aijaz, a Kashmiri militant, joined Lashkar-e-Taiba instead of Hizb and JKLF. He joined Lashkar-e-Taiba because the other Kashmiri militant groups had respect for the political leaders who "cheated and betrayed us... made their political careers on the bodies of Kashmiri" (228). Roy records the wretched condition of Kashmiri. They lived like prisoners in Jeremy Bentham's circular cell always watched by the unseen guard either by militant or by the Army. The people are consistently threaten at the gun point. We can understand their miserable condition when the Army officer, Armik Singh, uttered that sometimes they knocked on villagers' door "pretending to be militants from Pakistan asking for shelter. If they were welcomed, the next day the villagers would be arrested..." (335) The author's heart cries for the impoverish condition of the villagers, –

> How are unarmed villagers supposed to turn away a group with guns who knock on their doors in the middle of the night? Regardless of whether they are militants or military? (p. 335).

That kind of rigorous torture is enough to create another militant like Musa and Aijaz. Musa was arrested by the police because he was so calm at the funeral of his wife and daughter. His three years old daughter Miss Jebeen and his wife were shot dead. The ubiquitous death was hovering through the crystal white Valley. Here the person is not recognised by their personality, rather by their 'ID card', "our cards are more important than we ourselves are now. That card is the most valuable thing anyone can have" (p. 343). The Army personnel like Major Amrik Singh, Ashfaq Mir and ACP Pinky were enough to make the life of people horrible. Major Amrik Singh accosted himself as 'jannat express' who helped the Kashmiri to go to *Jannat*. He was a 'gambler, a daredevil officer, a deadly interrogator and a cherry, coldblooded murderer'. The men, like Amrik Singh want to prolong the war in Kashmir. Aijaz revealed the truth that he was trained in Kashmir. He never crossed the broader. He got everything in Kashmir. It was very shocking to know that the militants got arms from the very Army, who were appointed for the maintenance of peace. Aijaz disclosed the bitter reality by his revelation,

> Yes they (army) don't want the militancy to end. They don't want to leave Kashmir. They are happy with the situation as it is. Everybody on all sides is making money on the bodies of young Kashmiris. (228).

The Valley is presented as 'paradise' in earth by the Jammu and Kashmir Tourism Department, where indigenous people are made to sit on white snow, wrapped in warm clothes with their happy faces and shouting in an exhilarating voice, 'Jammu and Kashmir. So White. So Fair. So Exciting' (90) but in reality "Death was everywhere. Death was everything. Career. Desire. Dream. Poetry. Love. Youth itself. Dying became just another way of living." (314) The 'hyperreal' presentation of valley by the tourism department blurs the distinction between 'reality and imagined, reality and illusion, surface and depth' (Barry, 86). Baudrillard's association with 'the loss of real' is actually created by the influence of images from film, TV and advertisement. Arundhati Roy tries to interpret the depth of the surface which is misrepresented by the Media. In this novel, she tries to demystify those aspects of Media.

The police truculence were not only confined into Kashmir. The indigenous people of Central India were also the victim of the same truculence. Roy presents the Naxalite and Maoist uprising in Bostar district. The police tortured the men and sexually abused the female. It is presented through the experience of Comrade Revathy who was an activist. Some young girls and boys rose against the exploitation by the 'Class Enemy'. Operation Green Hunt was announced by the then Government in 2009. The forest was flooded by the 'police, Cobras, Greyhounds, Andhra Police' and Paramilitary Forces. They killed the adivasis and burnt the village. The villagers were plundered by them – "They take everything, burn everything, steal everything...They want adivasi people to vacate forest so they can make a steel township and mining" (p. 421). Comrade Revathy was unofficially arrested and unconsciously raped by six policemen. She was made pregnant by them. They fought for the rights of the poor, for their root but the Government labelled them as revolutionist or Maoists. So, the Government can do anything with them. The Government never try to assess their real problem, their poverty ridden situation.

The postcolonial scholar Partha Chatterjee observes that, "the image of woman as goddess or mother binds her to a form of subordination that is the exercise of dominance without hegemony" (Nyla Ali Khan, *The Woman Question in the Subcontinent*). As a postcolonial writer Arundhati Roy also exposes those patriarchal domination upon women. She projected Tilo against those domination. She does not inculcate the traditional feminine virtue in her. Tilo's insouciant lifestyle, her denial of being a mother, her daring attitude to love a Kashmiri Militant and her equanimity in front of Army interrogation were an another way of challenging patriarchy. The nationalist delimits the scope of women in larger spectrum by confining her in the trough of motherhood and assimilates her with the territory of a country. So, she should need protection. In this novel when Musa left Tilo finally he also suggested her to stay not alone because it's dangerous for a woman to live alone – "you need cover". Why she needs a cover, because she is a woman? But it's not easy to challenge the notion. Patriarchy demands traditional virtues in a woman. If she tries to go beyond, she should be regarded as a faithless, coquette women, and easily available object to anyone. When Tilo worked in an architectural firm she was going to be disturbed by the 'lewd suggestions' of a retired army officer. The man hammered on her door at midnight in a tipsy condition. But she never dared to complain against the man because "she was a lone woman" (p. 364). The whole society wants to teach women how to dress, how to live and how to behave. If she dares to go far from the traditional norms, she has to face such a cruel question repeatedly like Tilo, – "How many men do you fuck at the same time?" (p. 381) and the words are stinging like hell. So, when you are stigmatised as 'indecent' or 'immoral', you will lose all your legal rights of protest. That's why when the dead body of Rubina, the prostitute, was found with her eyes missing, the pimp Anwar Bhai did not dare to complain it to police. The author questions if there is any liberty for women. Women are always regarded as 'subaltern' that Gayatri Chakraborty Spivak argued in her path breaking essay "Can the Subaltern Speak?" As per Spivak's suggestion, a 'subaltern' cannot speak, who is only 'ventriloquised' or spoken for either by the colonial master or by the present postcolonial master.

Arundhati Roy is an acute commentator of Euro-American imperial policy and the impact of 'Neocolonialism'. 'Neocolonialism', was first introduced by Kwame Nkrumah. By this term, he proposes that the decolonised countries (previous colonies) have a small economic dependency. Their economic policies are basically controlled by the First World nation or by the super-national organisations (that are basically under control of First World nation). Like, ASPs, FDI, WTO, NATO, privatisation and other policies of these nations are also determined by the First World countries. This is the best way for the First World nations to retain their power in their previous colonies. "Exploitation of the natural resources of the former colonies continues through mining and cheap labour (sweat shop). Economic control is also very often accompanied by cultural imperialism... western models of dressing, eating and social interactions process begins to acquire a tenacious hold in the post-colonial nation" (*TPSD,* 115). Thus orientalism which is based on the seemingly cultural superiority of the West over the East paved the path for imperialism. Roy attacks these anglophile mentality of Indian people where American Army dogs live in five star hotel's AC room and native people sleep in street. The author addresses 'capitalism' a 'poisonous honey' that attracts people. The media as a medium of 'e-colonialism' colonised the mind of people. So, "English newspaper and the newest brand of skin whitening cream (selling by ton) said: Our Time Is Now. Kmart was coming. Walmart and Starbucks were coming..." (p 97) This tendency of inclination towards First World culture has made the Indian what Bhabha called a "mimic man".

According to P.K. Nayar, "Neocolonialism is furthered in the former colonies through the role of the elite...The elite who might be seen, not without reason, as supportive of globalisation, also occupy the places vacated by the former European masters. They became the new ruling classes..." (*TPSD,* 115). Thus the author's exposition of hidden ugly faces of American-imperialism, neo-colonialism, the failure of the postcolonial project of creating unified India, the wretched condition of untouchable, dalits, adivasis and transgenders are evident in this novel. The novel exposes the deplorable conditions of the colonised Indians in postcolonial India. Now, India is a Neocolonial state.

Works Cited

Abrams, M. H. & Geoffrey Galt Harpham. *A Hand book of Literary Terms.* 11th ed., Cengage Learning, 2015. Print.

Barry, Peter. *Beginning Theory: An Introduction to Literary and Cultural Theory.* 3rd ed., Manchester UP, 2008. Print.

Gandhi, Leela. *Postcolonial Theory: A Critical Introduction.* Oxford University Press, New Press, New Delhi, 1998. Print.

Khan, Nyla Ali. "The Woman Question in the Subcontinent". Daily Times, 21st August, 2017. Print.

Nayar, Promod K. *The Postcolonial Studies Dictionary*. John Wiley and Sons, 2015. Print.

____., *Contemporary Literary and Cultural Theory from Structuralism to Ecocriticism*, Pearson Books, 2010. Print.

____., *The Postcolonial Literature: An Introduction.* Pearson India, 2008. Print.

Roy, Arundhati. *The Ministry of Utmost Happiness.* Penguin Random House India, 2017. Print.

13

Food as a Metaphor for Identity and Isolation in Selected Stories of Jhumpa Lahiri

Dr. Prachi Priyanka

Food, as Jon D. Holtzman (2006) rightly observes in his essay "Food and Memory", is "an intrinsically multilayered and multidimensional subject – with social, psychological, physiological, symbolic dimensions." (362). Food becomes an important subject in diaspora writing especially because it is a "vehicle for memory" (365). Diasporic writings are often full of references to food, feasting and eating – nostalgic as they are – making food a veritable centre of attention for both the readers and the critics alike. (Chatterjee, 197) Frank Chin has opposed to this kind of diasporic writing by contemporary Asian American women where they dwell excessively on the culinary idiom. However, Supriya Chaudhury (2011) in her introduction to 'Writer's Feast', supports the idea of food description as a longing for a lost cuisine, or the attempt to recover it in a foreign kitchen, suffuses diasporic writing about food with a nostalgia that exceeds its object: it is as though the absent homeland, like the absent real, lies behind the imagined but unobtainable item of food" (x-xi).

In his essay 'Food and Eating: An Anthropological Perspective", Robin Fox (2015) talks about various ways food is associated with the emotional and sexual activity. The analogy between food/eating and sex/sexuality is abundant in academic and critical discourses. Malthus also holds that "the most powerful of all desires is the desire for food, closely followed by the passion between the sexes" Lahiri's stories invoke this association from different perspectives.

Jhumpa Lahiri recognises the importance of food on a global scale and she uses it as a consistent element in her short stories collection 'Interpreter of Maladies'. Lahiri recognises the potential of food in its ability to spark the exploration in and out of two cultures. In 'Interpreter of Maladies', food is used as a conduit between the English and Indian cultures; food serves as an expiatory offering, as a basis for assimilation, and as a source of cultural identity. (Garcia, 1)

In Mary Douglass 1972 article, Deciphering a Meal, she took Renaud's idea of food being a universal necessity and determined that food, for all practical purposes, is a "code" between different cultures that if broken, would unlock an entire history of any given culture. If food is:

treated as a code, the message it encodes will be found in the pattern of social relations being expressed. The message is about different degrees of hierarchy, inclusion and exclusion, boundaries and transactions across boundaries. (Douglass, 61)

Food and home are sometimes interconnected, in the manner 'food' serves as a bridge between the state of exile and the 'home' the migrant characters of Lahiri left behind. (Chaterjee, 200) Lahiri uses food in Interpreter of Maladies, as both a descriptor and lens, through which she explore the cultures of India and the United States. Lahiri is then able to maneuver through a neutral ground between two unique countries and cultures. (Garcia, 3)

In her essay 'Foodways and subjectivity in Jhumpa Lahiri's Interpreter of Maladies', Laura Ann Williams mentions that the culinary dishes and traditional gestures in multicultural stories such as the ones in this collection "create and stimulate an appetite in readers for the larger meal ahead.". Lahiri creates an enticing element within these particular stories through the constant introduction of different ingredients and dishes. She uses:

> Food as a symbol of a cultural anchor to distant/local/national/ethnic identities, as means to navigate tensions and anxieties and a vehicle to articulate the cultural construction of place/gender relations/(in)equality/class are topics well explored in the literature. (Smart, 158)

The first story of the collection 'A temporary Matter' is about a young couple who slowly drift apart after their baby is stillborn. The despair that characterises their relationship is conveyed through gastronomical imagery spilled all over the story. There is a visible strain in their conversations or awkward silences, which is evident in their avoidance of each other, food habits of the couple and the condition of their kitchen. The more Shoba stayed out, the more she began putting in extra works at work and taking on additional projects, the more he wanted to stay in, not even leaving to get the mail, or to buy fruit or wine at the stores by the trolley shop.

Even she wasn't this way before the miscarriage: She would put her coat on a hanger, her sneakers in the closet, and she paid bills as soon as they came. But now she treated the house as if it were a hotel. (6)

The disinterestedness that Shoba showed towards the house was not limited to the strained silence or negligence of the housework; but it extended to her aloofness from kitchen, cooking and food alike. Prior to her miscarriage, Shoba loved cooking and would keep the kitchen stores filled with surplus supplies: "There were endless boxes of pasta in all shapes and colors, zippered sacks of basmati rice, whole sides of lambs and goats from the Muslim butchers at Haymarket, chopped up and frozen in endless plastic bags (6-7). The overwhelming presence of food implies the emotional surplus in the couple's relationship. Dining together was a familial ritual and readers are told that the couple do not dine together anymore. In a study on the significance of the importance of family meals, De Vault argues that family meals are rituals of producing home and family (79). Charles also is of opinion that sharing of food is seen as indicating a close relationship (101). In the case of Shoba and Shukumar, not sharing meals indicates they are in the penultimate stage of separation.

It is also important to observe here how Shukumar and Shoba involuntarily interchange their roles. Shoba, who was a server and the cook, now becomes a passive consumer, while Shukumar becomes the active producer and facilitator in the kitchen (Garg, Lahiri 75). Cooking provides the solace that Shukumar needs, with the kitchen acting as a protective field that comforts him and does not act as a kind of confinement. Similarly, Shoba finds it relieving to escape from the constriction imposed by domesticity and spends more time in the impersonal space provided by the office. Her profile of a proof-reader also indicates that her work is more passive which involves more of reading, editing and correction as required. This is in sharp contrast to the activity of cooking which was satisfying, liberating and creative in many aspects. After the baby's death, Shukumar reflects, "if it weren't for him, he knew, Shoba would eat a bowl of cereal for her dinner." (8)

Whereas Shoba's emotional state is reflected in the abundance of her pantry, or the increasing emptiness of her shelves, Shukumar can be characterised by his consumption. ... Because Shobha no longer shops for the ingredients in the market, Shukumar plows through the surplus foods, "Her labeled mason jars lining the shelves of the kitchen, in endless pyramids, enough, they'd agreed, to last for their grandchildren to taste. They'd eaten it all by now. Shukumar had been going through their supplies steadily, preparing meals for the two of them, measuring out cupfuls of rice, defrosting bags of meat day after day" (7).

Shukumar's exhaustion of Shoba's well-stocked pantry, without replenishing it, therefore becomes a signifier of the way he has exhausted and emptied his wife, the way he has assumed their marital problems were temporary without investing any care in restoring or replenishing their relationship (Williams, 72).

When Mr. Pirzada Came to Dine is a story presented from the point of view of Lilia, a little girl whose parents are from India and then moved to the United States. Set in early 1970s, the story tells the family's interactions with a man coming from Dacca. Mr. Pirzada, who had received a one year scholarship in Botany in the

US, usually came to dine with Lilia's family. Dinner, thus, becomes an important part of interaction in the Asian-Indian kitchen where families share their private traditions and experiences and express their identities through food. Lilia is unable to understand what made Mr. Pirzada different from them when "they ate pickled mangoes with their meals, ate rice every night for supper with their hands. Like my parents, Mr. Pirzada took off his shoes before entering a room, chewed fennel seeds after meals as a digestive, drank no alcohol, for dessert dipped austere biscuits into successive cups of tea (25). Food in this story serves as a medium to bridge the differences regarding nationality and religion upheld in India and dissolved in America. Mr. Pirzada, a Muslim, visists the narrator's Hindu household and they have dinners together. Christensen views kitchen as 'repository for memory'. When eating mincemeat kebabs with coriander chutney, Mr. Pirzada recollects his memory about his homeland in Dacca, imagining how desperate and frightened his family might be, facing predicaments during Partition. Kebabs for Mr. Pirzada, besides a tool for memory and a strengthened identity as South Asian origin, also reflects his happy experience in the past in his homeland which is rather impossible for him to see that day due to the upheaval Partition.

Irma Maini observes. "Food is clearly an important part of the culture that binds them despite barriers of nation, nationhood, or nationalism." In this story, food plays not only as representative of local custom but also a symbol of a country. On the dinner occasions, Pirsada and Lilia's family discuss the social and political issues while rice, accompanied by some curry and vegetables is served as a mythic symbol of Asian cuisine. Indian homes, including the kitchen, also are a place to maintain the ethnic identity among the US community to protect, preserve, and strengthen the Indian national culture.

"The home was principal site for expressing the spiritual quality of the national culture, and women must take the main responsibility of protecting and nurturing this quality. No matter what changes in the external condition of life for women, they must not lose their essentially spiritual (i.e. feminine) virtues; they must not, in other words, become essentially westernised (Chatterjee qtd. in Mannur, 2010: 34)

A woman, therefore, plays crucial roles in preserving the Indian culture, and takes responsibility not only for the home and kitchen, but also on how people eat food in their own cultural construct. Lilia's mother also cooks various dishes like "lentils with fried onions, green beans with coconut, fish cooked with raisins in yoghurt sauce, followed by lemon and chilli peppers" that reflects also on how Indian homes with home-made food, tried to maintain their ethnic identity among the US community.

It can be argued that foodways are displayed and exchanged through kitchen, market and festivals. In this story too, the monthly activity of going to Chinatown is one way to keep the memory and identity alive. Not only as a place to buy and sell goods, Chinatown is also a place to recollect the memory since in the place people can interact with one another – things that differ from the self-service westernised supermarkets, make bargains, enjoy food cooking performance, and other Asia food and stuff activities.

Besides, the way food fuels waves of nostalgia, it also reaffirms the consumer's identity in terms of nationality and race. Each time Mr. Pirzada comes to dine at Lilia's place, he brings 'a small plastic egg full of cinnamon hearts' for her. He offers the candy both as a thank you and as assurance to be allowed to reciprocate. Liala recognises the importance of this gesture and even food as small as a piece of candy can create and solidify social relations as they evoke larger themes of gratitude, cooperation, and connection. Lilia's ritualistic consumption of a candy for the sake of Mr. Pirzada's well-being, gains significance where the act, according to Hindu practice of eating deity's leftover is 'prasad'. The magic of the candies worked, and hence the ritual becomes redundant as we find in the closing lines of the story, "Since January, each night before bed, I had continued to eat, for the sake of Mr. Pirazada's family, a piece of candy I had saved from Halloween. That night there was no need to. Eventually, I threw them away." (42)

Hell-Heaven, which appears in another short stories collection of Lahiri, depicts similar close bonding among Asian-Indian community in the US. Just like Mr. Pirzada, in this story we have another Bengali name named Pranab Mukherjee, who often visits Usha's family. Living in inappropriate constricted space in a small apartment, Pranab Kaku is relieved when he is served Bengali food at Usha's place. He thanks Boudi, Usha's mother, once when he says that "... this woman hosted my first real Thanksgiving in America. It might have been an afternoon in May, but that first meal at Boudi's table was Thanksgiving to me. If it weren't for that meal, I would have gone back to Calcutta" (79). Usha tells the readers how the visits of Pranab Kaku influenced her mother's routine, mood and even her involvement in kitchen. "Before we met him, I would return from school and find my mother with her purse in her lap and her trench coat on, desperate to escape the apartment where she had spent the day alone. But now I would find her in the kitchen, rolling out dough for luchis, which she normally made only on Sundays for my father and me ... she planned, days in advance, the snacks she would serve him with such nonchalance." Cooking for Pranab Kaku thus becomes a way to express her happiness at seeing him, for "she was in foul humor on the days he didn't materialise". As in Asian tradition, man becomes the breadwinner, responsible for external affairs, while women were expected to take care of the home and hearth, Usha's mother "had never worked, and during the day she watched soap operas to pass the time. Her only job, every day, was to clean and cook for my father and me" (76). Kitchen is a multiple area for women to deal with their feelings. When Boudi is burning with jealousy after she comes from the wedding ceremony of Pranab Kaku, she hides herself in kitchen, boiling rice for dinner, and dealing with her odd feelings in the comforts of the familiar space.

Like the other two stories, 'When Mr. Pirzada came to Dine' and 'Hell-Heaven', Mrs. Sen's is also told from a child's perspective. It depicts the identity crisis of a newly immigrated Mrs. Sen in America, who tries to adjust to the new life in a new country by clinging on to her old ways – including sartorial and culinary habits.

Eliot, an eleven year old ward under Mrs. Sen's day care, notices that the two things that made her happy were the arrival of a letter from her family in India and buying whole fish from the seaside. Food is immediately connected with Mrs. Sen as she serves tea with butter biscuits in a room carpeted in pear green. While in her care, Eliot enjoys watching Mrs. Sen preparing vegetables for dinner, and much of the story is occupied with lists of things she chops:

> She took whole vegetables between her hands and hacked them apart: cauliflower, cabbage, butternut squash. She split things in half, then quarters, speedily producing florets, cubes, slices, and shreds. She could peel a potato in seconds. At times she sat cross-legged, at times with legs splayed, surrounded by an array of colanders and shallow bowls of water in which she immersed her chopped ingredients. (114)

The story's listing of cauliflower, cabbage, butternut squash, potatoes, spinach, cucumber, eggplant, onions, chicken pieces, mackerel, butterfish, sea bass, and so on, draw attention to the parade of components but never the final dish. (Williams, 73) Her solitary chopping and the stories she tells Eliot of her past life are a means of crafting her identity. Food preparation, thus, is linked not only to Mrs. Sen's subjectivity but also her ethnic identity and her ability to forge a connection with others. As Anita Mannur points out, "Mrs. Sen returns to a world where she negotiates the pangs of loneliness and alienation that she feels as a woman located far away from her family with no real community to speak of besides her husband in the United States" (65). The story also brings out the loneliness of Mrs. Sen when her husband dismisses her yearning for fresh fish or the ways cooking provided solace and helped her shape identity in the new country.

Thus we can see how food connects with the word 'home' in diasporic writings like that of Jhumpa Lahiri. It forms a bridge between the state of exile and the home of migrant characters, which they had left behind in the process of accommodating their habits to the new lands. The stories of Lahiri cover different aspects of the significance of food – from nostalgia to subtle hints of sexuality, and taste of the exotic and cultural dichotomy.

Works Cited

Chaudhuri, Supriya. "Food and the Cultures of Representation" In Supriya Chaudhuri and Rimi B. Chaterjee (eds.), *The Writer's Feast: Food and the Cultures of Representation* (pp.136-145). Orient Blackswn. New Delhi. 2011.

Chatterjee, Kalyan. "Negotiating Homelessness through Culinary Imagination: the Metaphor of Food in Jhumpa Lahiri's *Interpreter of Maladies*". *Roopkatha Journal on Interdisciplinary Studies in Humanities*, V8N1, 2016.

Doughlas, Mary. "Deciphering a Meal." *Daedalus 101.1, Myth, Symbol, and Culture* (1972) pp 61-81. JSTOR. Web. 13 April. 2015

Garg, Shweta. & Khushu-Lahiri, Rajyashree. *Interpreting a Culinary Montage: Food in Jhumpa Lahiri's Interpreter of Maladies*. Asiatic. Volume 6, Number 1, June 2012.

Holtzman, Jon D. "Food and Memory". *Annual Review of Anthropology*. Vol. 35 (2006). Pp 361-378. Annual Reviews. 29 November 2012.

Kessler, Brad. *One Reader's Digest: Toward a Gastronomic Theory of Literature*. Kenyon Review. 27.2. 2005. 148-165

Lahiri, Jhumpa. *Interpreter of Maladies*. 1999. New Delhi. Harper Collins. 2006.

Maini, Irma. "The Politics of Home and Food in Jhumpa Lahiri's Interpreter of Maladies". *The Indian Family in Transition: reading Literary and Cultural Texts*. Eds. Sanjukta Dasgupta

Mannur, Anita. *Culinary Fictions: Food in South Asian Diasporic Culture*. Temple University Press. Philadelphia. 2010

Rahn, Millie. "Laying a Place at the Table: Creating Public Foodways from Scratch". *Journal of American Folklore*. Vol. 119 No. 471. Winter 2006. Pp. 30 – 46. 2013.

Williams, Laura Anh, *Foodways and Subjectivity in Jhumpa Lahiri's Interpreter of Maladies*, Melus. 32(4), 69-79.

Wulandari, Retno. *Food: Memory and Identity in Jhumpa Lahiri's When Mr. Pirzada Came to Dine and Hell-Heaven*.

14

Multi Approaches of Writing: V. S. Naipaul

Dr. Brajesh Kumar Gupta "Mewadev"

Sir V.S. Naipaul is a Trinidadian-British writer of Indian descent known for his novels set in developing countries. He won the Nobel Prize in 2001 for his novel, Half a Life. He is one of the greatest English writers of the Modern times. He has always resisted any attempts to be assigned either with national or political affiliations, causes which might limit his intellectual freedom. Naipaul has written about slavery, revolution, guerrillas, corrupt politicians, the poor and the oppressed, interpreting the rages so deeply rooted in our societies. His writing style is characterised by the use of simple yet strong words woven together in grasping narratives that reflect the dark realities of the world we live in. Naipaul very early experienced a profound alienation, both from the close-knit family life of his Brahmin ancestors and from the social and political life of his native Trinidad. He is famous for his early comic writings and later solemn and autobiographical works. The writer has found himself in an old situation as an Indian writer, writing in English for the English audience about non-English characters who talk in their English. Naipaul's prominent support for Hindutva has also been controversial.

Sir Vidiadhar Surajprasad Naipaul was born in Chaguanas in the Caribbean Island of Trinidad, on 17 August 1932, the eldest son of a second-generation Indian. He was the son of Brahmin parents; Droapatie and Seepersad Naipaul. His grandfather was a Banaras-trained Brahmin who had gone to Trinidad to teach the Indian cane workers. His father, was a reporter for the "Trinidad Guardian". He had also written some stories which were published under the title of 'Gurudeva and other Indian Tales' in 1943. His brother, Shiva Naipaul who was also a writer, wrote a novel under the title, 'Fire Flies'. V.S. Naipaul, often described, as a writer of the 'Colonial Literature', and with no other reference point, than the British Empire. He has always resisted many attempts to be assigned either with national or political affiliations, causes which might limit his intellectual freedom. Naipaul is of the opinion that an artist is to construct something meaningful out of brute reality. Many of Naipaul's fictional figures are at the mercy of social and political forces and also their own personal compulsions. Naipaul is a gigantic giant who has numerous fictions and non-fiction works to his credit which made him famous in many years.

Sir V.S. Naipaul is a Trinidadian writer of Indian descent best known for novels *A House for Mr Biswas* (1961), His novel 'In a Free State' (1971) is considered one of his masterpieces. The novel consists of three short stories set in three different countries, each exploring the concept of freedom and the price one has to pay for it, *A Bend in the River* (1979) and *A Way in the World* (1994). His novels, set in developing countries, are known for their pessimistic and cynical tone, often referred to as "suppressed histories." He received the Nobel Prize in 2001 for his novel *Half a Life,* a story about an Indian immigrant to England and Africa (which tells the tale of a fictional character, Willie Somerset Chandran, the son of a Brahmin father and a Dalit mother, who immigrates to England and then Africa borrows considerably from Naipaul's own life as the son of immigrant Indians). He has also written several works of non-fiction including *An Area of Darkness* (1965), *India: A Wounded Civilisation* (1977) and *Among the Believers: An Islamic Journey* (1981), as well as travel writing and several essays.

In all his writings Naipaul has focused on individuals attempting to escape fate. For him, fate belongs to a world of magic, myth and ritual where only the past exists but not history. His meeting with a college student, Patricia Ann Hale, helped him recover from his temporary mental illness. Naipaul has married Patricia Ann Hale in 1955 and decided to continue his work as writer during 1954 and 1956, he edited the weekly literary script of the B. B. C. programme 'Caribbean Voices'. He battles with the discovery that the 'real' England bears little or no relation to the one imagined and constructed in the colonial periphery. His work is of utmost relevance in today's world in which everyone is, in one sense or the other, an exile. Derek Walcott, a fellow 1992 Nobel winner and Caribbean poet has criticised his 'chronic dispiritedness' and called him 'V. S. Nightfall' in one of his poems. V.S. Naipaul tells stories which show us ourselves and the reality we live in. His use of language is as precise as it is beautiful. Simple, strong words, with which to express the humanity of all of us. Naipaul's prose is highly readable and his style is distinct to the point of being inimitable.

In Naipaul's vision of the world, pessimism may be said to be a central strain, while his commitment to truth is uncompromising. He is a writer who detests any kind of relationship based on the imposition of a so-called superior culture upon a so-called inferior one. Naipaul's first real achievement, House for Mr. Biswas, opens with the image of an old, derelict man completely at the mercy of what he believes is his destiny:

> Bipti's father, futile with Asthma, propped himself up on his string bed and said, as he always said on unhappy occasions, 'Fate. There is nothing we can do about it . . .' No one paid him any attention. Fate had brought him from India to the sugar estate, aged him quickly and left him to die in a crumbling mud hut in the swamplands; yet he spoke of Fate often and affectionately, as though, merely by surviving, he had been particularly favored.(1)

Describing the plight of slavery in Surinam in Middle Passage, Naipaul quotes Stedman to illustrate his own idea of slavery in the island:

> Yet one needs a strong stomach to read Stedman today. The Surinam he describes is like one concentration camp, with the difference that visitors are welcome to look around and make

> notes and sketches. The slave owner had less on his conscience than the concentration camp commandant: the world was divided into black and white, Christian and heathen. White might conceivably expected to show some scruples in his relations with black; but the Christian had no such inhibition in his relations with the heathen. (2)

Naipaul's writings in the post-independence period tends to be serious and reflective. His caricature of the dog in the novel Bend reads as follows:

> And then a large Doberman came bounding out at me. The man with the fork said, 'Don't worry. He'll miss you. He can't see very well. A foreigner's dog. He gave it to me when he went away'. It was as he said. The Doberman missed me by about a foot, ran on a little way, stopped, raced back and then was all over me, wagging his docked tail, beside himself with joy at my foreigner's smell, momentarily mistaking me for somebody else. (3)

The roots of thoughts coincide with Naipaul's in, reviewing the Press' book for The New Statesman, 24 September 1965:

> Things move so fast nowadays, even in the Literature Schools. Commonwealth writing, as we understand it is so new, and already it is being picked to pieces... it all seems to have been codified already. I know now, for instance, that the difference between the United States and Canada is that the United States had a revolution and Canada didn't. But I also get the impression that the point has been made so often before and has become such a received idea that it is now almost without meaning. Then there is the West Indian with his search for identity. (4)

He has dreamed of writing about the extremely painful experiences and suffering of the colonised caused by the European colonisation and imperialism from the beginning to the present day. However, he feels he could not do that.

The passage from Middle Passage illustrates his new technique clearly:

> Pursuing the Christian – Hellenic tradition, the West Indian accepted his blackness as his guilt. He never seriously doubted

> the validity of the prejudices from which he suffered, for he had inherited the prejudices of the culture to which he aspired. In the French territories he aimed at Frenchness, in the Dutch territories at Dutchness; in the English territories he aimed at simple whiteness and modernity, Englishness being impossible. (5)

Naipaul works in transparent modes, documenting concrete particulars in a spare style so that he provides his readers with immediate access to actual situations. He experiments along the boundaries of fiction and non-fiction in his travel-writings. The imaginative and creative use of caricatures remains an important feature of Naipaul's works. Theroux criticises Naipaul for his ethnocentric self that takes him far away from other post colonialist writers disabling him to establish his own standard and class of identity. He has focused primarily on non-fiction, he has returned in his most recent books *A Way in the World* (1994) and *Half a Life* (2001) to a more intimate semi-autobiographical voice.

The description of the organisation of the Hanuman house in the novel justifies the analogy:

> The organisation of the Hanuman House was simple. The daughters and their children swept and washed and cooked and served in the house. The husbands under Seth's supervision worked on the Tulsi land, looked after the Tulsi animals and served in the store. In return they were given food, shelter, and a little money; their children were looked after. (6)

His vision, thus, offers little hope to the third world societies that have been maimed beyond repair. As Naipaul's art matures, an increasing importance is given to ideas and he becomes more concerned with thought, meaning and philosophy. Simultaneously, style and structure lose importance. Naipaul's feeling is reflected through his sea of novels of living in a borrowed culture, needs to tell the writers of the world who is he and where he does stand. He says, "I have began to write, I am afraid, for no other reason than because I thought it would be nice to be a writer, I have nothing to say. My vision of writing and the life it meant was so childish really-writing articles and having them collected and all this sort of rubbish-which is nothing to do with writing. One has began with this very romantic vision of the writer as a free, gifted, talented, creative, admired person-with as a kind of social and cultural and sexual attribute." He describes his fiction related to an emergent country. He adds from colonialism to independence. Naipaul was not bound by his itinerary. His quest for understanding what he saw in India, and the interest in interpreting it to the west grew with every visit. N. Wong in showing the Hindu genesis of V.S. Naipaul's writings:

> The text that reverberates most influentially at the heart of V.S. Naipaul's *A House for Mr. Biswas* is not from the Western tradition. It is, instead, the Ramayana, one of the two sacred Hindu texts, the Mahabharat being the other. According to R.K.Narayan, all imaginative writing in India has its origins in these books. (6) (Talib, 66)

Naipaul is all praise for Indian sculpture and architectures. Originally, he intends to bleach his family history and cultural roots; Naipaul, intends to search for his self-identity and construct his owns subjectivity in the world via travelling. Naipaul's work has been described as an examination of "the clash between belief and unbelief, the unraveling of the British Empire, and the migration of peoples" (Donadio, 2005). Naipaul's literary output is of great literary value and is highly appreciable. Gramsci (1971) offers an understanding of identity in an environment shaped by hegemonic forces, sometimes exploitative, often brutal and capricious:

> When one's conception of the world is not critical and coherent but disjointed, one belongs simultaneously to a multiplicity of mass human groups ... The starting point of critical elaboration is the consciousness of what one really is, and is 'knowing thyself' as a product of the historical process to date which has deposited in you an infinity of traces, without leaving an inventory. (Gramsci, 37).

Although the subjects in Half a life (2001) and Magic seeds (2004) may "create an inventory of the past", it seems useful to distinguish between what JanMohamed (1992) describes as "syncretic border intellectualism" (recreating home in exile along the lines of what Fernandez-Armesto (445) terms as the "impulse to civilise"), and "specular border intellectualism" (reflecting on and registering discomfort with what home might mean). In Magic seeds (2004) its opposite is a wilful intervention, of the kind practiced by Sarojini, Chandran's sister, who goads lost individuals like Chandran into misguided action in the service of political causes:

> When I went out to Africa … I never wanted to stay. I thought something was going to happen and I would never unpack. Yet I stayed for eighteen years. And it was like that when I joined the guerrillas. The first night in the teak forest. It was too unreal. I wasn't going to stay. Something was going to happen and I was going to be liberated. But nothing happened, and I stayed seven years. (Naipaul, 178).

In Naipaul's novels the people who become unemployable are educated migrants with skills, refuting a mantra of globalisation that these two elements, irrespective of race or gender, enable mobility. In A Bend in the River, Naipaul suggests a way out of that problematic situation for the immigrant groups of Indian origin that settled in East Africa more than a thousand years ago, or that were brought there by the region's British colonisers at the turn of the nineteenth century to work on the Kenya-Uganda Railway. Examined from this perspective, the true nature of globalisation becomes readily understandable. Proponents of the phenomenon routinely represent it as the outcome of global realignments that are manifesting themselves in an emerging "global village," a utopian environment where everyone puts in their fair share and all are rewarded accordingly. But the reality of globalisation makes one wonder whether globalisation might be nothing more than the ongoing substitution of the more economically powerful European (and particularly American) cultures for their less hegemonic counterparts in the developing world. Could this in part be the explanation behind the increasing uniformity among the world's peoples in terms of their appearances, tastes, and general world-views? It could be argued that perhaps the common denominator here is their increasing proximity to European culture.

These concepts given and illustrated by Said and Bhabha can be found in many of Naipaul's novels. Naipaul's importance is not only in postcolonial studies, but he has now become equally important in the modern studies since he sketches characters that are victims of Profrokian symptom. In his essay "Prologue to an Autobiography" from Finding the Center, Naipaul has written:

> Half a writer's work . . . is the discovery of his subject. And a problem for me was that my life had been varied, full of upheavals and moves: from grandmother's Hindu house in the country, still close to the rituals and social ways of village India; to Port of Spain, the negro, and G.I. life of its streets, the other, ordered life of my colonial English school, which is called Queen's Royal College, and then Oxford, London and the freelances' room at the BBC. Trying to make a beginning as a writer, I didn't know where to focus. (V.S. Naipaul, *The Art of Fiction* No. 154; Interviewed by Jonathan Rosen, Tarun Tejpal).

V.S.Naipaul has depicted a protagonist in a society that is pan demonic and lacking in ideas and creativity. The rootlessness is a prominent theme found in almost all of Naipaul's writings. The concept of "home" and "homelessness" has always been a recurring theme of Diaspora literature, especially, the literature of the Caribbean. V.S. Naipaul himself experienced, and repeatedly described in his fiction, this particular heart feeling urge. Throughout his life he has desired a place to identify with. However, a rereading of A House for Mr. Mr. Biswas suggests that it is an extraordinary narrative which evokes the memory of indenture and the post-indentured unaccommodated man with psychological acuteness and emotional truth. Naipaul as a postcolonial novelist with a diasporic contemplation, recording and analysing various nuances of the colonial as well as diasporic people, situates his novels in colonial, ex-colonial and diasporic settings and provides a perceptive account of the complexities and intricacies inherent to such societies. Naipaul's writing is sufficient with a great melancholy and loneliness, and feels about him that he is "under the volcano, homesick". As Naipaul points out in *Finding the Centre* (1985: 49), it was the life of the clan that gave the East

Indians, "a caste certainly, a high sense of the self." Cultural identity in the diasporic discourse has to be defined in terms of a shared culture, a sort of collective 'true self hiding inside other, more superficial or artificially imposed selves, which people with a shared history and ancestry hold in common.

Other qualities that may be typical of many Diasporas are thoughts of return, relationships with other communities in the Diaspora, and lack of full integration into the host country. Nevertheless, one important touch of diaspora feature, that of longing for homeland, is obvious in the novel. In fact, the narrator confesses that on his arrival in England, he loses his "dream of future". Naipaul describes about his migrate experiences in life and his diasporas ideas of Britain, USA, India etc from A House for Mr Biswas. Naipaul, for the concept of 'homeland' is a complex one in his life as well as his works, since he has been frustrated by the cultural failure of his homelands, both Trinidad and India, to transcend to a standard level of sophistication. Thus, Naipaul tries to display, through his work, the nature of his diasporic identity, which often seems paradoxical, because he lives in a voluntary Diaspora in metropolitan London.

V. S. Naipaul, considered the leading novelist to emerge from the English-speaking Caribbean, has long been tipped to win the award. His hard work paid off and he received a scholarship to study at the prestigious Oxford University. By this time he has realised that his true interest was writing and began writing earnestly. Naipaul shows that, it is important to become successful in Trinidad, does not matter by what means, because people will not bother at all. He is a private man, who lives in the country in order to have the solitude for thinking and writing. Both his fiction and his travel writing have been criticised for their unsympathetic portrayal of the third world. He has made a characteristic observation. 'Everything' he said, 'of value about me is in my books....I am the sum of my books.... I feel that at any stage of my literary career it could have been said that the last book contained all the others'. At present, the most rational debate characterises, West Indian literature, as a tradition within a tradition, an outgrowth and extension of the western mode of writing. Naipaul's achievements outstrip his inadequacies. Many of Naipaul's fictional figures are at the mercy of social and political forces and also their own personal compulsions. He strongly believes that literature is an expression of society. His fictional world is concerned with the realistic portrayal of individuals, cultures and societies. This way in the world, in Ralph and Naipaul's idea, is a model of constructing an authentic and dignified identity. His success lies in the fact that he has convincingly forged a distinct authorial voice of his own through his eclectic, experimental play with various literary forms. Naipaul's literary creation adopts an outgrown and extended mode of writing that can certainly be said as sine qua non of his Identity shows his writing as a literature as a tradition within a tradition. Therefore, there can be no denial of the fact that, Naipaul's writings cover different settings and characters, but a single strain always can be found that is based on rootlessness and alienation. Conclusively, it can be said that it is V. S. Naipaul's serendipity and his writing skills which make him the prominent author across the world.

Works Cited

"A Nobel for Mr. Naipaul." *The New York Times.* October 12, 2001.

Adams, Robert Martin. "V. S. Naipaul." *Hudson Review* 33 (1989).

Allen, Walter. "London Again." *The New York Review of Books* 2.3 (1964).

Bala, Suman, V. S. *Naipaul: A Literary Response to the Nobel Laureate*, New Delhi: Khosla Pub. House, 2003.

Chaudhary, Helga. "V. S. Naipaul's Changing Vision of India: A Study of An Area of Darkness, and India, a Wounded Civilisation." *Literary Half-Yearly* 23.1 (1982).

Ciolkowski, Laura. "Books in Brief; Nonfiction (V. S. Naipaul)." *The New York Times Book Review* (2000).

Clemens, Walter C. Jr. "The Third World in V. S. Naipaul." *Worldview* 25. Sept (1982).

Cocks, Joan. "A New Cosmopolitanish? V. S. Naipaul and Edward Said." *Constellations: An International Journal of Critical & Democratic Theory* 7.1 (2000).

Cohen, Robin. *Global Diasporas: An Introduction*. London: Taylor & Francis, 2001.

Donadio, R. 2005. *The irascible prophet: V.S. Naipaul at home*. The New York Times: 5, 7 Aug.

Dr. Pandian I. B. *Life and Works of V. S. Naipaul: A Critical Study*. Kanpur: Bhaskar Publications, 2009. Print.

Evans, Adrian Rowe. V.S. Naipaul (Interview), Transition, 8, No. 40 (December 1971), http://www. jstor.org/stable/2934130.

Farred, Grant. "Out of Contexts: Thinking Cultural Studies Diasporically." In *The African Diaspora and the Disciplines*, edited by Tejumola Olaniyan and James H. Sweet, 257. Bloomington: Indiana University Press, 2010.

Gerhard Stilz (2007). *Territorial Terrors: Contested Spaces in Colonial and Postcolonial Writing*. Wurzburg: Konigshausen & Neumann, Print.

Gourevitch, Philip (August 1994). "Naipaul's World," *Commentary*, Vol. 98, Issue 2.

Gupta, Suman, *V. S. Naipaul*, Northcote House, 1999.

Landeg White, in V. S. *Naipaul: A Critical Introduction London: Macmillan*, 1975.

15

The Colonialism and the Changes in the Postcolonial World

Sujoy Barman

It is certain that there are many changes that have come with the colonial movement. If the movement is generally explained, it would be found that the movement is simply identified as an extortion and domination of one weak country by other powerful country, basically for the economical profits, utilisation of the natives natural resources by the settlers. This is the short and simple definition of colonialism. But the movement has brought a lot of changes in all the formations of the world. It has influenced world's economy, cultures, languages and politics etc. Its impact has been noticed both former colonial and colonised countries in the twenty first century. Both sometimes search for the loss of their inherited cultures, traditional values, lost identities or sometimes they maintain their new identities, new practices of conventional life etc. Colonialism is not only a struggle between hard powers like arms, forces, militaries, weapons but also a struggle between soft power like education, language, cultural practices etc. Through these actions and reactions, every culture in the world changes continually and simultaneously. Sometimes, it solves some big problem, for example the spreading knowledge among the dark civilisations and sometimes it has created unending critical problem like "Kashmir Issue" between India and Pakistan. The colonialism has both its positive and negative feedbacks in the societies after colonialism.

The greatest Victorian cultural critic Matthew Arnold defined the term 'culture'. He used the term 'culture' for 'perfection', culture stands for the "passion of perfection" that forces one towards the pure knowledge and at the same time, the cultured man also forces or pushes others to the purity or perfection of knowledge. The universe doesn't possess a single pure culture, it has multiple cultures according to the geographical, ethical, diversities. The geographical factors in India, Africa, and Europe are not same. These three lands have three different geographical, natural atmospheres. And these natural and geographical environments impact on the lives of the people. Besides this, the every country has its own geographical, ethical, mythical stories about the origin of the country. These geographical, ethical, mythical ingredients influence the culture of a particular society. In India, the Hindu people practice the Hindu culture based on the Puran, the Bads, and epics like "the Ramayan" and "the Mahabharat'. They take lord Ram as the ideal male figure, on the other hand devi Sita, Draupadi are the ideal women figures who are copied by all the Hindu people. In the Muslim culture, their ideal mythical figures for their lives are 'Muhammad' and 'Fatema'. Likewise the Christian society also maintains same system for the domestic lives. And the Africans are not the exception of this system. Everyone loves to practice own culture and manipulates the importance of that culture. But some norms become big controversy among these diverse cultured people. For example the position of 'wine' in the Christianity and the Islam is different. For the Islam, it is known as anti-religious, sinful and for a Christian it is usual. This individuality of every culture has been collapsed at the rise of capitalism, industrialism in the European countries who migrated out of the Europe and dominated rest of the world and thus colonialism began.

It has already said that the colonialism has begun with the hand of industrialism in the Europe. The excessive growth of industry, technology, capitals, enabled the European countries to discover the world and also to spread their capitalist markets and they formed a huge consumer society through the world for their industrial products. The basic motto of colonialism was the economical profits. The European countries utilise the natural resources of the native countries and the natives who were exported to Europe as labours in the European factories; known as slave trade. In this economical domination, the European colonial countries used arms, weapons, soldiers as their supporting powers. This is the one side of colonialism, but it has impacted the cultural, socio-political, religious life both of the colonial and colonised people. Hybridism is found in cultures, literatures, politics, and social life. Indian Constitution is a hybrid constitution in the world because it has its ingredients from the constitutions like England, America etc. After colonialism, there has come anti-colonial movement i.e. 'decolonisation'. Decolonisation denies the power of settlers over the natives; it suggests a local governing body for the local people. But decolonisation is itself a movement of violence, a programme of complete disorder, it is so because it brings order, peace after colonialism; as the colonialism is also a movement of violence: "In the colonies, the foreigner coming from another country imposed his rule by means of guns and machines" (*The Wretched of the Earth,* 31). And decolonisation is also: "Decolonisation, which sets out to change the order of the world, is, obviously, a programme of complete disorder." (*The Wretched of the Earth,* 27)

At the present time, all countries are free, but domination over one nation by another is still but in different ways. This time no brutal powers like army, weapons are used. The influence of one nation over other nation is through the economical power, technology, and the world market is the field for competition for the developing and developed countries. This is known as "the Neo-colonialism" by the first president of Ghana, Kwame Nkrumah. He defines it in his book "*Neo-colonialism: The Last Stage of Imperialism.*" According to him "...the former colonial powers and the new super powers, such as the United States, and China, use new forms of domination over the formerly colonised countries even after they gain independence". (*The Penguin Dictionary of Literary Terms and Literary Theory,* 466) This domination is indirect, subtle, with the soft power. For example, the international treaties between China –

Pakistan, India-Russia, India-America are based on neo colonialism and its concepts.

Colonialism and Colonised Countries

There are a lot of changes in the colonised countries with the establishment and abolition of the colonial power. Its effects on the natives are clearly visible. The basic trends of life of the natives that are hereditary have been changed as the settler's government imposed their new trends over the natives. Settlers believe that they follow the good traditions, good cultures, and high quality norms of life, and on the other hand the practices of natives are out of culture, back-dated, wild. The natives are regarded as creatures like animals, or wild beasts. And the Europeans think that they are the centre of the world for culture, technology, science, and industry, and others move around this centre. This 'Eurocentric idealism' forces all the Non-Europeans to imitate the Europeans. There are many reasons for a native to copy the life a European. First, he thinks himself uncultured man and the settlers are cultural people. In order to be a cultured man, he imitates the Europeans. Secondly, he, as a native, follows this new cult of life in order to avoid the humiliation. Next, colonialism has brought the conflict on the basis of casts, the Europeans are superiors and the natives are inferiors in the native lands. And being categorised to a lower class, the settled higher class of people thinks the natives as dogs and humiliates them. And not to face this humiliation, a native accepts the European way of livings. Indian novelist Mulk Raj Anand in the novel *Untouchable* through his hero Bakha very beautifully has pointed this situation of colonised life. Bakha, as an illiterate Indian boy, has the fantasy of English way of life-style. And he thinks to civilise himself; wants to save from the humiliations, practiced by the Hindu culture. He is the model for all the young Indian children who have the fantasy for the Englishness:

> He had been told they were sahibs, superior people. He had felt that to put on their clothes made one a sahib too. So he tried to copy them in everything, to copy them as well as he could in the exigencies of his peculiarly Indian circumstances. (*Untouchable,* 3)

The third important reason behind the imitation of the European culture, ways of living is the economical benefit. All the commercial systems are controlled by the Europeans in the native land and for the employments or any other services to live, a native has to depend on the colonial personals. And the natives are indirectly forced to practice the colonial languages, manners which enable the natives to be an employee. Besides this, the natives who imitate the European cult also feel some proud, think themselves superiors to the rest of the natives:

> In the French colonial army, and particularly in the Senegalese regiments, the black officers serve first of all as interpreters. They are used to convey the master's orders to their fellows, and they too enjoy a certain position of honour. (*Black Skin, White Masks,* 18/19)

These are the basic reasons for a native to copy the European settlers.

Colonialism has created a mimicry class of people among the natives, such mimicry has also negative effects on the native cultures and trends. By imitating settlers, the natives are capable for the employments, belonging to civic society, but at the same time they lose their interest for their own inherited cultures, languages. They avoid their own systems, neglect these systems and as a result these native cultures and languages become useless, worthless to them and as well as to the world. So the decay or decline of culture is the negative side of colonialism:

> The middle class in the Antilles never speak Creole except to their servants. In school the children of Martinique are taught to scorn the dialect. One avoids Creolisms. Some families completely forbid the use of Creole, and mothers ridicule their children for speaking it. (*Black Skin, White Masks,* 20)

Another dark side of colonialism over the colonised or natives people, that is the most vital, is racism. The society is divided into compartments i.e. the native's compartment and settler's compartment. And these two compartments are totally different from each other regarding their maintenances. The settlers think themselves superiors and enjoy every facilities of life. And on the other hand, the natives are recognised as inferiors and also excluded from all the facilities. For this racism, a few number of settlers rule over a huge number of natives. In their own land, the natives are many in numbers to the settlers and yet they belong to the minority class:

> In Martinique there are two hundred whites who consider themselves superior to 300,000 people of color. In South Africa there are two million whites against almost thirteen million native people, and it has never occurred to a single black to consider himself superior to a number of the white minority. (*Black Skin, White Masks,* 92-93)

But this racism shapes a different look in the colonial countries from the colonised where minority becomes majority and majority becomes minority. In the countries like England, France, the minor colour people are always minor and inferior. They are humiliated. They then start to think about their own culture, organise black cultural campaigns. The Black Arts Movement, Harlem Renaissance are such activities in the colonial countries. The responsibility is to find out the reasons for the hateness of a colour by a white because from the very childhood, he has been taught to hate the colours. Through the TV shows, magazines, the white children are taught to think themselves superiors from rest of the world and the rest of the people in the world are inferiors and uncivilised. Generally, when they become grown up men, hate the rest of the people:

> This is the purpose of games in children's institutions, of psychodramas in group therapy, and in a more general way, of illustrated magazines for children – each type of society, of course, requiring its own specific kind of catharsis. The Tarzan stories, the sagas of twelve-year-old explorers, the adventures of Mickey Mouse, and all those "comic books" serve actually as a release for collective aggression. The magazines are put together by white men for little white men. (*Black Skin, White Masks,* 145-146)

In short the seed of the racism is growing up from the very childhood.

"Language carries culture, and culture carries, particularly through orature and literature, the entire body of values by which we come to perceive ourselves and our place in the world." (Norton anthology of English literature, 2740) The identity of people with their cultural practices and the use of language is also influenced by the colonialism. It has a vital result over language related culture. And the colour people face this problem. In their own land, they are forced, directly or indirectly, to avoid their own language. Without knowing the settler's language, for a native, the success in life is rare. And the settlers dominate the whole natives without using a bullet because of the power of language. This is the soft power domination. Thus the natives are forced to accept the settlers' language and their culture. And on the other hand this has a devastating negative result over the natives. To be master of colonial language is a successful prosperous life and not to be a mastership means nothing in life:

> All the papers were written in English. Nobody could pass the exam who failed the English language paper no matter how brilliantly he had done in the other subjects. I remember one boy in my class of 1954 who had distinctions in all subjects except English, which he had failed. He was made to fail the entire exam. He went on to become a turn boy in a bus company. I who had only passes but a credit in English got a place at the Alliance High School, one of the most elitist institutions of Africans in colonial Kenya. (*Norton Anthology of English Literature,* 2739)

This is the story of the native dialect in the native land during colonialism, but after colonialism, the influence of the colonial language is still, for India has its own regional languages and English is the language from England, but in the independent India, English is practiced as the main language rather than the other dialects in offices, administrative sections and academic sections etc.

Such domination also brings resistance among the colonised people. Some colonised people think about the value of their own language, culture and start activities for these values. For example, Négritude is a movement by the French-speaking African writers like Aimé Césaire to maintain and hold the values of the traditional African culture and sensibilities. Creoleness is another movement for the African cultures and traditions. In the last quarter of the twentieth century, there is a long list of African originated writers who through their writings, express their roles for the African images and attempt to make a global reputation for their own inherited cultures and traditions:

> We African writers are bound by our calling to do for our languages what Spencer, Milton and Shakespeare did for English; what Pushkin and Tolstoy did for Russia; indeed what all writers in world history have done for their languages by meeting the challenge of creating a literature in them... (*The Norton Anthology of English Literature,* 2741)

In the colonised countries, the native intellectuals think of the centering of their own cultures and languages. They push their own systems to the centre, replacing the settler's language:

> The aim, in short, should be to orientate ourselves towards placing Kenya, East Africa, and then Africa in the centre. All other things are to be considered in their relevance to our situation, and their contribution towards understanding ourselves. (*The Norton Anthology of Theory and Criticism,* 1996)

So they think to glorify their own literatures, own languages, own cultures rather than the settler's:

> We'll have argued the case for the abolition of the present Department of English in the college, and the establishment of a Department of African Literature and Languages. This is not a change of names only. We want to establish the centrality of Africa in the department. (*The Norton Anthology of Theory and Criticism,* 1999)

Sometimes, such resistances have some faults. The leaders among the colonised people argue about the existence of their inherited values but some leaders do different things. They send their sons and daughters to abroad to learn English; and for the rest of his fellows in their native land, they give advice for the regional languages. Jyoti Basu, the former renounced Marxist chief minister of West Bengal in India organised a State led movement against English literature. But he included English literature in his personal life and educated his next generation; according to the English curriculum:

> My son won't learn English; your son won't learn English; but Jyoti Basu will send his son abroad to learn English. (*The Norton Anthology of English Literature,* 2750)

Colonialism and Colonial Countries

It is wrong if it is accepted that the colonialism has influenced only the colonised atmosphere; but colonialism is also effective for the colonial atmosphere. For colonialism, the colonial countries not only increased economical power but there are some minor or major changes in the socio-cultural fields. Most of the times, they are not so much vital like in the colonised countries. With the slave trade, colour people from African countries, Indian continent etc. entered into the European countries where they were faced the inhuman activities, and also treated as animals not as human beings. Later the number of these slave people has gradually been increased and they have felt some security regarding their existence. The second generation of the slave trade has faced problem regarding their identities. They have double consciousness; first they are blacks and they belong to the Non-European countries. So their cultural practices and ethical backgrounds are different. This is the one conscious of their minds. Secondly they belong to such societies where these norms and ideas are not valued. They find, in practical, a new culture is practiced and dominates their surroundings. In such duel situations they can't select the one for their lives:

> Jean Veneuse is a Negro. Born in the Antilles, he has lived in Bordeaux for years; so he is a European. But he is black; so he is a Negro. There is the conflict. He does not understand his own

> race, and the whites do not understand him. (*Black Skin, White Masks,* 64)

Some colonised rationalists support their own cultures, and practice them, and these movements are sometimes known as 'Negritude', 'Harlem Renaissance', or 'Black Arts Movement'. These minor class of people try to equalise with the local people for the civic rights, political rights etc. Sometimes the local politicians use this issue for their political benefits in the colonial lands. There are of examples in the history of politics how the European political leaders, for the victory in elections use this policy.

It has already said that the colonised people are inferiors and excluded from the main body by the colonisers. But at the present time, some incidents are happened and they prove how a black becomes white. In the chapter, named *The Man of Color And The White Woman* in the theoretical text *Black Skin, White Masks,* Frantz Fanon shows how a black is accepted in white society, how a Negro belongs to the Europe. If a black lives for a long time in white country, he becomes white; or if a black possesses excellent qualities of life and if he is the master of science, literature, and technology; then he is gladly identified as a European and a white brother is ready to marry his white sister with this talented black man:

> When the question is put directly, then, the white man agrees to give his sister to the black – but on one condition: You have nothing in common with real Negroes. You are not black; you are "extremely brown." (*Black Skin, White Masks,* 69)

With colonialism, both the European and Non-European countries have come into contact with each other and the Non-Europeans copy the Europeans as they are considered as superiors. But at the same time, the Europeans also imitate the Non-Europeans. They follow the indigenous cultures, religions, myths. There are a lot of English families in India who have come during the British rule in India and they did not leave India after 1947, the year of Indian Independence. After the British rule in India, the succeeding generation of these English families has adopted the Indian culture. Ruskin Bond is the renounced writer in English literature. His parents were Europeans who had come India and after their deaths, uncle of Ruski asked Ruskin to lead a European life. But from his very childhood, Ruskin showed his interest for Indian life. In his auto-biography *The Room on the Roof,* Ruskin describes his tussle with his uncle Mr. Harrison regarding the European and the Indian contexts of lives:

> It's the truth. I've tried to bring you up as an Englishman, as your father would have wished. But, as you won't have it our way, I'm telling you that he was about the only thing English about you. You're no better than the sweeper boy! (*The Room on the Roof*, 29)

Besides this, during the colonialism, the Christian missionaries have converted the natives into the Christianity because their religions are corrupted and the gods are false gods. But after the colonialism, the situation is quite different. The Europeans have come into contact with the religious trusts of natives and some of them show their interests for these holy practices. They divert themselves towards these practices. 'The International Society for Krishna Consciousness', shortly known as 'ISKCON' is an example of this category. It has been established in New York City in 1966 by A. C. Bhaktivedanta Swami Prabhupada in order to develop the Krishna spiritualness among the people. This spiritual philosophy is now practiced in India as well in the European countries by the Europeans. It is noticed that the Non-Europeans are uncultured, beast like creatures. And the Europeans have taken it is their moral duty to educate and civilise the rest of the world. This moral duty is identified as 'The White Man's Burden'. Rudyard Kipling expresses it as:

> Take up the White Man's burden –
> Send forth the best ye breed –
> Go bind your sons to Exile
> To serve your captives' need;
> To wait in heavy harness
> On fluttered folk and wild –
> Your new-caught, sullen people,
> Half-devil and half child
>
> (*The Norton Anthology of English Literature*, 1880-81)

But this moral duty to civilise the Non-Europeans is not correct. The history tells many times about the cruelty, barbarity of the colonial people by presenting such acts. If one becomes uncivilised, it should be remembered that it is not his fault. It is the environment in which he lives, forces him to be uncivilised. The environment plays the basic role behind it. William Golding, in his novel *Lord of the Flies,* shows how civilised children become uncivilised when they have come into the contact of the wild nature.

The Non-Europeans are uncultured and uncivilised; and the Europeans are cultured and civilised' are the concepts of colonialism. But, are these concepts true and correct? And what are the sources of these concepts? And why such ideas are practiced? First thing should be remembered that every culture has its specific qualities for its uniqueness and it has some great practices and some corrupted practices. For example, in the Hindu mythology, women are identified as 'mother' and in the same society, they are treated same. But in the English culture, the position for women is different. They are 'other' to the men. So most of the Europeans adopt the good practices of the Non-European's cultures likewise the Non-Europeans do. If Europeans think that the Non-Europeans are uncultured, illiterate, and creatures like animals, it is not their fault. It is the fault of the representatives who through their informations provide them these vague or fake informations. These representatives are very crafty and performing such misleading acts in their informations, they popularised themselves to their readers. Or it is the demand of the readers who want to know the Non-Europeans as uncultured and uncivilised, so the representatives do so. Joseph Conrad is one of these representatives who represent the Africa for the Europeans. And his work *Heart of Darkness* is as popular as an elite work as a mirror for the Congo culture to the Europeans. But the "*Heart of Darkness*" and Joseph Conrad later have been charged by the African writer Chinua Achebe. He said that Conrad's information of Africa for the Europeans is not perfect. Some are based on Conrad's own romantic ideas of Africa. Chinua Achebe in his work *An Image of Africa: Racism in Conrad's*

Heart of Darkness has pointed out the faults, performed by Joseph Conrad during his writing *Heart of Darkness.* He said:

> In the final consideration, his method amounts to no more than a steady, ponderous, fake, ritualistic repetition of two antithetical sentences, one about silence and the other about frenzy. (*The Norton Anthology of Theory and Criticism,* 1614)

So the post-colonial resistance is not found in the cultural, political, and civil atmospheres but in literature and in theory the resistance is available. If one wants to know any culture, it would be better if he goes through the representatives of that culture. If one wants to know about India, he must read Indian writers rather than the other because the information is first hand. For Africa, Chinua Achebe, Wole Soyinka, Elechi Amadi should be given the priority for the African concepts.

Colonialism is the power relation between the two or more countries. The power is manipulated by one country to another for several pursuits. Through the utilisation of, the countries are changing continuously. The economical condition of the colonial countries is gradually developing and on the other hand, the condition of colonised countries is gradually decreasing. Colonialism has brought, besides the economical changes; cultural, socio-political, religious, literary changes. These changes will never stop in future, as all the countries in the world are related with one another, they depend to one another for several grounds like war-weapons, commercial markets etc.

Works Cited

Anand, Mulk Raj. *Untouchable.* Gurgaon: Penguin Random House India Pvt. Ltd., 1935. Print.

B. Leith, Vincent. *The Norton Anthology of Theory & Criticism.* 2nd. New York: W. W. Norton & Company Inc., 2010. Print.

Bond, Ruskin. *The Room on the Roof – Vagrants in the Valley – Two Novels of Adolescence.* Gurgaon: Penguin Random House India Pvt. Ltd., 1993. Print.

Cuddon, J.A. *The Penguin Dictionary of Literary Terms and Literary Theory.* Pengiun Books, 2014. Print.

Fanon, Frantz. *Black Skin, White Masks.* Trans. Charles Lam Markmann. London: Pluto Press, 1986. Print.

____ ., *The Wretched of the Earth.* Trans. Constance Farrington. London: Penguin Books, 2001. Print.

Greenblatt, Stephen. *The Norton Anthology of English Literature.* 9th. New York: Norton & Company Inc., 2012. Print.

Singh, Khushwant. *Kipling's India.* The Lotus collection. New Delhi: Roli Books Pvt. Ltd., 2012. Print.

16

Awakened by Darkness: An Exploration of Shamanic Archetypes, Voicing Female Experiences in Selected Novels of Margaret Atwood

Alik Jha

Before exploring speckles of Shamanic Archetype in Atwood's selected novels, I slightly would like to torch upon the considerations regarding *shamanism*. The richness and diversity of the field of study called *shamanism* is obvious in many ways. Researchers in the field come from areas diverse as history, anthropology, religious studies, sociology, medicine, humanities and art. The phenomena studied are equally diverse. The use of the term *shamanism* might give false impression that the phenomenon, so labelled is a single fixed religious system, which exists in various societies in the world. In reality, the term *shamanism* covers a number of beliefs and rituals, which are continuously changing and evolving as new historical and religious situations arise in different societies. Scholars of many different disciplines in the eighteenth century were fascinated by *shamanism*. Whether they were philosophers, missionaries, writers, archaeologists, physicians, botanists or ethnographers, these observers from different backgrounds in the West reported their perceptions of *shamanism*, despite their limited understandings of the religion and culture of the peoples they observed. This trend toward broad interest in *shamanism* continued into the nineteenth and twentieth century, and the framework for discussion about *shamanism* widened, as shifts in methodology occurred. One of the major shifts was that both anthropologists and psychologists in Europe and America entered with full force into the study of *shamanism*. Ake Hultkrantz considered the issue of *shamanism* as a religio – magical cultural complex: that is magic with an ingredient of established religion, though without a priesthood. He considered *shamanism* instead of genuine religion. According to classic definition proposed by Hultkrantz, a shaman is "a social functionary, who with the help of guardian spirits, attains ecstasy to create a rapport with the supernatural world on behalf of his or her group members" (Hultkrantz, 1973). It is the very root from which humanity's various disciplines have issued. When Shamanic Archetype is activated, it precipitates a deeper part of the psyche to become mobilised. As people enacting the Shamanic Archetype, journey deep inside themselves, flying on the wings of their creative imagination to become familiar with and address what has got activated within them.

If we try to cast the Shamanic Archetype into a theoretical model, it may be said that in Nietzschean sense, the connotation of Shamanic Archetype is a transition from Apollonian to Dionysian, from the form to the formless, from the rational to irrational, from the fixed to the fluid. As archetypal symbols or representations are variable, polysemic and tuto-gorical, it stands not as the representation of something else, but for itself. Cassirer thus states:

> Whereas empirical thinking is essentially directed towards establishing as unequivocal relation between specific "causes" and specific "effects",... archetypal projections, even when it raises the question of source-points as such, 'has a free selection of causes at its disposal. Anything can come from it because anything can stand in temporal or spatial contact with anything. (Philosophy, 46)

C.G. Jung asserts that the entire archetypal manifestation could be taken as a sort of projection of the "Collective Unconscious". The "collective unconscious" is a part of human psyche which consists of primordial images that are different to understand for modern man, and these primordial images –

archetypes are conveyed by the "collective unconscious" and present themselves in dreams, fantasies, instincts etc. For Jung, archetypes are universal archaic images and are inherent in humans as the contents of "collective unconscious":

> "Archetype" is an explanatory paraphrase of the Platonic *eidos.* For our purposes this term is apposite and helpful, because it tells us that so far as the collective unconscious contents are concerned we are dealing with archaic or – I would say – primordial types, that is, with universal images that have existed since the remotest times. The term "*représentations collectives*", used by Lévy-Bruhl to denote the symbolic figures in the primitive view of the world, could easily be applied to unconscious contents as well, since it means practically the same thing". (Basic, 288)

The psyche, which accounts for the total personality for Jung, is comprised of several interacting systems and archetypes; such as 'anima-animus', 'shadow' and 'mother'. The archetypes of 'anima-animus' are of special importance since most post-Jungians, including the feminist archetypal theorists have some problems with them in terms of their problematic nature which depends on binary oppositions between the female and the male psyche. Although feminist thinkers benefit from Jungian theory of archetypes, their standpoint is entirely different from Freud's and Jung's, as this is mainly because of the logocentric thinking that works at the background of the idea. Feminist theorists make use of Derridian and Lacanian theories to reveal and subvert the binaries. By disconnecting the bond between signifier and signified and then by subverting the hierarchy of speech over writing, Derrida deconstructs not only "Word" but also the structurality of history, science, religion, politics, economics, techniques, law and art namely "the myth of origin".

Feminist archetypal theory is "an interdisciplinary re-visioning that makes use of Jungian archetypes. It began to nourish in late 1970s; but feminist archetypal theorists were brought together in the collaborative work, entitled "Feminist Archetypal Theory: Interdisciplinary Re-visions of Jungian Thought", edited by Estella

Lauter and C.S. Rupprecht in 1985. In contrast to traditional Jungian feminism, feminist archetypal theory is not related to Jung to form a 'Grand Narrative' concerning culture and gender issues. When talking about her approach to archetypes, Maria Warner, like the feminist archetypal theorists, underlines the point where her approach is different from Freud and Jung. Warner is of the opinion that the characteristic of archetype as an interactive and changing medium in shaping people's lives can be used to correct the negative and false qualities attached to women and leave room for genuine female experience. The aim of feminist archetypal theorists is to establish a theory that will help them to study and analyse the patterns found in women's thoughts and images to clarify conspicuously female concerns that have been persistent throughout human history. By applying this theory to a broad range of works by woman writers, they seek to unpack a set of reference points that would serve as an expandable framework for defining female experience. The aim of feminist archetypal thinkers is to express multiple female experiences which prompt them to depart from Jungian archetypal concept as an inherent fixed image. To impart voice to women who have been oppressed by male-dominated myths and archetypes for centuries is the concern of many women writers like Margaret Atwood.

Margaret Atwood uses archetypal elements to tell women's quest stories and the basic ingredient of the quest is the search for a Shamanic voice, – a voice which will work as healing balm to overcome the present turbulent situations. In most of her novels, Atwood frequently uses the Shamanic archetypes of heroine's journey towards 'self-recognition' and 'rebirth' and by such way tries to record the experiences of women who have somehow lost their sense of belonging and true nature.

Atwood's "Surfacing" is a story of a nameless female protagonist who takes a trip back to her homeland, – her past. As the protagonist of the novel searches for her father and (M)other, she also searches for her childhood, her memories, and the point which split her body from the head. Alienated from the world and from her boyfriend and two other friends who she has taken trip with, she tries her utmost to reconnect to nature and to wilderness like a Shaman with an attempt to get rid of 'the Americans' and the language they use. The end of the novel signifies the metamorphosis; the protagonist goes through by reconnecting to her past and by bringing forth the healing balm to overcome her present state of crisis, just as the Shamans do usually.

In "The Edible Woman", the narrative point of view shifts from first to third person, accentuating the protagonist Marian's slow detachment from reality, which suggests her utmost efforts to lay bare meanings and significances which lie buried beneath the heavy weight of life. Throughout the novel, the protagonist Marian carries on her exhaustive quest for her identity which she perceives to be exterminated. This struggle becomes more explicit when one of Duncan's (with whom Marian has an affair) roommates expounds on "Alice's Adventures in Wonderland" as having a 'sexual-identity crisis' and then goes on to describe the situation of both Alice and Marian. Following Marian's engagement, the switch to third person narrative shows that Marian's story is controlled by someone other than Marian herself, following Marian's regaining of identity Atwood returns to the first person narrative again. The narrative shifts from first to third and again at the end to the first person which projects conspicuously Marian as a representative of Shamanic Archetype who by way of her experiences (while recounting the story from third person narrative) gains the divine knowledge which works as a touchstone to prevail over the chaotic state of life.

In "The Penelopiad", Atwood projects the entire narrative of the novel from slightly different perspective. Here, both the text and the protagonist of the novel are the representatives of Shamanic Archetype. It may be said that the narrative follows Arnold's 'touchstone method', as Atwood projects the narrative of the novel in deference with 'Odyssey Myth'. "The Penelopiad" is a retelling of 'Odyssey Myth' from the perspective of the protagonist of the novel Penelope. The novel, by so far, is an attack on society and literature, which through archetypes subordinate women as virtuous, domestic beings who do not know how to assert themselves. Employing the twelve maids of Penelope, who slaughtered by Odysseus and Telemachus for their 'infidelity', as the chorus, Atwood once more problematises victimhood and patriarchal violence. Moreover, Penelope's comments on her experiences from the underworld in her disembodied state and the analogies she makes between course of things in ancient times and in today's world enable Atwood to impart Penelope the stature of a Shaman.

Becoming a Shaman is not for faint-hearts. The initiates has to go through a death experience, whose other side, if all goes well, is rebirth. The suffering is nothing but a kind of purification. A key part of the Shaman's initiation is to come to terms with evil and to diminish it. In Atwood's novels, the female protagonists, as I have already discussed, is an acute representatives of Shamanic archetype, who struggle against the powers of evil and brings forth the healing balm to come to terms with chaotic state of life.

Works Cited

Atwood, Margaret. *The Penelopiad.* New York: Canongate, 2005. Print.

____ *Surfacing.* New York: Quality Paperback, 1990. Print.

____ *The Edible Woman.* Toronto: McClelland and Stewart, 1969. Print.

Bockman, Louise, and Ake Hultkrantz. *Studies in Lapp Shamanism. Stockholm Studies in Comparative Religion* 16. Stockholm: Almqvist and Wiksell, 1978. Print.

Lauter, Estella and Carol Schreier Rupprecht, eds. *Feminist Archetypal Theory: Interdisciplinary Re-Visions of Jungian Thought.* Knoxville: Tennessee, 1985. Print.

Nietzsche, Friderich Wilhelm. *The Birth of Tragedy.* Oxford: Oxford, 2000. Print.

Sharp, Daryl. *Digesting Jung: Food for the Journey.* Toronto: Inner City Books, 2001. Print .

17

Glocalisation through the Lens of Postcolonial Mimicry and Hybridity: A Study of Amitav Ghosh's *The Shadow Lines*

Rabindra Sutradhar

The term 'glocal' and the process noun 'glocalisation' are formed by combining and blending the words 'global' and 'local'. The concept of glocalisation is important to postcolonial studies because it can be understood in terms of the transcultural relationships pertaining between colony and imperial centre in imperialism. The relationship between the local and global has been of particular interest to postcolonial theorists such as Arif Dirlik, Appadurai, Homi K. Bhabha and Spivak. As a phenomena of post colonialism the ambition of both globalisation and glocalisation is to transcend the boundaries of the nation state, and to provide new vistas for understanding cultural flows. Glocalisation explains the relationship between 'the homogenous factors of globalisation and the heterogeneous factors of local communities' (R. Burton, 25-44). It is the interpretation of the global and the local resulting in unique outcomes in different geographic areas. As we go through the novel *The Shadow Lines*, we observe that almost all the characters of the novel confront and conflict with their Local, global or universal identities in the context of mimicry, hybridity and identity crisis as the consequences of colonisation especially in the period of decolonisation and as a result of the post-partition communal holocaust in Bengal. Ghosh's endeavour throughout the novel to synthesize various strings of local and global culture into a glocal culture has been a considerable matter of observation and study.

The novel serves as mental web criss-crossing physical and mental boundaries through linking past and present memories and inviting reader to create personal memories or imaginations that presents or promotes various shades on same experiences. The novel recalls historical events as Swadeshi Movement, Second World War, Partition of India, and riots of 1960s in Dhaka and Calcutta. It spans and centers round three generations of the narrator's family living in Dhaka, Calcutta and London. It manifests and assimilates a wide-range of characters picked up from diverse religions and cultures put beside each other in a unified and comprehensible setting. The novel is an attempt by Amitav Ghosh to show the blurring of lines or borders between East and West, castes and religious beliefs which shows the colonised travelling and moving to and from the coloniser's territory.

The connection and relationship between the local (native colonised) and the global (coloniser) is suggested in the very opening line of the novel; "in 1939, thirteen years before I was born, my father's aunt, Mayadebi, went to England with her husband and her son, Tridib." (Ghosh, 1) The line indicates Mayadebi's visit to London and her intimate contact with the Price family which is recounted by Tridib more than two decades later to the unnamed narrator, an eight years old inquisitive child. Tridib teaches him (the narrator) to use his imagination with precision to release himself from the boundaries surrounding him. They both (narrator and Tridib) enjoyed mental journey to locations they had not visited at all. It is the space of memory and imagination that link them together emotionally. "Tridib had given (him) worlds to travel in." (Ghosh, 20)

Using this power of fancy and imagination, the narrator is able to see various places or spaces. It enables him to travel in real and imaginary places in 'fading photographs' (Ghosh, 60), reading maps in his "tattered old *Bartholomew's* Atlas" (Ghosh, 231), the old newspapers, 'faint recollections' (Ghosh, 19) of childhood memories and games.

Memory as an abstract entity exceeds the bounds, transcends the time scale, and moves beyond any kind of restrictions. So, constant shift of time, going back and forth, and incessant transfer from present to past are important factors attracting our attention to understand the writer's effort to project glocalisation in the novel. In addition to Tridib and narrator, Ila despite her numerous travels around the world, is unable to invent a place in her mind as she believes all places are the same. To her, just the physical existence of a place is a matter of importance. She is mentally unable to remember the past and when asked the reason, she replies: "It was a long time ago – the real question is, how do you remember?" (Ghosh, 19-20). We observe that both narrator and Ila experience displacement and dislocation from their native homelands across the globe, but in different ways: one physically, the other imaginatively. The narrator holds the belief that " a place does not merely exist, that it has to be invented in one's imagination; that [Ila's] practical, bustling London was no less invented than [his own], neither more nor less true, only very far apart." (Ghosh, 21)

Ghosh describes many places in his narrative to be 'a part of history' (Ghosh 104). Tridib had lived in their old family house in Ballygunge place with his aging grandmother in Calcutta, England, Banaras, America, London, and Delhi. (These places have identity, a present, a past and a future. Place represents a geographic Locale.) Ila spent her times in Cairo, Algeria, Brisbane, London, Calcutta, Colombo and America, Lionel Tresawsen in Malaysia, Fiji, Bolivia, Ceylon, Calcutta and in London, Thamma in Dhaka, Calcutta and London, Nick Price in London and Kuwait and so on. The mention of numerous places and spaces in the narrative highlight the significance of location both local and global with better understanding of self, identities, language, culture, surroundings, environments and the world around. The displacement of characters, both practically and imaginatively, makes one being engaged in World and familiar with new findings. So the writer's effort to project the theme of glocalisation is noticeable here.

'Mimicry', in general connotation refers to the imitation of one species by another. It is a critical term in Homi K. Bhabha's criticism of Postcolonial literature. What Bhabha contains is that the colonised, after a long relationship with the coloniser has ambivalent feelings toward the coloniser: some good feelings, some good desire for they have; some bad feelings, some repulsion at what they are. Bhabha contends that this ambivalence – this duality that creates a metaphorical lesion in the identity of the colonised other – is apparent in colonial and post-colonial literature and that it creates beings who are a hybrid of their own cultural identity and the coloniser's cultural identity. As a result, mimicry occurs on various levels both from the side of colonised as well as the colonisers. In Bhabha's use of the term, mimicry occurs when colonised people imitate the culture of the colonising power. The imitation or mimicry is always meditated by the fact that the colonised person is not one of the colonisers. The colonised subject, therefore, develops a double vision, recognising both the culture of the other and his own alienation from it. Mimicry is thus an attempt to attain some of the power of the coloniser through adoption of his culture. The double vision brought about by dual identities is the impact of divided sense of self as a result of mimicry. Thus we find that in postcolonial studies 'mimicry' is considered as unsettling imitations. It is a desire to severe the ties with 'self' in order to move towards 'other'.

Ila, the narrator's cousin, in the novel *The Shadow lines* expresses her penchant for colonial mimicry when she wishes to severe her inherited cultural bond with the East:

> "Her hair cut short, like the bristles on a toothbrush, wearing tight trousers like a free school street whore." (Ghosh, 80)

She feels uncomfortable in Calcutta and finds its social environment tough and unbearable. She adapts nothing from Indian culture – "I want to be free…free of your bloody culture and free of all of you." (Ghosh, 88-89). In quest of freedom she flees Calcutta to seek a home in London, marries an Englishman Nick Price, buys a house, finds a job and tries to settle down there, but all in vain because later it is found that Nick is allegedly having an affair. Nick proves to be unfaithful to her. Later we see that Nick works in Kuwait for a brief period of time, quits his job and it is implied that he may have been fired for embezzlement. So, we find that Ila's freedom brought rootlessness for her. Due to this ambivalence and rootlessness both Ila and Nick develop a double vision and identity which establishes their hybridity. They felt themselves neither coloniser nor colonised and hence in-betweeness and a third space identity of culture as per Bhabha produces here as a result of mimicry and hybridity.

In the novel mimicry is occurred from both coloniser and colonised's side. We see that May price responded to the vehement passion of Tridib to her. Despite their distance the romantic love between them remains deep and ardent. May Price showed respect to other cultures as is found at the Railway Station where she felt sorry and ashamed of hurting the culture of India by kissing Tridib openly there. She rushed to save Tridib from the fanatic mob. After Tridib's death by their hand, she blamed herself for his death. Her loving and kind nature elevated her beyond any border of country, class, creed or colour. After Tridib's death she joined in philanthropic activities.

Mr. Lionel Tresawsen of middle-age leaves his home in North London and comes to Calcutta, after Malaysia, Fiji and Ceylon, establishes his business and finally settles his life here. Travelling a large part of the globe, he tried to set up a homeopathic hospital in a village near Calcutta. He had also developed an interest in spiritualism and begun to attend the meetings of the Theosophical Society in Calcutta where he met and earned the trust and friendship of a number of leading nationalists. This had, of course, estranged him and his wife from most circles of British society in the city and led to innumerable colourful slights and insults at clubs and tea parties, but that had made very little difference to Lionel Tresawsen. The double, hybrid and unstable identity of Mr. Tresawsen is emphasized here in terms of his rootlessness and identity crisis as a result of globalisation. He emerges to be a third culture space identity, i.e., neither coloniser, nor colonised.

Hybridity, in literal speaking, refers to the state of being mixed. It denotes the mixture of culture, religion and state etc. The term 'Hybridity' has been associated with the work of Homi K. Bhabha whose analysis of coloniser/colonised relations stresses their interdependence and the mutual construction of their subjectivities. Bhabha contends that all cultural statement and systems are constructed in a space that he calls the 'Third Space Enunciation'. Cultural identity always emerges in this contradictory and ambivalent space, which for Bhabha makes the claim to a hierarchical 'purity' of cultures untenable. It is this 'in-between' space that carries the burden and meaning of culture, and this is what makes the notion of hybridity so important. Hybridity has frequently been used in postcolonial discourse to mean simply cross-cultural 'exchange'.

In the novel *The Shadow Lines* hybridity is marked not only in characters' identity but also in Language, place and time. The narration hovers between Bengali (that of narrator) and English. The narrator holds a hybrid identity, as he is born in India but received English education. So the whole story moves back and forth between India and England. Even Thamma, the most ardent figure of nationalism, seems swinging between two identities: Whether she belongs to Dhaka or is a citizen of Calcutta. She is caught between memory and nationality, between belonging and citizenship. Naturally, the grandmother's unbelonging can be ascribed to the product of the circumstances of her life and history. In the novel hybridity is traced in love and politics also. The positive outlook of male characters to the concept of love is contrasted with the negative attitude of females as Ila and Thamma that finally lead to an unsuccessful relation. In the story we find that the female characters like Ila and Thamma are interested in political movements and feel they should actively participate in events to remain permanent in the course of history. On the contrary, male characters like Tridib and narrator remain passive and just as observers of political events rather than being participant.

The collection of characters chosen from two opposite extremes provides novel a quality of hybridity that corresponds to a heterogeneous society, as India and Bangladesh. The elements of the novel such as, illusory national borders, the omnipresence of time and space fluctuating between reality and non – reality, are examples of a hybrid microcosmic world that is not merely limited to one geographical area. It seems to us that there is no separate or isolable spot of time and place in the story. Ghosh's diasporic identity is mirrored in the novel which illustrates that diasporic displacement is a source of creativity and a new polyglot and cosmopolitan culture evolves as a result of Diaspora and cross-cultural exchange.

To conclude, Ghosh's endeavour to project the issue of glocalisation throughout the novel *The Shadow Lines* can best be comprehended from postcolonial approach and framework. Through the postcolonial elements of mimicry, hybridity, identity crisis, Diaspora, displacement and unbelonging the novel not only moves beyond the boundaries of time, but also mingles and merges diverse characters, memories, nations, locations and history. It fuses past, present and future, fact and fiction, reality and unreality to magnify the aftermath of colonisation. The novel starts and ends with migration which represents life in crisscross cultural spaces. In *A Reading of The shadow Lines*, Prof. A. N. Kaul righty observes, "Crossing of frontiers – especially those of nationality, culture and Language – has increased the world over, including India. Of this tendency *The Shadow Lines* is an extreme example…" (Kaul, 299).

Work Cited

Ghosh, Amitav. *The Shadow Lines*. New Delhi: Oxford University Press. 2015. Print.

Kaul, A. N. "A Reading of *The Shadow Lines*". Amitav Ghosh. *The Shadow Lines* (11th Ed.). New Delhi: Oxford University Press, 2003. Print.

Roberton, R. *Glocalisation: Time-space and Homogeneity-Heterogeneity.* Eds. M. Featherstone, S. Lash and R. Berton. *Global Modernities.* London: Sage, 1995. Print.

18

Home and beyond, between National Identity and Culture: A Reading of Basharat Peer's *Curfewed Night*

Amrita Datta

Nation and its identity is frequently questioned in the purview of global and postcolonial culture. Globalisation which is often termed as neo colonialism gradually takes over the local culture. People within the nation state belong to diffused, unidentifiable, unrecognisable culture which attempts to build a coherent homogenous national identity. Multi-layered social, political, military and economic issues across national borders invoke a kind of new identity, a quest for self among the people in global culture. Dominance of the majorities in respect of race, religion and community over the minorities create a sort of post-colonial tension and anxiety by projecting the majority and its culture as national culture. In certain places people are treated as 'outsiders' in their own place even if they are living within their territories. They are not treated as men of their home but of the beyond. It is a discourse of conflict of location, paradox of global and local culture, emergence of metaphoric and imaginative space by subjugating the material reality of spatial location.

Basharat Peer's *Curfewed Night* is a memoir of war torn Kashmir, of militancy in Kashmir of 1990s, violence and vigilance, life and death shows that nation is not a myth of 'unity in diversity' but rather a bundle of contradiction . People of Kashmir who reside in the different geopolitic locations from the rest of India are unable to feel the nation like the rest of the countrymen. They have their own perception and expression. A sense of collective unity is sustained by national flag, songs, films, cultural and traditional practices (celebrating Diwali and Eid) etc. The collective national unity is basically an act of imagination and fantasy rather than material reality.

> After all, in all the thousands of years of Indian history, there never was such a creature as a united India. Nobody ever managed to rule the whole place, not the Mugals, not the British. And then, that midnight, the thing that had never existed was suddenly "free". But what on earth was it? On what common ground (if any) did it, does it stand? (*Imaginary Homeland: Essays and Criticism*, 27)

Benedict Anderson maintains in his book Imagined *Communities* that a nation "is imagined because the members of even the smallest nation will never know most of their fellow members, meet them, or even hear of them, yet in the minds of each lives the image of their communion."[1] People of one part of the country can never meet their fellow members but always forced to identify themselves as the part of the same nation. Perception of Kashmiri people regarding rest of India is ambiguous and paradoxical. They do not feel in their minds any image or affinity with the whole part of the nation.

> Despite the rather sleepy existence of our village and my ignorance about the political history of Kashmir had a sense of alienation and resentment most Kashmiri Muslims felt and had against Indian rule. We did not relate to the symbols of Indian nationalism –the flag, the national anthem, the cricket team .We followed every cricket match India and Pakistan played but we never cheered for the Indian team. If India played Pakistan, we supported Pakistan; if India played the West Indies; we supported the West Indies if India played England, We supported England. (*Curfewed Night,* I. 11)

To the Kashmiri Muslims, game is not a game especially when it played between India and Pakistan. It is also the symbol of hatred, resentment and alienation. Cricket becomes an extraordinary game while it takes place between India and Pakistan. Kashmiri Muslims always supported Pakistan though they lived in Indian Territory. Basharat Peer shared in his memoir 'grandfather sat facing Mecca on a prayer mat, seeking divine help for the Pakistani team', (p 12) 'people hugged each other, jumped around, and shouted over the din of the celebratory crackers'(p13) It seems to be ironical and anti-national that Kashmiri Muslims love Pakistan more than India . They do not relate themselves to Indian nationalism – the flag, the national anthem, the cricket team .Living in one place but praising the other has become a code for Kashmiri Muslim Identity. From his childhood days like other Kashmiri children the author also internalised by the environment that Indian government always responded ruthlessly towards them, treated them brutally, inconsiderate towards Kashmir in every respect. But in case of rest of India, the national sensibility of the Muslims is completely opposite to the Kashmiri Muslims. Transformation of identity accompanies change of place or location. In his days in Aligarh Basharat observes 'most of my Indian Muslim friends seemed quite patriotic...Whenever a cricket match was screened in the television room of our hostel, my Indian Muslim friends cheered, sang and rooted for the Indian cricket team. The Kashmiris cheered for Srilanka or whoever else was in the opposite team.' (*Curfewed Night,* IV.66)

A sense of place has tremendous influence in building up the physical, environmental, spiritual and even psychological set up of a human being. Basharat Peer's *Curfewed Night* shows the author's powerful and deep attachments with his own birth place. It is not at all an uncommon human behaviour but have a serious effect on each human psyche.

> I might have forgotten Kashmir – it might have turned into a place I visited every two or three months – but I could not. Kashmir was the text and subtext of my professional, personal and social worlds in Delhi. (Curfewed *Night*, V. 70)

"A sense of place" suggests a sense of home which requires boundaries and a sense of outside the boundaries is beyond one's sense of place. Peer's *Curfewed Night* is a novel on Kashmir, of Kashmir and Kashmiri life. The author begins the novel by introducing the place from where he belongs to:

> I was born in winter in Kashmir. My village is the southern district of Anantanag sat on the wedge of a mountain range. Paddy fields, green in early summer and golden by autumn, surrounded the cluster of mud and brick houses. In winter, snow slid slowly from our roof and feel on our lawns with a thud. (*Curfewed Night*, I. 1)

Kashmir is the place with which the author connected by the environment – the flora and fauna; family, friends and relatives; the slogans of Aazadi ('*War till victory*', '*self-determination is our birthright!*'), army vigilance, violence and trauma, frisking crackdown, bunker, search, interrogation, identity card, arrest, torture, mine blasts on the roads, the smell of dead bodies, the machine guns, conflict between Indian army and militants etc. These experiences are quite natural to the man who feels comfortable in his own place even if these experiences sometimes may be negative or undesirable. One cannot neglect it, it remains in the subconscious.

> I wasn't scared of being scolded; I felt a part of something much bigger, unknowingly making a journey from I to We. I let myself go, fly with the crowd. *Aazadi!* (*Curfewed Night,* I .11)

The influence of a place where someone was born, grown up develops one's identity, the place has made an impact consciously or unconsciously and one responds according to it.

> I was training myself for the one story I wanted to tell the most: Kashmir. And then my editor said, 'Basharat! You are going to Kashmir'. It was hundred times the rush of graduation, I was tossing my hat far, far into the air .My excitement dwarfed my experience and competence. I was going home as a reporter, I took stories of Kashmir to the world. (*Curfewed Night,* VI .79)

This eternal search for connection for one's own place, home which connects one to oneself or others is not a part of place as the physical landscape one inhabit only but more than that it crosses the

separatist slogan. "August 14 and August 15 are the Pakistani and Indian Independence days. Pro-Pakistan militants held celebratory parades on August 14 and a day later, the Indian Independence Day was declared a 'Black Day'." (*Curfewed Night,* 38).Shared history of India and Pakistan asserts violence and suffering haunted by memory, imagination and material reality. There are examples of ill-fated bride facing extremities of inhumanity on her wedding night, about the torture chamber of Papa II, about a boy who forced to hold a bomb when it is exploded etc. "The journey was not over, it will never be. The sky has been red, the days fear – filled, and the nights curfewed since 1990." (*Curfewed Night,* 234).Understanding Kashmir in respect of home and beyond culture is only possible by restoring the stories of present and past and also by searching for a personal identity(closely connected to the sense of self) crossing the boundaries not for the writer only but for the readers also. Duality of Kashmiri life and existence redirects us to the laws of universe; retelling and reclaiming "the naive hope of a new world about to be born." (234).

Works Cited

Abraham, Taisha. *Introducing Postcolonial Theories and Debates.* Delhi: Macmillan Publishers India Limited, 2007.

Anderson, Benedict. *Imagined Communities: Reflections on the Origin and Spread of Nationalism.* (Revised and extended.ed.) London: Verso. ISBN 978-0-86091-546-1.1991. Retrived 15 December, 2017.

Ashcroft, Bill, Griffiths Gareth and Tiffin, Helen. *The Postcolonial Studies Reader.* New York: Routledge, 2001.

Ashcroft, Bill. *Postcolonial Transformation.* London: Routledge, 2001.

Bose, Sumantra, *Kashmir: Roots of Conflict, Paths to Peace.* New Delhi:Vistaar Publications, 2003.

Dr. Himadri Lahiri, Former Professor, Burdwan University (Advices and information).

Dresse, Donelle N "Eco Criticism, Sense of Place". *Ecocriticism: Creating Self and Place in Environmental and American Indian Literatures.* New York: Peter Lang Publishing, 2002.

Gandhi, Leela. *Post Colonial Theory: A Critical Introduction*. New Delhi: OUP. 1998.

Ganguly, Sumit. *Conflict Unending: India Pakistan Tensions since* 1947.New Delhi: OUP.2001.

Matindra Debnath, Mind Scientist, Life Coach and Mentor for his lectures at Khalisamari, Alipurduar (W.B) during Eagle Rebirth Retreat (26th Dec'17 to 31st Dec'17).

Mongia, Podmini. Contemporary *Postcolonial Theory: A Reader*. New Delhi: OUP. 1997.

Nayar, Promod K. *Contemporary Literary and Cultural Theory*. India: Dorling. Kindersley (India) Private Ltd. 2010.

Peer, Basharat. *Curfewed Night*. Gurgaon: Random House Publishers India Pvt.Ltd. 2008.

Rushdie, Salman. "Commonwealth Literature" Does Not Exist'. In *Imaginary Homelands: Essays and Criticism* 1981-1991, P61-70. London: Granta. 1991.

19

Postcolonial Dilemma of Language: A Study of Male Protagonist in Anita Desai's *In Custody*

Tinku Das

The term postcolonial takes our thoughts back to the colonial period. It reveals the act of domination over the colonised by the colonisers. The imprint and effect of colonisation that is still fresh after the period of colonisation reveals and comes to light through action and thoughts in the postcolonial period. That is the reason that, when we study the postcolonial literature we find the colonial influence heavily working underneath. Anita Desai's *In Custody* is also no difference in this regard. The characters of her novels feel the same breath that the victims of colonisation do. The very title *In Custody* itself shows a sense of under control, lack of liberty and being passive or helpless. It recalls the sense of being colonised. It also means you are under bindings. You cannot do anything according to your will. You are in custody.

In *In Custody*, Anita Desai has presented her weak and feeble hero as a post-colonial person. He is a failure in every side but has a great goal of life. His sole aim is to re-establish the once royal language 'Urdu' to its place that it used to enjoy. But his struggle for Urdu seems quite imaginary when we find that Devan himself is a teacher of Hindi language in real life. Hindi is the language which is thought to be the prime responsible for the pathetic condition of Urdu. Though his first language is Urdu but he could not study that for long. As a result he becomes a part time lecturer of Hindi in a college and proved himself to be failure in that profession also.

Desai has introduced her two prime characters Devan and Murad in the very beginning of the novel. Devan and Murad are two contrasting personalities and belong to different family backgrounds. They meet and try to explore lots of probabilities in the future. Murad is also like Devan, an Urdu lover. He runs an Urdu literary journal *Awaj*. But his belonging to a business family and his using Devan for *Awaj* without paying any payment brings his love for Urdu under question. We meet Murad as Hindi hater. For him,

> The language that is raised on radishes and potatoes......it flourishes, while Urdu language of the court in days of royalty now languishes in the back lanes and gutters of the city (*In Custody*, 15)

It shows how much rage and anguish he is having against Hindi. Murad's complaint against Hindi is actually a complaint against the colonisers. It is the British colonisers that have come to India, ruled more than two hundred years, gave more importance to Hindi and spoiled status of Urdu. So the postcolonial theme begins from the very beginning.

Murad, the tactful businessman knows very well that Devan harbours a great love for Urdu language. He has used Devan for many a times for his magazine *Awaj*. Once again Murad wants to use Devan for his purpose. Murad outrages his hatred for Hindi language. He blames Devan for neglecting his mother tongue 'Urdu' and nourishing its rival language 'Hindi' with his professional abilities. He inspires Devan by saying that Urdu language will not survive if they do not come out to support it whole heartedly. He names Hindi as monster and calls it a language of peasants. He encourages Devan to start his action for the upliftment of Urdu. For Murad, it is the high time to start action rather than just loving and keeping it as a hobby. He questions Devan,

> Can you serve a language by taking it up only as your hobby? Doesn't it deserve more? Doesn't it deserve a lifetime's dedication like mine? (*In Custody,* 16)

Being hit by such arrows of questions, Devan agrees to work for Murad. Now, Devan who is a hope for the upliftment of Urdu language is actually a great failure in personal life. He cannot fulfill his duty as a good husband and father in the family and as a successful teacher in profession. Devan's wife Sarala shows him his inability to buy anything for his son. Devan asks,

> Where is Manu? I don't see him. Manu! His wife arrogantly replied – He has gone to neighbours to show them his new clothes ...My parents have given him... (*In Custody,* 194)

The response of Devan's wife shows his position in the family. He has failed to maintain his place in home. Devan's inability to keep his position as a good teacher, proves him to be a failure in every field. In his college, Devan is,

> A boring teacher, who could not command attention, let alone regard of his unruly class. (*In Custody,* 194)

The reason behind being failure as a teacher is his love for Urdu. Though he has become a Hindi teacher, he could never love Hindi. It always remains as a second language for him. He suffers a lot by seeing the dying condition of his first language Urdu. He cannot realise that his love for Urdu language is an illusion but his job as a Hindi teacher is the reality. The illusion may take him to a dreamy poetic world but his job gives him the bread that his family eats and the home where they sleep.

Devan as a typical postcolonial character chooses to live his life under illusion. He valorises the past glory of Urdu and gets pain by looking back with nostalgia. He comes under the influence of Murad and accepts his project of interviewing the famous Urdu poet Nur Shahjehanabadi. Murad knows that Devan has a great liking for Nur and he will never reject that proposal which he has already planned to print in the next edition of *Awaj* to make a good profit without paying anything.

Devan, the failure, begins a new journey to re-establish Urdu to its glorious position. He begins to live in a world of fantasy – a world where Nur is holding the position of lord.

> He had pictured him living either surrounded by elderly, sage and dignified literatures or else entirely alone, in divine isolation. (*In Custody,* 51)

The more Devan thinks about Nur, the more he becomes poetic. His imagination gets wings. He feels as if a new world is waiting for him and

> He casting away the meanness and dross of his past existence and steadily approaching a new and wonderous illuminated era. (*In Custody,* 40)

But as Devan goes near to his ideal poetic hero Nur, all his dreams begin to shutter. The first blow to Devan's imaginary world comes in the shape of Nur's residence. Nur's residence is located past a gutter over flowing with garbage released from a gloomy hospital. Devan cannot accept the fact that his great bard lives in such a pathetic condition. Nur's dwelling severely disappoints Devan. It pains him.

The second blow that Devan gets is about Nur's companion. He finds his ideal hero is sharing his time with "…shopkeepers, clerks, bookies and unemployed parasites." (*In Custody,* 50).

Before coming to meet Nur, Devan has expected that he will meet his poetic hero, speak with him, discuss about his poems and his sound will enter into his heart through his ears. But in contrary he finds Nur to be surrounded by some parasitic langers, who want to expose themselves as poets. The harsh reality becomes very hard for Devan to digest.

Here we can see the real picture of the position of Urdu language. The language of royal palace is now suffering near gutter. It cannot breath properly for the foul smell that the parasites are spreading. That is the reason behind the dying condition of Urdu language. But Devan, the postcolonial hero needed some more evidences to accept the influence of modernity and the change it demands from everything even from language.

After a lot of preparations, Devan succeeds to meet his poetic hero just to meet another harsh reality to break his world of illusion. The meeting which is a long waited event for Devan proves to be a disturbing moment for Nur. The latter says, "Who gave you permission to disturb me?" (*In Custody,* 41) The question shakes Devan but he expresses his own feelings that he has for Nur: "It is a great honour for me sir, a great privilege." (*In Custody,* 41)

It shows how one's privilege turns to be others disturbance. The literary discussion over Urdu language calls no interest for such a great Urdu poet. As the discussion somehow begins, Nur shows Devan the real picture of Urdu language in the present literary scenario. He says,

> Urdu poetry? ... How can there be Urdu poetry when there is no Urdu language left? It is dead, finished. So, now you see its corpse lying here, waiting to be buried. (*In Custody,* 42)

Here the colonial feature comes out very clearly. The Urdu language speaker thinks themselves to be colonised by the coloniser Hindi speakers. They think that the royal position of Urdu is snatched away by Hindi. The pain of the loss of position gives birth to a sense of hatred for the coloniser Hindi. They think Hindi to be a usurper who usurped the glorious position of Urdu.

It is a fact that Hindi replaced Urdu in India. Before British colonisation, Urdu has enjoyed a royal status. All official activities have been done in Urdu language. As the days passed the colonisers have started to give more importance on Hindi. Later, as the struggle for Indian independence has begun, Hindi turns into a medium through which the whole India is united. But in the process of freedom struggle and with the passage of time, Indians start to accept Hindi more than Urdu. One more thing that has hampered the language is the religious tag. Urdu language carries a Muslim tag with it. It is generally believed that Urdu language is harboured and nurtured mainly by the Muslim people. This religious sense has hampered the language at its worst. As a result, after colonisation and partition, Urdu does not find a good position in independent India. Gradually it starts to lose its past glory. Urdu writers also have failed to grasp the attention of the readers with their literary inventions. Slowly but steadily it has lost all its previous status and has earned a colonised position in the postcolonial era.

Devan, the helpless hero finds it very hard to accept the position of Nur and Urdu language. He is a modern hero. He has many thoughts but little action. Devan is bound by many bindings. Bindings of the family needs professional duties, social obligations, mental urge and so on. Being in all these pressures, Devan feels himself in a "kind of zoo from which he could not hope to find freedom." (*In Custody,* 131)

It means that Devan is living his life according to others' will as the animals in a zoo lives according to the zoo keepers' wish. At home, he is in custody of his wife and in college he is in custody of his head of the department. In both the fields, he proves himself a great failure. He cannot become a good husband, a good father, and a good teacher. He remains invisible in the crowd. It is not that Devan has become such after any incident. He has always been passive and submissive.

> All through his childhood and youth he had known only one Urdu to deal life and that was to lie low and remain invisible" (*In Custody,* 20)

Now, this invisible man hopes to revive Urdu language out of its death bed. Desai has very nicely presented the postcolonial theme of identity crisis through her hero Devan and Urdu language. Both are facing the same problem. Devan wants to re-establish the identity of Urdu language but in disguise he is searching a way to establish his own identity, gain a position at home and at work place.

As Devan meets the Urdu poet Nur, the latter charges him for his becoming a Hindi teacher by ignoring the call of his mother tongue Urdu. He explains,

> I studied Urdu sir, as a boy, in Lucknow. My father, he was a school teacher, a scholar, and a lover of Urdu poetry. He taught me the language. But he died...I was sent to the nearest school, a Hindi medium school sir." (*In Custody,* 48)

Here Desai has drawn a good link between Devan's Urdu learning and his father's death. For Devan his father, worked as a life line for Urdu language learning. As his father dies, Devan's Urdu learning also stops. After his father's death Devan studies in a Hindi medium school and becomes a Hindi teacher. Now Hindi has become the means of livelihood for him and his family. Though Hindi has become his source of earning, his love for Urdu still remains in his heart. He explains to Nur,

> I took my degree in Hindi, sir and now I am temporary lecturer...it is my living sir. You see I am a married man, a family man. But I still remember my lessons in Urdu..." (*In Custody,* 40)

This shows that Devan loves and keeps Urdu safe in his heart, but to maintain his household duties he is bound to deal with Hindi language. The very terms like 'married man' and 'family man' shows how much burden he is carrying with him. Still he has preserved the lessons of Urdu that he learned in his childhood. It shows his love and respect for the language.

Devan's love for Urdu language and his trying to uplift its position brings problem to his professional life. His head of the department has a good problem with Devan's interest in Urdu. He informs Devan,

> I'll get you transferred to your beloved Urdu department. I won't have Muslim toadies in my department; you will ruin my boys with your Muslim ideas, your Urdu language. I'll explain to the principal, I'll warn the RSS, you are a traitor. (*In Custody,* 163)

Thus the family man gets entangled into his family responsibilities, professional obligations and his love for mother tongue Urdu. The struggle for regaining the lost position of Urdu becomes tougher for Devan. Here Desai has very rightly explains the condition of Devan,

> ...he must look like a caged animal in a zoo...And that was all he was ...a trapped animal. In his youth, he had the illusion of having free will, not knowing he was in a trap. Marriage, a family and a job has placed him in this cage; now there was no way out of it. The unexpected friendship with Nur had given him the illusion that the door of the trap had opened and he could escape after all into a wider world that lay outside but a closer familiarity with the poet had shown him that what he thought of as the 'wider world' was an illusion too. (*In Custody,* 131)

Devan thus becomes a trapped animal where there is no way to escape. The life has become a zoo for him where he is free within a boundary. The outside world is mere illusion for him. Though with Nur, a ray of hope has come to his dwelling but it also proves to be just a flattering reality. It pained him more than solace. His sense of being in trap grows the urge to be free and ultimately suffers, more and more.

Anita Desai has very rightly projected Devan as a postcolonial hero who suffers from every side. He has no position at home and at his work place. His friend Murad uses him for his own purpose and blames him for keeping Urdu only as a hobby. His head of the department calls him a traitor for nurturing the rival language Urdu. Again, Nur, the ideal Urdu poet for Devan, calls him a 'slave', 'a spy' and 'a destroyer', of Urdu language.

> ...you are its slave. Perhaps a spy even if you don't know it, sent to the universities to destroy whatever remains of Urdu, hunt it out and kill it. (*In Custody,* 40)

So, from every side, Devan has a problem to face, a blame to bear. Though, with Mr. Siddiqui's decision to sell his house to the builders, Anita Desai has shown a probable solution to the identity crisis of Urdu language and Devan himself. Mr. Siddiqui's decision shows his acceptance that to survive, one has to adapt to the new ways of life and leave the useless tendency to cling to the glorious past only. The same thing is applicable to Urdu language and Devan both. Both need to be modern and up-to-date to cope up with modern time to establish self-identity and maintain one's position.

Works Cited

Desai, Anita. *In Custody*. New Delhi: Penguin Books, 1994. Print.

Sharma, Anjali. *Anita Desai's In Custody – A War. The Criterion: An International Journal in English.* Vol. II Issue III (Sep. 2011): 1-4. Web.

Subha, V. "Anita Desai's *In Custody*: A Clash between Reality and Illusion". *The Ashvamegh International Journal & Literary Magazine.* Vol. III Issue-XXIV (Jan. 2017). Web.

Yaquin, Amina. *The Communalisation and Disintegration of Urdu in Anita Desai's 'In Custody'. The Annual of Urdu Studies.* Vol. 19 (2004): 1-22. Web.

20

Revisiting the Colonial Discourse: A Study of Chinua Achebe's *Things Fall Apart*

Saurabh Debnath

Introduction

Chinua Achebe, one of the major writers from Africa, has depicted the colonial encounter between the Africans and the British in all his novels. *Things Fall Apart* (1958) happens to be his earliest novel which captures the spirit of the African society during the transitional period. The clash between Nigeria's white colonial government and the traditional culture of the indigenous Igbo people is the keynote of this novel. Okonkwo stands for the Igbo culture. Inspite of his poor family background, he worked very hard and became a prosperous and one of clan's men of his community. The very beginning of the novel depicts how Okonkwo rises from humble origin to become a powerful leader in Umuofia, a rural village in southeastern Nigeria:

> OKONKWO WAS WELL KNOWN throughout the nine villages and even beyond. His fame rested on solid personal achievements. As a young man of eighteen he had brought honour to his village by throwing Amalinze the cat. Amalinze was the great wrestler who for seven years was unbeaten, from Umuofia to Mbaino. He was called the cat because his back would never touch the earth. It was this man that Okonkwo threw in a fight which the old men agreed was one of the fiercest since the founder of their town engaged a spirit of the wild for seven days and seven nights. (Achebe, 5)

In this novel Achebe endeavours not only to increase awareness about the cultural traditions of Igbo society but to remind his own people of their past and to assert that it was of great value. He takes two things into consideration. First to recreate the past of Africa and secondly, to counter the European version of Africa. What Achebe wants to say is:

> The African people did not hear of culture for the first time from Europeans, that their societies were not mindless but frequently had philosophy of great depth and value and beauty, and they knew poetry above all, they had dignity. (Achebe, 160)

Significance of the Title

The title *Things Fall Apart* was adopted from William Butler Yeats' poem *The Second Coming* (1921). The poem foresees the end of the present age and the world's approach to another phase that is completely different:

> Turning and turning in the widening gyre
> The falcon cannot hear the falconer;
> Things fall apart; the centre cannot hold;
> Mere anarchy is loosed upon the world,
> The blood-dimmed tide is loosed, and everywhere
> The ceremony of innocence is drowned;
> The best lack all conviction, while the worst
> Are full of passionate intensity.
>
> (Yeats: 1921)

As the title suggests, *Things Fall Apart* is concerned with the dislocation of the Igbo society (representative of African society) caused by the colonial impact which is felt and experienced in three main spheres of social-cultural activity-religion, trade and legal system. The events in the novel move towards a stage until "Things fall apart" and to its utter helplessness "the centre cannot hold". Achebe assimilates into his narrative a general history of the colonial impact directly and empirically, through his depiction of how it changed and scarred local lives in places like Umuofia, Mbanta and Abame. The knife of British administration supporting the cause of missionary campaign fell on the culture of happily living Igbo people and cut it to bleed and die. Achebe is preoccupied with "Things fall apart", the breakdown of the old order under the relentless onslaught of the new order.

The Three Major Segments of the Novel

Things Fall Apart can be divided into three parts. The first part is devoted to the depiction of life of the inhabitants of Umuofia in terms of their political, cultural and sociological aspects. The second part is a sort of formless darkness on account of the intrusion of European missionaries in the land of innocence. The third part assumes the shape of anarchy let loose on the Umuofian world to destroy the native institutions and traditions. This is a stage where the missionaries collaborate with the coloniser.

The First Part of the Novel Reflects the Following Aspects before the Coming of the White Man

Life of Igbo People

The life of Igbo people in general as existed before the coming of the external forces into Igbo land has been illustrated in the first part of Achebe's novel. People led a happy life without bitterness of any serious kind. They were contented with what they had. They live in co-operation with one-another. Their main occupation was farming. During sowing and harvest seasons they worked hard in their fields from morning till evening. They were quite unaware of what was happening in African continent around them. They did not have knowledge of advanced technique of farming. Their agriculture was limited to hoe cultivation. They were hospitable by nature. They always gave a warm welcome to their guests. They offered them kola-nuts and palm-wine to eat and drink and rejoiced in their company. Telling funny, ethical and adventurous stories to their children, composing new poems, taking delight in music, playing and gossiping in the silvery light of the moon were the other simple joys of the primitive people.

Festivals of Igbo People

Before the planting season, Igbo people observed 'A Week of Peace' to please 'Ani', the goddess of earth so that she might bless them with good crops. During this week people did no work. They went to their friends and spent most of their time in talking, gossiping, eating, drinking and merry-making. Saying a harsh word to anyone was a sin.

Another important festival observed by Igbo people was 'The new yam festival'. It was observed every year after the harvest to honour the earth goddess and the spirits of the ancestors. Man, woman, young and old were happy at the arrival of this festival. These festivals not only catered to the needs of eating, drinking and merry-making but also developed intimacy among the Igbo People. This was the occasion when they got an opportunity to exchange their views for a better understanding.

Sources of Recreation

Igbo people were very fond of wrestling. It was the most popular play of recreation for them. People from nine villages gathered to see wrestling matches held in Umuofia yearly on the second day of the new year just after the festival of new yam. There was a beating of drums which created a feeling of sensation among the people. They rushed to the wrestling ground dancing to the beating of the drums. Old men nodded to the beat of the drums and remembered the days when they wrestled. The way in which Achebe describes the setting of the wrestling events and the wrestling tricks applied by the wrestlers is quite realistic.

Igbo people taught their children by telling stories so that they might become promising when they were grown up. They had collected in their memories, stories, proverbs and poems, which were passed on from one generation to another by words of mouth. There were story-tellers, poets and priests to inculcate interest of young children in this artistic heritage, youths loved to sing poems and songs. Masculine stories of violence and blood-shed, female stories of tortoise and birds of earth and the sky of vulture and others as referred to in *Things Fall Apart* were told to children.

On the moonlit nights the children came out of their houses and played in the open fields. They were mad with glee at their play. While playing they made joyful shouts resounding in the atmosphere. Old men and women would recall to their minds their youths and the happy times of their lives. They all were happy and enjoyed the beauty of the silvery light.

Igbo people were fond of music. After the harvest village musicians played upon their musical instruments. Unoka was one of them. This was the way how the Igbo people enjoyed their lives unmixed with bitterness of any kind before missionary interference in their peaceful life.

Political Life of Igbo People

An important aspect of Igbo society was the lack of centralised political structures. The Igbo people lived in autonomous villages and towns, ruled by their elders with a few exceptions, they organized themselves in patrilineages – lineage groups organized along lines of descent from father to son. Relationships were based on blood ties, and each person traced his or her descent to three groups. First, a person belonged to the smallest social unit known as Uno, or house. This was a natural family, consisting of a man, his wife or wives, and their children. The second group was the Umuhha, or lineage, composed of a number of related houses. Finally, a group of lineages formed a compact village or town, Obodo. This was the highest territorially defined authority of the Igbo people.

The Igbo people subscribed to the principle of direct participation in government. Their entire social and political structures revolved around the idea of cross-cutting ties. The five most important cross-cutting institutions were the councils of elders, age-groups, councils of chiefs, women's associations, and secret societies, without them, the Igbo society would be starved of its essence and would disintegrate. As we shall presently see, the traditional Igbo communities did indeed fall apart in the twentieth century when the Europeans destroyed their cross-cutting ties in the process of colonial rule.

The Religion of Igbo People

The religion of these primitive people had a powerful influence on their life. Violation of the rules of conduct as provided for in their religion was treated as a vice endangering the existence of the whole clan. The people believed in the supremacy of one God whom they called Chukwu. They had belief in many gods and goddesses, oracles, evil spirits, priesthood, medicine men and magic etc. To sum up, they were happy with their religious life inspite of certain traditional evils like throwing of infant twins, killing of innocent boy like Ekemefuna for other's fault, throwing of people suffering from serious illness to Evil Forest to rot and die and banning of burial by the clansmen of the dead bodies of the men (like Okonkwo) who happened to commit suicide even for a great cause. When Okonkwo's dead body was dangling from a tree, Obierika uttered the following words:

> We cannot bury him. Only strangers can. We shall pay your men to do it. When he has been buried we will then do our duty by him. We shall make sacrifices to cleanse the desecrated land. That man was one of the greatest men in Umuofia. You drove him to kill himself, and now he will be buried like a dog... (Achebe, 145)

So we find that Achebe explores the good and evil prevailing in the native culture as well as in the foreign culture. In this regard David Cook writes:

> Achebe prefers to reveal the darker side of both the traditions as well as the better side and leaves us to draw our own conclusions. (Cook, 142)

The Second Part of the Novel Shows the Intrusion of European Missionaries in the Land of Innocence

The second part of the novel shows how the external forces stepped into the Igbo villages such as Umuofia, Mbanta and began to create havoc in their life. At first the missionaries appeared. They built their churches in different villages. They propagated the gospel of Christianity and attracted a large number of Igbo people to their religion. The number of converts went on increasing day-by-day. Thus the missionary factor was successful in dividing the primitive people among themselves.

The converts turned bitter enemies of their brothers and the conflict between the two had become a matter of routine. In this context Obierika remarked:

> Our own men and sons have joined the ranks of the stranger. They have joined his religion and they help to uphold his government. If we should try to drive out the white men in Umuofia we should find it easy. There are only two of them. But what of our own people who are following their way and have been given power? They would go to Umuru and bring the soldiers, and we would be like Abame. (Achebe, 124)

James Smith, the successor of Mr. Brown, was a hard task master. Mr. Smith's policies turned the upside down and disturbed the peaceful life of the native people. After his arrival in Umuofia, he found everything topsy-turvy. He saw things as black and white. He believed in slaying the false deities of the Igbo people. He was opposed to Mr. Brown in thought and action. His approach was dictatorial and not humanitarian like that of Mr. Brown.

The Third Part of the Novel Highlights the Disintegration of Igbo Culture

However, the missionaries by themselves fail to destroy the Igbo culture. The real process of disintegration began when the colonial power had set up its government, courts of justice, prisons and agencies for trade and commerce. The government began to enforce its laws. Igbo people who did not abide by the white men's laws were thrown behind the bars. Even the members of the council of elders were not spared. They were insulted, beaten and tortured. They were released only after the people had paid the penalty of 250 cowries. The people had no moral courage to face the challenge exposed to them.

In this part of the novel Okonkwo becomes a spokesman of his own cultural values. After his exile of seven years when he returns to his native place Umuofia, he finds that various changes have taken place in Umuofia due to the entry of the Christian missionaries and the establishment of colonial government. Okonkwo finds himself at cross-roads and fails to reconcile with the new society, new religion and new generation. He tries in vain to rouse his clan to take action against the foreigners and their institutions. In frustration he kills an African employed by the British and then commits suicide. Thus his death means the defeat of the traditional Igbo culture and the victory of the white man's religion and political power.

The Essence of the Novel: Conflict between Traditionalism and Modernity

The conflict between traditionalism and modernity is the essence of the novel, Okonkwo representing traditionalism and Mr. Smith and Mr. Brown representing modernity. The conflict shows the inability of the natives to welcome and at the same time accept the changes that accompany colonialism. With the appearance of the white man in Africa and with the introduction of his religion, the existing order is disrupted. Towards the closing of the novel Okonkwo kills an African employed by the colonial government and then commits suicide, a sin against the tradition to which he had long clung. Here Achebe tries to achieve a balance in recreating the tragic consequences of the clash of two cultures. Thus we can conclude that in showing the Igbo society before and after the coming of the white man, Achebe avoids the temptation to present the past as idealised and the present as ugly and unsatisfactory.

The Design behind the Emerging Imperialism

The design behind the emerging imperialism was one of empowerment of colonial culture and denigration of African culture. The imperialist arrogance, working on the presumption of cultural superiority undertook the mission of civilising the uncivilised world of the native. But Africa was itself versicoloured in culture and tradition to which the whites were ignorant. Through his novel *Things Fall Apart* Achebe makes an attempt to present and highlight the cultural heritage of the African tribes. Okonkwo thus becomes a spokesperson of his culture and its values and tries to resist the colonial power of the British.

However, it is part of the irony of life that Okonkwo's resistance and sacrifice do not help to retain the unity and solidarity of his society and culture in the context of colonial conflict between two cultures. His society and culture disintegrate inspite of his opposition because of the British religious, administrative, legal and economic forces which are more powerful than the native ones.

Conclusion

Things Fall Apart is an assault to the superiority of the whites. The imperialists considered themselves to be supreme in their religion, culture and traditional values. By via the medium of his novel, Achebe reveals the rich culture of the so-called blacks. Instead of critically rejecting the cultures of the so-called black societies, the imperialists need to acknowledge certain positive attributes of the native culture which Achebe has endeavoured to illuminate in *Things Fall Apart*. This novel achieves the quality of a parable and the stature of a classic by projecting an almost archetypal picture of the Calibanesque resistance to the presence of Prospero in his cultural island.

Works Cited

Achebe, Chinua. *The African Trilogy: Things Fall Apart, No Longer at Ease,* Arrow of God. UK: Everyman's Library, 2010. Print.

____ ., "The Role of the Writer in a New Nation", Nigeria Magazine, No. 81 (June 1964). Print.

Cook, David. *African Literature: A Critical Overview*. London: Longman, 1977. Print.

Finneran, Richard J. Ed. *The Collected Poems of W.B. Yeats*. New York: Scribner, 1996. Print.

21

Interrogating National Identity: A Postcolonial Study of Mahesh Dattani's *Final Solutions*

Dipak Giri

Apart from having own personal identity, every human being has a sense of having another identity that relates him or her to the larger community in the form of nation. This very sense of nationhood brings him or her close to a certain group of people and their culture to which he or she belongs since his or her birth. Etymologically the term 'Nation' came into English from the old French word *nacion* – meaning 'birth' after being originated from Latin word – *natio*, also meaning birth. In this sense nation is a birth right irrespective of caste, religion and sex. However, contrary to conventional outlook as to what nation is, postcolonial study posits a different idea as regards national identity. Nation now has become a critical study from postcolonial perspective. In postcolonial study, nation has taken the form of supposition – a myth that finds its reality only after holding over a certain elite and privileged class of people belonging to a certain community from which non-elites and underprivileged are kept aside. This very idea of binary has made its original meaning biased and contaminated and now it is no longer a birthright, rather it has become the right and privileging power of majorities over minorities. In his celebrated book, *Imagined Communities*, Benedict Anderson defines nation as 'an imagined political community':

> In an anthropological spirit, then, I propose the following definition of the nation: it is an imagined political community – and imagined as both inherently limited and sovereign. It is *imagined* because the members of even the smallest nation will never know most of their fellow-members, meet them, or even hear of them, yet in the minds of each lives the image of their communion. (Anderson, 5-6)

This definition of Anderson has given rise to debate and criticism regarding the validity of nation. Many postcolonial writers have openly criticized this very idea of nationhood. Under this criticism, the very notion of united India as a nation that emerged suddenly after its freedom has also taken critically by postcolonial writers. Salman Rushdie looks this sudden emergent idea of united India as a mere fancy:

> After all, in all the thousands of years of Indian history, there never was such a creature as a united India. Nobody ever managed to rule the whole place, not the Mughals, not the British. And then, that midnight, the thing that had never existed was suddenly "free". But what on earth was it? On what common ground (if any) did it, does it, stand? (Rushdie, 27)

In colonial period, people of our country identified themselves as Indians against the identity of their British oppressors. Being fostered by a shared resentment against the British colonial power, at that time, they had a strong feeling of communal, national identity. But thing did not remain same. It underwent a radical change after India got its freedom. National, communal identity slowly started to weaken. Bit by bit India's populace fell apart into more and more divided factions in post-colonial era. Validation and promotion of one religion at the expense of others has given birth to the problem of communalism in postcolonial India. Putting on the mask of secularism, the nation-state India in postcolonial period has held the real face back from public. India as a community taken birth in this period has appeared more an imagined community for Hindus than a united community for other religions. The discourse of religion has made national identity more exclusionary than inclusionary. At the centre of this discourse, Hindus stand head and shoulders above Non-Hindus. "...in Hindustan exists and must need to exist [sic] the ancient Hindu nation and nothing else but the Hindu nation. All those not belonging to the national, i.e. Hindu race, religion, culture and language, naturally beyond the pale of real 'National' life... so long, however, as they maintain their racial, religion and cultural differences, they [minorities] cannot but be only foreigners." (Golwalkar, 45-46) Such rise of nation out of discursive basis of power has stirred questions to many. Many postcolonial writers have come openly to challenge this. Still the way Dattani has done this in his play *Final Solutions* is an achievement in itself. What Chakraborty has remarked is true to the context of the play:

> These discursive frameworks and the kind of actions they instigate are integral to the process of postcolonial subalternisation as a result of which the new subaltern begins to feel a sense of unbelongingness owing to the multiple deprivations and injustices that he is subjected to and they may well generate a sense of hostility towards the nation-state in question, This is precisely the context that Dattani seeks to explore in the play. (Chakraborty, 181-182)

With the fine blend of past and present through Daksha's reading of her diary forty years ago when she was merely a girl of fifteen in her father's household and her appearance as Hardika after finishing it as a mother of Ramnik Gandhi and a grandmother of Smita, Dattani opens his play *Final Solutions* in communal stress and unrest that has been still persisting in the same way as it was forty years ago:

> HARDIKA. After forty years...I opened my diary again. And I wrote. A dozen pages before. A dozen pages now. A young girl's childish scribble. An old woman's shaky scrawl. Yes, things have not changed that much. (Dattani, 167)

The past experience of Daksha that she had that night in Hussainabad in her ancestral house after partition finds no mismatch with her present one that she has now in Amargaon after disruption of 'rath yatra'. Since then many years have elapsed but no change has come upon the mentality of men. The play concentrates on the theme of 'transferred resentments' that are always on shift from one generation to other generation:

> As I see it, this is a play about transferred resentments. About looking for a scapegoat to hit out at when we feel let down, humiliated. (Padamsee, 161)

Due to this transferred resentment, mentality always lies there where it has been for years, though the wheel of time unstoppably moves on. "The demons of communal hatred are not out on the street...they are lurking inside ourselves." (Padamsee, 161) Encompassing three generations that saw Daksha's transformation from being daughter to grandmother, the play focuses on how transferred resentments remained rolling on through the mentality of the characters

The sense of transferred resentment coming down generation by generation can well be perceived through the relational study of Javed and Bobby with other characters in the play. The food and shelter offered to them by Ramnik Gandhi on being followed after by a fanatic Hindu mob, though apparently appears as a humanitarian act from the part of Ramnik Gandhi but only at the end we are made realise that it was not out of love but out of guilt related with his past action with his kinsmen in getting the shop of a Muslim burnt down in order to buy it at a low price. He could not help suppressing the sense of superiority that is still apparent in some way or other on his facial impression and the way he moves and behaves. Being well aware of the body language of Ramnik, Javed taunts him,

> JAVED. But, sir, it is in your every move. You must know. You can offer milk to us. You can have an angry mob outside your house. You can play the civilised host. Because you know you have peace hidden inside your armpit. (Dattani, 192)

Similarly Daksha, the past self of Hardika also feels the same resentment transferred to her by her father.

> DAKSHA. My father had fought for that hour. And he was happy when it came. He said he was happy we were rid of the

> Britishers. He also said something I did not understand then. He said that before leaving, they had let loose the dogs. I hated to think that he was talking about my friends' fathers...But that night in Hussainabad in our ancestral house – when I heard them outside – I knew that they were thinking the same of us. And I knew that I was thinking the same, like my father. (Dattani, 167)

Her sense of hatred and resentment aggravate the situation when she is brutally beaten up by her husband due to her visit to her Muslim friend Zarine:

> Hardika, the grandmother, builds up a hatred for Zarine, her best friend, and her community because she herself can't stand up to her own in-laws. (Padamsee, 161)

Her traumatic past forces her to muse over the entry of Javed and Bobby:

> HARDIKA. Why did he do it?
>
> DAKSHA. Oh God! Why do I have to suffer?
>
> HARDIKA. Didn't he have any feelings for me?
>
> DAKSHA. I just wanted them to be my friends!
>
> HARDIKA. How could he let these people into my house?
>
> DAKSHA. Oh! I hate this world!
>
> HARDIKA. They killed his grandfather! (Dattani, 179)

Living by the strict code of the Hindu scriptures, Aruna, Hardika's daughter-in-law and Ramnik's wife treats Javed and Bobby as untouchables. When Ramnik asks her to "bring them a glass of water" (Dattani, 184), she "stares at him as if she has asked her to go and kill someone." (Dattani, 184) When they finish glasses, "Aruna holds the glasses with her thumbs and index fingers, on the sides which have not been touched by their lips. She takes them away and keeps them separate from the other glasses." (Dattani, 185) Later Ramnik uses "the same glasses they drank water from" (Dattani 191) to serve them milk. Aruna stands strongly against water to be filled into brass pot by them:

> ARUNA *(to Javed)*. We don't allow anyone to fill our drinking water. No outsiders.

...

ARUNA. We bathe our god with it, Smita. It has to be pure. It must not be contaminated. (Dattani, 209)

Besides main characters, the chorus also plays a very effective role in the dramatic frame work. Through this device Dattani presents the thinking of the two communities. Through this device, the very fact that Muslims are looked upon as 'others' in the imagined community of India, is brought out from domestic atmosphere of Hardika's household to public place and thus the issue has been given the widened shape making it public out of four walls. In this connection, Jeremy Mortimer's observation is mention worthy, "Mahesh's plays often feature characters who are questioning their identity, and who feel isolated in some way." (Mortimer, 4) The hard fact that Muslims are still looked upon as foreign in the very structure of national identity in spite of being born on the vey soil is brought home through their speech:

CHORUS 1. What must we do? To become more acceptable?
Must we lose our identity? Is that what they want?
Must we tolerate more? Does our future lie in their hands?
Is there anyone more unsure more insecure than us?
Oh what a curse it is to be less in number! (Dattani, 208)

The policy of intolerance from the part of Hindu chorus is also noticed.

CHORUS 1. Why did they stay?

CHORUS 2. This is not their land. They have got what they wanted. So why stay?

CHORUS 3. They stay to spy on us.

CHORUS 4. Their hearts belong there. But they live on our land.

CHORUS 5. They are few. They can't do much harm. (Dattani, 176)

The hard fact that Muslims being marginal community is treated under uneven law in the imagined community of India is revealed through Javed's speech when Aruna suggests to Ramnik to call the police instead of handing them over the fanatic mob:

> JAVED. Yes, call the police! Do you think they care? They will say we started it all! They will lock us up! Not them! (Dattani, 180)

Noorani presents the situation in concrete words:

> The foreign races in Hindustan must either adopt the Hindu culture and language, must learn to respect and hold in reverence Hindu religion, must entertain no idea but those of the glorification of the Hindu race and culture, i.e., the Hindu Nation and must lose their separate existence to merge in the Hindu race, or may stay in the country wholly subordinated to the Hindu nation, claiming nothing, deserving no privileges, far less any preferential treatment – not even citizen's rights. (Noorani, 20)

Being driven by the fear of exclusion, minorities are forced either to become counteroffensive or to hide their identity. Javed, after being humiliated as an untouchable by a man whom he was to deliver a letter as per the direction of a postman became counteroffensive. Bobby, on the other hand, being not as resolute as Javed strives to hide his identity from Babban to Bobby. Keeping Javed and Bobby at the centre of his story, Dattani leaves no stone unturned to bring into surface the plights and sufferings of minorities as non-ethical beings in the concept of nation. Stripping off the false layers of India as a united nation, the play successfully shows India as an imagined community to our full view. "Theatre can't change society but you can make society aware of issue and the complexities of issues", and in this regard Girish Karnard thinks, "*Final Solutions* was superb". (Dattani and Karnad, 4)

However, the popularity of Dattani's play *Final Solutions* lies not on its theme of 'transferred resentments' of one community against another as regards question to national identity but on the possible solution that the playwright tries to find out in order to end such violence and animosity. Along with dealing with the question of national identity arising out of hostile binaries existing between Hindus and Muslims, Dattani's *Final Solutions* also works as a searchlight for that 'third-space' or 'in-between space' (Bhabha, 1) from where the bond of 'horizontal comradeship'(Anderson, 7) that

Benedict Anderson takes essential for national identity can be achieved. The play "forces us to look at ourselves in relation to the attitudes that persist in the society. Since it is an experiment in time and space and relates to memory, it is a play which involves a lot of introspection on the part of the characters in the play and thus induces similar introspection in the viewers." (qtd. in Datta, 265) Apart from feeling of 'otherness', the feeling of 'oneness' is brought home at the end of Act III when Javed, Smita and Bobby, youth of present generation prefer 'forgetting' in place of 'transferred resentment'. Unless we forget we cannot dream of a united India, free from resentment and intolerance as it is "a crucial factor in the creation of a nation." (Renan, 11) We cannot reach to the goal of a new nation as long as we walk on the beaten track. The question that Alyque Padamsee has raised in the introductory note of the play should be the question of every Indian if we wish to see our nation in altered shape: "Is life a forward journey or do we travel around in a circle, returning to our starting point? Can we shake off our prejudices or are they in our psyche like our genes? Will we ever be free or ever-locked in combat...Are they any final solutions?" (Padamsee, 161) The play indeed, takes a serious turn when Bobby places the statue of Krishna on his palm disregarding Aruna's prejudices and forces to rethink everyone over his speech:

> BOBBY. See, Javed! He does not humiliate you. He does not cringe from my touch. He welcomes the warmth of my hand. He feels me. And He welcomes it! I hold Him who is sacred to them, but I do not commit sacrilege. (To Aruna). You can bathe Him day and night, you can splash holy waters on Him but you cannot remove my touch from His form. You cannot remove my smell with sandal paste and attars and fragrant flowers because it belongs to a human being who believes, and tolerates, and respects what other human beings believe. That is the strongest fragrance in the world! (Dattani, 224-25)

Through mutuality of love and respect among Javed, Smita and Bobby, Dattani suggests 'forgetting' as the solution of all kinds of anger and resentment. Lack of forgetting leads a nation to "a luminal signifying space that is internally marked by the discourse of minorities, the heterogeneous histories of contending people, antagonistic authorities and tense locations of cultural difference." (Bhabha, 148) Through Bobby's final concluding speech, Dattani shows that there is still spark of hope for communal understanding amidst ashes of communal violence if we forget our past: "If you are willing to forget, I am willing to tolerate." (Dattani, 225) The sense of 'horizontal comradeship' is achieved through Javed, Smita and Bobby in the play. Together they try to subvert the hierarchies of power in order to establish 'in-between spaces' which, according to Homi Bhabha, "provide the terrain of elaborating strategies of selfhood-singular or communal – that initiate new signs of identity," (Bhabha, 1) free from binaries of communal violence and animosity.

Works Cited

Anderson, Benedict. *Imagined Communities: Reflections on the Origin and Spread of Nationalism*. London: Verso, 2006. Print.

Bhabha, Homi. *The Location of Culture*. New York: Routledge, 1994. Print.

Chakraborty, Abin. *Dattani's Final Solutions and the Quest for Horizontal Comradeship*. Ed. A.S. Kaushik. *Indian Drama in English: Some Perspectives*. New Delhi: Atlantic Publishers, 2013. Print.

Datta, Ketaki. "Mahesh Dattani's Final Solutions: A Reconstruction". *Indian Drama in English*. Ed. Kaustav Chakraborty. New Delhi: PHI Learning Pvt. Ltd., 2011. Print.

Dattani, Mahesh. *Collected Plays*. New Delhi: Penguin Books, 2000. Print.

____ ., Karnad, Girish. 'Two Faces of Indian Drama'. *Indian Review of Books* 8.6. 16 March-15. April 1999. Print.

Golwalkar, M.S. *We, or our Nationhood Defined*, New Delhi: Bharat Publication, 1939. Print.

Mortimer, Jeremy. "A Note on the Play". *Collected Plays.* Mahesh Dattani. New Delhi: Penguin Books, 2000. Print.

Noorani. A. G. *The RSS and the BJP: A Division of Labour.* New Delhi: Leftword, 2000. Print.

Padamsee, Alyque. "A Note on the Play". *Collected Plays.* Mahesh Dattani. New Delhi: Penguin Books, 2000. Print.

Guru Gobind Singh College of Commerce, Delhi University, Delhi.

9. **Samiksha Sharma** is a Research Scholar, Department of English, Baba Ghulam Shah Badshah University, Rajouri, J&K.

10. **Shweta Verma** is a Research Scholar, Department of English, University of Lucknow, U.P.

11. **Tabish Wani** is a Student of M.A., Department of English, Kashmir University, Kashmir.

12. **Rumana Nisar** is a Student of M.A., Department of English, Kashmir University, Kashmir.

13. **Ragini Kapoor** is a Ph. D. Research Scholar, Department of Modern Indian Languages and Literary Studies, Delhi University, New Delhi.

14. **Surabhi K.** is a Ph. D. Research Scholar, Department of English, University of Hyderabad, Telangana.

15. **Supriya Mandal** is an M.Phil Research Scholar, University of Gour Banga, Malda, West Bengal. She was formerly Guest Lecturer in Malda Government DIET College, Malda, West Bengal.

16. **Dr. Prachi Priyanka** is an Assistant Professor, School of Languages & Culture, Sharda University, Greater Noida (U.P.).

17. **Dr. Brajesh Kumar Gupta "Mewadev"** is the Head and Assistant Professor, Department of English, Eklavya Mahavidyalaya, Banda (U.P.).

18. **Sujoy Barman** works in Bhatun Junior High School, Bhatol Hatch, Raiganj, Uttar Dinajpur, West Bengal.

19. **Alik Jha** is a Ph. D. Research Scholar, Department of English, Raiganj University, Raiganj, Uttar Dinajpur (W.B.).

20. **Rabindra Sutradhar** is an Assistant Teacher, Khirerkote High School (H.S.), Alipurduar, West Bengal.

21. **Amrita Datta** is an Assistant Teacher in Mowamari Tattanath Vidyapith (H.S), Cooch Behar and a Ph. D. Research Scholar, Department of English, Raiganj University, Raiganj, Uttar Dinajpur (W.B.). She is an Academic Counsellor, Cooch Behar College Study Centre, NSOU, West Bengal. She was formerly Part Time Lecturer, Vivekananda College, Alipurduar and Academic Counsellor, A.B.N Seal College Study Centre, IGNOU, Cooch Behar, West Bengal.

22. **Tinku Das** is an Assistant Teacher, Uttar Khapaidanga High School, Cooch Behar, West Bengal. He is an Academic Counsellor, Netaji Subhash Open University, Cooch Behar College Study Centre, Cooch Behar, West Bengal.

23. **Saurabh Debnath** is an Assistant Teacher, Pundibari Ramgopal Lakhotia High School, Cooch Behar, West Bengal. He is an Academic Counsellor, Netaji Subhash Open University, Cooch Behar College Study Centre, Cooch Behar, West Bengal.

24. **Dipak Giri** is an Assistant Teacher, Katamari High School (H.S.), Cooch Behar, West Bengal and a Ph. D. Research Scholar, Raiganj University, Raiganj, Uttar Dinajpur, West Bengal. He is an Academic Counsellor, Netaji Subhas Open University, Cooch Behar College Study Centre, Cooch Behar, West Bengal. He was formerly a Part-Time Lecturer, Cooch Behar College, Vivekananda College and Thakur Panchanan Mahila Mahavidyalaya, West Bengal and a Guest Lecturer, Dewanhat College, Cooch Behar, West Bengal.

Index